To Sharon
Best wishes
David Beasley

ASPECTS OF LOVE

HELEN CARAVETTI ADAM

BY DAVID BEASLEY

DAVUS PUBLISHING

Published by Davus Publishing
150 Norfolk St. S.
Simcoe, ON N3Y 2W2 Canada
and
P.O. Box 1101
Buffalo, N.Y. 14213-7101

Beasley, David, 1931-
Aspects of Love: Helen, Caravetti, Adam

ISBN 0-915317-11-7

I. Title

PS8553.E14A86 2000 C813'.54 C99-901561-3
PR9199.3.B43A86 2000

"Davus: 'He's either insane - or composing poetry.'"- Horace, *Satires* II,7

Davus sum, non Oedipus.

HELEN

The doorbell rang startling me from my chair. I had been waiting for Helen so eagerly that I had fallen into dreaming of her as she appeared in this first week of our love - sinuous hips, her cries of pleasure in hot breaths upon my ear. The stale odour of fried eggs struck at me as I passed the kitchen. Dampness coated the wood of the hall. I pictured the wet London street and Helen shivering, waiting for me. The hollow thump of my descending footsteps resounded throughout the three floors of the house. My hand shook as I tried to fit the key in the lock. Little shoots of pain sprang up from my stomach. I could scarcely breathe. Pausing, I watched the keyhole and gasped nervously for air. The glabrous feel of Helen's skin passed over me, weakening me. I exhaled and fitted the key firmly in the hole.

Helen looked up. She stuck out her hip and smiled naughtily. The fragrance of her body poured out in that gesture as if she had tipped the top off a bottle and waved its scent under my nostrils. Seizing her wrist, I pulled her in from the street, slammed the door and pressed her tightly against me. My hands sought her form, caressed, gripped, told my need as our mouths clinched. A door slammed somewhere in the house. We tensed and listened. My hands rested upon her hips seeming to soak up the animalism in her. My knees quivering, I stepped aside and allowed her to push by me up the stairs. Her behind wiggled on a level with my eyes. When she reached the landing, I seized her legs. She laughed over her shoulder and broke away. In a few short strides she was in my room and pulling the drapes across the high Victorian windows. Grabbing a straight-backed chair, I wedged it under the doorknob. My fingers clamped the wood as if to mash it, and, for a moment, I could not release them. With my other hand I pried away my thumb and rubbed my wrist until the muscles relaxed, and my fingers slipped to my side.

Helen had slung her coat across the table. She undressed, a feverish excitement alight in her eyes; her short energetic body wrestling with her blue sweater and her plaid skirt; her flesh mysteriously luminescent in the pale light that fell through the high cracks at the sides of the drapes.

I dropped my clothes as she stepped to the bed, arching her back in a way that reminded me of college girls at gymnastic exercises. The bedspread flew up and circled to the foot of the bed, wafting a breeze over my nakedness. She rolled to one side as I went to her. I picked up the sheet but, trembling, dropped it. Smiling, she pulled it back and ran her eyes over me as I got in beside her .

Warm and firm, she pressed towards me, the two small breasts nestling against my chest, and I steered impulsively into the wet haven, offered as if it had been waiting a long time for this moment.

A gasp of relief escaped us both. Our pain, our tension fused into an ecstatic wonderment. I saw the curl of her lips and the rhythmic motion of her shoulder. The soft lines of her body began to break up, and I moved over them to help destroy, to enjoy every crumbling piece of beauty that strove beneath me.

Suddenly she groaned. Her head stretched back and the tendons came out upon her neck.

'Gently,' she whispered.

Chastened, I kissed her lips and lay my cheek alongside hers. I cuddled the curve of her shoulders into me and ran my hand over her back, treating her body as part of me. Slowly I recommenced the pleasure. Her arms pushed up against my shoulders. Eyes sparkling, she squirmed over on top of me. She snapped her fingers by her haunches and leaned forward. 'Giddyup.' Then grinning, she sat back and began to ride, gradually spiraling me into a violent heat, consuming my senses. Lost in the enjoyment of her flesh, I felt her suddenly take my heart with the cords of my being and grappling them tightly, jerk them so that I went rigid, then weak beside her.

I opened my eyes to the black and gray of her hair. Several very white strands curled low over her ear. Moving my arm from under me, I brushed them back.

She turned her head and gazed dreamily at me. 'How do you feel?'

'Great.' My voice came out in a breath.

The lines of her face were sharpened by the white background of the pillow. Was she forty really?

'What are you thinking?' Her eyes widened in alarm.

'Nothing.' I looked away guiltily.

'Why were you looking at me like that?'

I sensed her anger working behind her brow.

'Should you be worried?' I laughed.

Her frown disappeared. 'I thought you were criticizing me. Your face shows your thoughts.' She relaxed.

'What did it show that time?'

'That I am old and you are young.'

I smiled. 'Twenty-one isn't young.'

She sat up, allowing the sheet to fall about her middle and turned, rumpling her side, to look back. Her breasts stuck out with the warm look of honey cones. I started with pleasure and reached out, but amused, she brushed my hand away.

'If I'm too old, don't touch me.'

'You'll never be too old. Oh brother!'

She pushed away the sheet and threw her legs over me, but before I could seize her, she wriggled away and stood up. My dressing gown hung on the back of the door. She didn't see it because this was the first time we made love in my room. She stretched, her arms planed back and her legs tightening as she rose on the balls of her feet. In an instant, I was beside her, kissing her neck and shoulders and arms, a titillating sensation drawing me to her inescapably.

She pushed me back and, catching sight of the gown, made a ballet leap to it and threw it about her shoulders.

'Did you learn that in acting school?' I said with interest, for the movement incited me to make love again.

She nodded roguishly. 'I've only found ballet useful for getting away from men.' She stuck out her tongue and pushed her arms into the sleeves of the gown. 'Let's hope I don't meet either of the boys.'

'Someone's in,' I warned, 'but I don't know who.'

Opening the door slowly, she listened and then stepped quickly out. The dampness of the room slapped my skin as if with a wet cloth. The gas fire had gone out. Picking up my clothes, I threw them onto the bed and searched the pockets of my trousers. My skin was tingling from Helen's caresses. The cold of February could not penetrate to the inner glow, although its dank personality had settled upon the air of the room. I found a shilling. Sticking it in the meter I lit the fire and crouched for a moment in front of it.

I thought of the dirty yellow look of the street door and the wet street bending away in a line of houses in both directions.

Suddenly Helen's legs gripped my back, the pubic hairs tickling my skin. Her hands, small and square, rubbed over my arms possessively.

'Let's get dressed,' she said. 'When we've had tea we'll go for a walk, shall we?'

'Okay.'

She rocked against me, flooding me with a sensation of physical agreeableness, then stood up and strode over to her clothes as if she were taking a stance for her next exercise.

I dressed with an effort for I felt drawn in limb and organ. My strength seemed to stand away from me.

'I'm glad I've moved out of this old house,' she said with a shiver.

'It's not bad,' I grinned, 'especially when the landlady's your lover.'

'Yes,' she nodded seriously, the strong lines of her Celtic features giving her a determined expression. 'Be sure you don't say a word to the others.' She paused and added, 'Have you seen Eric?'

The lean face of nonchalant Eric had not appeared on the stairs, in the kitchen, or at the bathroom door, not since the morning I stormed into Helen's room. The previous evening we kissed for the first time and tamely went to our own beds to dream. It had taken a full night to bring about a violent reaction.

'Not since he knocked at your door,' I said. 'Imagine asking for your radio at that hour.'

She wasn't amused. 'He wasn't the one to waken me out of a deep sleep,' she complained. 'I told you that I have to have my sleep. I need my strength.'

A high pitch came into her voice as if she were under nervous tension. If her agent hadn't telephoned as promised, she would complain of her poverty. Now she was annoyed at the mention of Eric. The voice of the young man had sounded hesitant and choked at the time, perhaps owing to my alarm at being apprehended in the act of love, but I remembered that it was unlike him to be emotional. A radio announcer, he seemed always most controlled.

Helen, seeing that I was disturbed, smiled in the way that made her look eighteen. 'Come along, darling. You'll catch cold.' Clothed, she came up to me and raised her mouth.

As I kissed her, I wished that my powers had not been drained away. Her lips provoked lust even when it had no strength to rise.

'I think the kettle's boiling,' she said, pulling away.

There was a sound in the hallway.

'Who's that?' she whispered, pausing with one hand on the doorknob.

I threw on my shirt and buttoned it hastily. 'Pretend we're talking.'

She held my sports coat out and shouted, 'You wretched boy, when are you going to pay your rent? I'm tired of your excuses.'

'Don't take that,' I pleaded. 'My lunch money is in one pocket.'

'Oh ho,' she cried rounding her eyes devilishly and plunging a hand into the coat.

'You'd strip a man of all he's got,' I said.

We laughed and came together as I circled a scarf around my neck. A quiet knock upon the door alerted and then amused us because it sounded timorous in the face of our bravado. Carefully lifting the chair from under the handle, I opened the door wide enough to emit my head.

'Oh,' Eric's thin face simulated surprise. 'Do you think you could let me have some sugar? I'm all out of it.'

'Sure.'

I sensed his curiosity and kept the door close behind me.

'I say, is Helen in there?' he blurted. 'I thought I heard her.'

I paused wondering whether a lie would be possible under the circumstances.

'I'm sorry,' he stammered. 'I don't mean to be curious.'

The door was pulled from my grasp. Helen stood beside me and put her arm about my waist. 'Yes, I'm here,' she said.

Intimidated, Eric glanced down, swallowed, and looked up again.

'Do you wish to tell me something?' Her eyes were cold.

Eric frowned and stared back at her. 'I have nothing to say to you.'

The reproach between them cooled the air. Their anger was meaningless to me. I stirred uneasily and Helen took her arm away.

'We were going to have tea,' she said in a milder tone. "Will you have a cup?'

Eric nodded. 'I was just about to have one.'

'At least you English can always get together for tea,' I smiled.

They grinned spontaneously, finding my simple statement funnier than I meant it to be.

Helen stepped into the kitchen. The swing of her skirt caught my eye. Eric, watching me, smirked as if I had unwittingly revealed my familiarity with Helen. Pretending that I hadn't understood his look, I stepped back into my room.

'The sugar is in the cupboard,' I said.

His smile vanishing, he nodded and went into the kitchen.

My bed was not yet made. I picked the blankets off the floor and threw them on the bed, then sat down and pulled on my cold socks and shoes.

Musty London encaged a loneliness in my room. The large table strewn with papers reflected the half-light. I drew back the drapes and watched the windows evenly spaced in the houses across the street. The sky jutted out from the flat roofs. I had been without work for a couple of months. My savings were almost gone.

Helen's voice cried out in anger. Its harshness frightened me. I listened to Eric's low mumble. A suspenseful pause spoke its own language from the kitchen. I entered the kitchen but did not want to get involved.

'Your rent is three pounds,' Helen was saying as I entered.

'But it's always been two pounds ten,' Eric retorted, his face pale.

'If you don't like it, move!' she snapped.

I looked at the blue and white square of linoleum rather than see the desolate expression on Eric's face. An ugly somberness overcame me as I looked up and recognized it. Anxious to stay away, I took a cup from the cupboard and looked at the pattern on its side.

'Cups are on the table,' Helen said.

'Oh.' I moved quickly to a chair and watched Helen pour the tea. 'Are you arguing about the rent?'

Helen sighed. 'I just haven't enough money to run the place. Eric has to pay his share.' A quiver of hysteria lined her voice.

'Aren't you going to rent your old room?' I asked.

She grimaced, almost in tears. 'I'm trying.'

Eric shifted his brown eyes to me expectantly. With a lump in my throat, I took Helen's hand.

'There, there, don't worry about the house. You're just upset over nothing.'

'I'll pay the extra ten shillings,' Eric said grudgingly.

Helen moaned and sat down. 'This house isn't worth it,' she said.

'Well, don't get rid of it until we've found somewhere else,' Eric warned.

'Isn't he just like a man?' Helen glared at him. 'You always have to be considered first.' She looked about her quickly. 'Oh damn, I left my purse in your room.' Her eyes looked sweetly into mine. 'Do you have a cigarette?'

'No,' I stood up, 'but I'll get them.'

Eric pulled out a packet and handed it to her. 'Take the whole thing; it's my last one.'

Helen took out the cigarette and leaned on one elbow for me to light it. I took a kitchen match and scraped it over the stove. I felt Eric's eyes looking for any sign of intimacy. Helen glanced up at me as she put her cigarette in the flame, and, when I smiled, Eric stirred restlessly.

'I needed this,' she said, picking up her cup and sipping. 'I needed something to calm my nerves.'

She looked down, blew out smoke, and fidgeted with her dress. Eric drank his tea and stared over his cup rim at the tablecloth. I wished he had not caught Helen in my room. His resentment had given way to wistfulness which made me feel even more uncomfortable. It occurred to me that he could have been Helen's lover. The hurt in his eyes was genuine. Yet the idea seemed preposterous. She wouldn't have looked twice at him! But perhaps he just cherished a secret affection for her, and she, detecting his disapproval, was angry that he should pretend to be upset.

'Why don't you tell us a story, darling,' Helen was saying. 'You write plays.'

Eric smirked and brought his cup down with a clatter. I frowned in surprise at the bitterness in his face.

'Don't call me a writer until I've staged something, otherwise it's embarrassing,' I said.

'You'll have to marry a rich woman if you want to be a writer,' Eric advised.

I glanced at Helen. She pursed her lips with a shrewd look at Eric.

'Like money, they don't grow on trees,' I said. 'Anyway, who wants riches if you have to spend your time looking after money?'

Eric nodded. 'A discussion on money is the last thing I want at this moment.' He glared at Helen and stood up. 'Be seeing you, dear.'

'The next quarrel you start with me will be your last in this house,' Helen called after him.

Wheeling, Eric pointed a shaking finger. 'You take care or you'll be having an extra room to rent, and then, God help you, you can quarrel all you like with the wallpaper.' He stepped out and slammed the door.

Helen laughed into her fist as we heard him climb the stairs.

'What was the matter with him?' I asked.

She bent forward and rested her arm on the table. 'He's furious at me for raising his rent.' She straightened up and took a long drag on her cigarette.

'Is that all?' I asked.

'That's all,' she said sharply.

I drank my tea and watched Helen fidget. The slight movements of her hand, the twists and shrugs of her torso, the compact look of her hips entranced me. The luscious tones of her body came through her clothes. Her sophistication added to the attraction; when dreaming in my room, I could hardly believe that a woman who had starred on the stages of London and New York had given herself to me. My personality seemed to have become infused with her in the giving.

'Any word from your agent?' I asked.

'Oh no.' She glanced at the window which gave out on the wall of the house three yards away. 'Finished your tea? Let's go out. This place is as gloomy as hell.' She stood up and put her arms around my neck, the fuzz of the wool smoothly caressing my skin. 'I'm looking forward to our walk, darling. I was thinking of you all the way down on the bus, and of walking with you in the park.'

'You're always in my thoughts,' I said, feeling the woolly warmth of her breasts upon the back of my head. 'Honest, I feel you in my skin. I can't think of anything but making love to you.'

Brushing her cheek in my hair, she laughed with pleasure and then stepped away as I tried to seize her. I followed her into my room and we put on our coats.

'I wonder,' Helen was looking at me thoughtfully, 'how long will it last?'

'What?' I frowned.

'I mean our affair,' she said seriously.

I laughed, happy that she could think of losing me.

'Forever, I hope.'

She smiled. 'I'd be a better companion if I weren't worried about expenses.' Taking up her purse she went to the door and rolled her eyes back at me. 'But you make me forget.'

The front doorbell rang. Helen's fingers jumped to her lips. 'Is it four o'clock?'

My desk clock signaled two minutes to four.

'Oh dear, I think it's the man to see the room. I'd forgotten the time.' She stripped off her coat and threw it on the bed. 'You let him in.'

The picture of the two of us walking in Regent's Park against a background of creamy Regency architecture came poignantly to my mind.

'But when are we going for our walk?' I protested.

She looked up blankly. 'We'll go after I've shown him the room, dear.'

Reassured, I slung my coat over hers and stomped down to the door. The stranger glanced at a card in his hand. His fedora had a used but smart look. He squinted at me.

'Does Miss Browning live in this...' he paused for a word, 'house?'

'Yes.' I wondered whether Helen could be attracted to this man of her own age. There was a seasoned air about him. His face was tanned and handsome. 'She's been expecting you.'

The corners of his mouth sank when he saw the dinginess of the hallway. The garbage can should have been set out for the last collection, but, after Helen moved, none of the roomers remembered to do it.

Helen was waiting for us at the top of the stairs. She smiled charmingly and held out her hand as if she were welcoming him to the Queen's drawing room.

He smiled and mumbled his name. As he followed her to the second storey, I saw his eyes deftly take in the shape of her legs.

'The bathroom is right across the hall, doctor,' Helen said confidently. 'You didn't have trouble finding the house, did you?'

The doctor's mumbled reply died away into the inaudible distance. I listened in the hall for a few minutes. The banister crackled once and the floor boards squeaked as I shifted my weight. The silence from upstairs was disquieting. I wondered if Helen could be attracted to this doctor, but then I remembered that she met many handsome actors. She had passed everyone by in order to be in love with me. The thought was beatific.

With cool assurance I went into my room and over to the table, cast an eye on the very little work I had done since I had moved in, and resolved to come to terms with my obsession for Helen. She was using up every waking hour and my every thought. Just as now, I spent my days waiting. I heard voices on the stairs. Helen was escorting the doctor to the door. I went to the window but I couldn't see the sidewalk directly below. The front door thudded shut and I went into the hall to meet Helen. She ran up the stairs watching her breasts jiggle without seeing me at first, then her eyes rounded at me.

'He liked it at three pounds,' she said happily. 'That solves one problem, darling.'

'Where is he from?'

'Central Europe. He's been naturalized and works in the Colonial Office. He's just come back from the Falkland Islands.'

'He's got a nice tan,' I eyed her. 'Do you like him?'

She wrinkled her brow in amusement. 'Being nice to one boarder is all I have energy for, thank you.'

Satisfied, I helped her on with her coat.

'Do you mind if we don't go for the walk, dear? It's got so late, and I have a dinner engagement,' she said casually.

I stiffened in spite of my attempt to appear nonchalant. 'Dinner? Who with?'

'Just an old friend.' She ticked my chin with her finger. 'I knew him in the Bristol Stock fifteen years ago.'

I bit my lip.

'You don't look pleased.' She drew a long face.

'Well, I was hoping you'd have dinner with me.'

'Poor darling, we'll eat together tomorrow evening. I'll take you to one of my favourite restaurants.'

We kissed. My sadness lingered as we parted. When she reached the end of the hall, she turned and came running back to throw her arms about me tightly. 'I'm sorry, dear, I really am. If I had known it was so late I wouldn't have suggested going out. But ring me tomorrow afternoon, won't you?'

The feel of her in my arms compensated for the disappointment. She snatched a hurried kiss and I watched her run down the stairs. When the door closed I went to the window of my room and gazed at her standing by the side of the street. She held up her arm and posed with one hip angled out. I stirred restlessly, regretful that I couldn't spend the evening with her. A taxi took her into its blackness and out of my sight.

The telephone rang and rang at Helen's number. I decided she had gone to the store for a few minutes. I rang ten minutes later. No answer. I paced the room and thought of her small apartment being empty.

We had made love for the first time in it. She asked me to help her move a couple of lamps from the room upstairs to her new place. As I set them up, I sensed her presence, powerfully overwhelming. My legs trembling, I felt for a stool and sank back onto it. My stomach tightened as if in a nervous nausea. She bent over me and in an impulse we embraced. We wanted to go to bed immediately, but first, at her insistence, I had to run to the store for prophylactics. I asked if I should stay the night and she said, 'We may as well be hanged for sheep as well as for a lamb.' I laughed outright whenever I remembered it. That particular expression gave me bewitching enjoyment as if it signified my baptism into the adult world.

Unable to work I went to the Park and walked between the trees sheered like umbrellas left upright in the wet. The rock gardens rose in levels of rusted weeds and mud-splotched stones. I stopped at the fountain in Queen Mary's Gardens and gazed at the slim green mermaids wickedly glancing over their shoulders. Their bodies glistened lustily, reminding me of Helen. Since the fountain was not running, the mermaids had the appearance of being suddenly stripped naked and deserted.

I thought of Helen deserted. She had promised to be home. She asked me to ring. I dashed out of the Gardens to a telephone booth in the street. The wood was wet and rain drops fell over my hand as I pushed on the door. The pennies clanked metallicly. There was no answer. Feeling nauseous again I leaned back in the booth and watched the autos pass in the road. Occasionally they slapped the sidewalk with muddy water. I winced and pushed dejectedly onto the street. Then in the back window of a passing cab I saw the back of a woman's head. I stood still and watched as the cab turned the corner. Helen's profile was clearly visible through the glass. My heart leaped. I ran to the corner and shouted and waved just as the cab turned into the next street and in a split second disappeared, as if shunning my nervous cry, my call for recognition.

Cutting back through the park on the double, I guessed that she was headed for the house. Branches caught at my head and shook rain on my collar. Breathless, I arrived at the yellow door, clutched my key and with shaking hand turned the lock. I pictured Helen sitting in my room, her coat over the back of the chair and the heater glowing. In a spasm of energy I leaped up the stairs and burst through the door. The emptiness of a vacant bed-sitting room confronted me. No feminine figure vanquished the drabness. I was alone.

Throwing off my coat, I stretched out on the bed and tried to breathe easily. It was a while before I could admit to my heart that Helen was not in the room. The dankness of the street remained stuck in my nostrils. The long blue drapes hung in mourning. I began to feel cold and wondered if I could spare another shilling for the meter. Helen emptied it of coins monthly. I reached up to put my hand where she put hers on the black tin box when she emptied it.

The telephone rang jarring me to my feet. Half-fearing that it wasn't Helen ringing me, I waited for someone else to answer. Then fearful lest I miss her, I seized the arm.

'Helen?'

'Darling,' her voice called. My whole body relaxed. 'I have news.'

'Where have you been?' I asked anxiously.

She paused, then said with annoyance, 'Don't you want to hear my news?

'I called your apartment,' I insisted.

'I'm here now.'

I didn't believe her because how could she be at home when the taxi was taking her in the opposite direction?

'Didn't I just see you in a taxi?'

There was a long pause, making me bristle with suspicion.

'No, you did not see me in a taxi. Are you cross-questioning me? Because if you are, I won't stand it.'

'No, Helen, I just thought I saw you. I swear I saw you. Just the back of your head.'

She laughed. 'Well, dear, that wasn't my head. Now do you want to hear my news?' she added pleasantly.

My spirit brightened. I was wrong after all. 'Yes.'

'Television has offered me a role. Rehearsals begin next week.'

'Wonderful!'

'Its only a small part, but it pays.'

'Oh darling, I'm glad. This will bring you back to a wide audience and you may get popular again.' I felt somehow that I was connected with television through her.

'I have a death-bed scene in the first act, dear. I don't know how popular that will make me.'

As we chatted I heard a receiver being put down on one of the extensions. Either Eric or the doctor had been listening, probably Eric.

Helen's voice soothed me. Her personality came over the wires as refreshingly as a dream. I wanted to hold her close and smell the perfume of her skin.

'Are you coming by here tonight or shall I meet you someplace?' I asked.

'Dear, look, I can't meet you. I have so much to do. I have my role to learn and, oh, I don't know, odds and ends to wash. Let's see each other tomorrow, shall we?'

I swallowed hard, feeling a stone in my throat. 'All right. Sure, we'll make it tomorrow. Don't call me in the afternoon, though.' I wanted her to feel that I was not always easy to reach. 'I'll be looking for a job. My money's getting low.'

'Aren't you writing?'

'Not much.'

'Dear, there's a cinema with Danny Kaye. I think he's funny. Meet me at six outside the Oxford tube. Do you want to?' Her voice carried a plaint in an intimate undertone, speaking directly to the desire bottled up inside me, asking me to protect her.

'Don't be late, dear,' she said and I pictured her cutely wrapped in her coat, rubbing her legs in the cold.

The Oxford Tube Station took in tributaries of pedestrians and molded them to one great stream flowing down its throat. All afternoon I had been making the rounds of employment agencies in Soho. There had been one job open: typing. An actor had just taken it. Sorry, call tomorrow. Would you like to test your speed? I hurried nervously onward until night fell and the homeward-bound stir in the streets reminded me of Helen. It had turned very cold. The newspaper vendor clapped his gloved hands and shouted out loudly for attention. At ten minutes past six, Helen came wearily out of the tube. Her face was pale, revealing her tiredness. She lifted her lips for a quick peck and shifted her eyes to the neon sign of a restaurant down the street. I took a webbed string bag with a couple of books in it from her hand and gave her my arm as we walked.

She leaned against me as if depending on my strength yet at the same time exciting me.

'The air in the studio was so tiring. I told them to open the windows, but they wouldn't.'

A couple, of cold and senior disposition, regarded us strangely. Instinctively I moved a little away from Helen and she straightened.

'Oh dear, I must try and look fresh before we go in. B.B.C. people often eat here.'

She glanced at herself in a darkened store window and licking her finger, wet under her eyes, then lightly touched her hair as if coiffeuring it into position.

'That'll have to do.' She dropped her eyes over me. 'Comb your hair, dear. Oh, don't you have a comb,' she frowned. 'You should always carry one.' She gave me hers. 'Quickly.'

I handed it back to her as we came to the door.

'Keep it for now,' she said, irritated.

We stepped inside. Helen braced her shoulders back and radiated charm at me. Escorting her to a small table from where we could see the counter and the other tables leading back into the room, I witnessed the effect of her entrance on several interested male faces. At first startled, then admiring, some began to smile when Helen looked their way. She threw small 'hellos' to the back and front of her. I began to feel shy. I didn't belong to this world of Helen's and probably looked as awkward as I felt.

Two men were whispering and regarding Helen with knowing expressions which I didn't like. She knew them and nodded in their direction.

'Who are they?' I asked.

'Producers,' she said casually, and fingering her fork seemed to reflect on it. Helen in a dream was lovely. A softness tinged her features and her eyes emoted love and sympathy.

I put my hand over her moving fingers, experiencing the magnetism of our touch. 'Helen darling.'

She gazed at me and then her eyes seemed to lift over my shoulder to a happy recognition. Her mouth opened in a surprised half-smile.

'Helen Browning!' The smell of hair tonic came to my nostrils as a threat. 'Darling! How many years?' The voice warbled affectedly. 'Two? Three?'

'As long as that?' Helen laughed and held out her hand.

The visitor kissed it with a little swing of the shoulders. His act of continental charm seemed like showmanship. Ignoring me, he concentrated on Helen.

'It was when we were doing "Life's Last Wonder," wasn't it?' she asked.

'I can't remember, dahling, so much has happened since those days,' he smiled.

Helen winced just slightly. 'I heard about you - doing films.'

'Hollywood's dying on its feet,' he shook his head. 'I've come back to have a look here.' He raised his eyebrows and puckered in a mischievous way.

Since I was stirring impatiently and glaring in annoyance at our visitor, Helen introduced me to J. J. Jarvis.

'Don't get up, please,' he shook my hand at such an angle that I had to remain seated. He turned to Helen. 'When am I going to see you?'

'Join us now,' she answered as if highly delighted.

'Uh well,' he held up his watch, 'it's getting onto half-past. My wife... uh,' he nudged his lower lip with a knuckle.

'Oh yes,' Helen said quickly.

'But I'll call you. We'll have,' he looked at me, 'lunch together.' He waved and jauntily strode out.

Helen was amused at me. 'He's only an old friend. Come on, cheer up, dear.'

'But are you going to see him?' I demanded.

'Maybe. I'll see him for lunch but that's all.'

The waitress arrived. Helen sat back with a consolatory smile. I saw her dart a look at the waitress and sensed that they were laughing at me. We ordered, and the waitress went away.

'If I appear jealous,' I said, "I'm not. It's just that I don't like four-flushers.'

'Will you stop it!' Helen said. 'He's an old friend. When you've worked in this business for a number of years you know quite a few people.'

'I'm sorry. I just want you so much I don't like anybody else wanting you.'

She cocked her brows. 'You don't! Well, I shall have to warn everyone not to make eyes at me, shan't I?'

Blushing, I wished there were some way to grow sophisticated suddenly so that I could spar verbally with her.

'I don't mean to sound possessive. Your life is your own to lead.'

She put out her hand and wriggled her fingers for me to place my hand over them. I fitted my palm over hers. She gripped hard transferring the impulse of her attraction into me. Staring with hardened eyes into mine, she seemed to want to clutch onto me yet at the same time reject me. Then her expression changed, and a sad look of pity took its place. She seemed sorry for me, even sorry for herself and the situation we had found ourselves in.

'Let's not talk about it again,' she whispered.

'Okay,' I smiled, encouraged by this show of attention. The pressure of her hand on mine had squeezed sympathy from me as well. I thought of myself as a jealous ogre enflamed over an innocent friendship between Helen and her fellow actors.

Minestrone arrived, steaming. Gratefully we spooned it. With food in us we began to regain our good spirits and Helen told amusing incidents in her acting career. We ordered wine and laughed together, our pairs of blue eyes twinkling at each other, as if we were alone in the restaurant as in bed. Although she was catty about actresses, she spoke of males with deference. Lowering her voice when mentioning an actor's faults or a director's waywardness, she gave the impression that they were all good fellows and apparently rather dear to her.

'Oh darling!' she cried. 'Look at the time.'

I wheeled round to catch sight of a wall clock pointing out eight-thirty.

'Too late for the cinema,' she smiled. 'I don't want to go to a late showing, do you?'

I shrugged. 'What are we going to do?'

She leaned forward and hinted. 'You can take me home.'

The sexual intimation made me grin.

We paid the bill, she more than I because he said she was earning. She didn't ask me whether I had found a job as I expected she would, but she inquired about my finances.

'Now that I have the doctor's rent, you can pay me ten shillings less,' she offered. 'I can afford it, I think.'

I looked gratefully at her. She was constantly brushing against poverty, more recently than in her younger years when her beauty won her roles as the teen-age daughter. And now when the threats of landlord, the harassment for rent money on her new apartment (so much down, so much per month) and the subtle but sure denouement of her career drove her into crying jags of helplessness, she was prepared to stint for my sake.

'Are you sure?' I asked.

She took my arm and directed us toward the bus stop.

The drive northwards took us away from coal-smudged buildings to the residential quietude of old homes and modern apartment houses. A small triangular lawn in front of Helen's red-bricked building of six floors, hastily constructed as a wartime necessity. The switchboard operator called out to Helen as we came in the door. There were messages for her. She read them as we ascended in the lift; a couple she pocketed quickly, the others she mumbled about, 'I must call him first thing tomorrow, this one's useful, this is radio.'

Her door opened onto a tiny hall and straight into the bathroom. To the left was her bedroom, a blue square, and hooking off it to the right by the window was a kitchenette.

She hung my coat in the cupboard which meant that I was to stay the night. If she left it over the back of the chair, it meant that she had to rise early and wanted me to catch the last bus home. Then she came into my arms and we lay upon the bed comfortable in the aura of one another.

'It's a long time since I have known peace like this,' she said.

'I've never known it,' I said, truthfully, for until then I had only snatched love from frivolous girls my own age or younger.

We kissed and petted, gradually inspiring desire in our movements and heat in our skins.

'Let's make love now,' I suggested.

'Oh darling, I was so enjoying just lying here, resting. Wait a while.'

Twisting with impatience, I reached for cigarettes and lit us two. We smoked them to the end, not speaking, just thinking, dreaming, listening to the sighs of wind at the window and sensing the nearness of each other. I pushed my lips over her ear and ran my tongue round and round the orifice and pecked at her neck and smelt the ripeness of her body, mature and molded to be held in my hands.

'All right.' She jumped up abruptly. 'Get undressed.'

She went into the bathroom. I hung my clothes over the back of the chair and climbed between the sheets. My mind seemed to separate from my body as I waited. The ego became a thought solid and self-sustaining. It hovered over my body which lay in fever, waiting to be cured by a touch.

Helen approached, her naked figure lithely moving through the dim lamplight. She stooped to pick up a magazine, her back bent in beautiful symmetry. Her small breasts quivered as she straightened up and tossed the journal onto the seat of the chair which held my clothes. Then smiling wickedly she placed hands on hips and slunk toward me so that I caught the full impression of her firm belly and strong white calves. Clicking off the light she descended on me.

The thought disintegrated as we worked out our passions, as we strove to enflame each other with our want and gradually became infused in one subconscious urge spinning us into blank unawareness of ourselves. At moments we stopped, gasped, and had visions of lovers embracing before we plunged again into mutual annihilation. Her voice called out as if she had been pushed into a void and was falling past the frontiers of reason, until I dove after her, caught her in my soul and carried her back to the safety of our bed.

Turning on her side with her back against me, she put my arm over her tummy and we fell asleep.

In the morning, I tip-toed across the chilly floorboards, closed the window and set the water kettle on the burner. Helen awoke by degrees and managed to sit up as the kettle sang. We stayed in bed to keep warm while Helen made us toast and Nescafe on a stool beside the bed. After breakfast we made love as energetically as in the night and then lay together while Helen told stories of her past lovers in that affectionate tone she employed when speaking of males.

I was never jealous of these phantoms of the past because they seemed to have been superseded by me, as if they were the preceding generation lost on the battlefields of Europe. They were romantic figures and never stepped out of character in Helen's narrations. They were all obviously more adept at love-making than me. But their exploits gave me the ambition to make an impression upon Helen so that when our affair was finished, I would take my place amongst these fallen heroes.

As we grew used to making love to each other, Helen would incite me to try newer ways of expressing our passion. At first amused, then fascinated by her techniques, I felt myself being enveloped with a strong desire for lust which seemed unable to be satisfied, and which drove us on to further experiments, until the whole meaning of our being together was contained in this search for physical pleasure.

For the first weeks when we spent long mornings in bed, I was not aware of our decline from the natural joy of being together to an incontinent pleasure-seeking. Our attraction had remained so powerful from the beginning that it was difficult to notice just when our personalities were completely immersed in our physical need. She kept a spark of jealousy alight in me while circumstances sent her into neurotic tantrums, both moods being superficial replacements for genuine personality. We would come into violent contact under the spell of one of these moods and believe ourselves dynamically involved with each other.

For instance, the man in the apartment above had the habit of walking the floor at nights. His footfalls creaked across the ceiling exasperating Helen who believed that she needed sleep more than life itself. She employed the switchboard and lift operators to stop the man - in vain. She telephoned him one evening and angrily threatened to send the management marching against him. The footfalls continued. In a fit of rage Helen leaped from bed, seized a broom, and thrust its handle in smashing drives against the ceiling until we had silence.

'He has a prostitute with him every night,' she said climbing in next to me. 'I've seen them in the morning going down on the freight elevator.'

When the telephone rang in the mornings Helen might speak for half an hour while I sat propped in bed beside her. The long wait for the call to end was hard to bear. I wondered who she was calling 'Darling' in stage lingo. She would rarely tell me and became upset if I questioned her. Once on impulse I answered the telephone and heard the doctor's voice asking for Helen.

When she finished speaking with him, she showed her annoyance that I had answered by demanding that we get dressed and go about our daily business directly.

'What did he want?' I asked.

'He's going to the country for the week-end and will leave his rent money with you,' she said sharply.

I frowned. She sounded as if she were including me to conceal the reason for the call. 'Have you been seeing him?'

'Would you like me to?' Her eyes blazed. 'It would be quite easy.'

The challenge intimidated me. I couldn't dare risk losing her to another man simply through stupid reasoning. When we parted in the street, she for the studio and I for my writing desk, I realized that emotionally I was deeply dependent upon her. Our love-making had become a way of life, a constant wish-fulfillment. When she limited our meetings to thrice weekly, my waking moments were spent in anticipation of her telephone calls.

If she said she would ring on a specific morning, I would wait all morning and part of the afternoon until she called. I couldn't reach her for I didn't know where she was. I was tied to my room and to the telephone whose wire stretched like an umbilical cord.

There seemed no hope of finding work and so I forced myself to write the play. Helen said that I could owe her rent and save what money I had to buy food. 'Just finish the play,' she said.

The play became a dream of my success, a financial bonanza to spring me out of debt. But with my desire for Helen foremost in my thoughts, I found it impossible to concentrate on writing for more than a few minutes a day. When the four brown walls of my room became unbearable I went into the park, sat on benches, strolled through the long grass, visited the zoo and gazed on caged animals whose suffering corresponded with mine. There seemed no way to get closer to Helen; she kept me distant by telephone. I had no wish to meet other girls or go anywhere without her. My room was my cage and the park was like the open quarters of a zoo where I was allowed to run about for exercise.

The doctor seemed to stay in his room a good deal also. He was waiting to be posted to another British possession. An unhappy exile, shifted from place to place on the outskirts of civilization, he was friendly with me in his sad way. Although once I picked up the telephone to call, and overheard him talking to Helen, I could not believe there was any special friendship between him and my loved-one. Occasionally his girl from the country stayed overnight and took him away for the week-end. I used to discover them having breakfast in the kitchen.

Eric and the other roomer, one of Eric's colleagues at the B.B.C, who shared the top floor, became like strangers. Although we lived in proximity, I rarely saw or heard them. Eric spoke derogatively of Helen when he had the occasion. 'Has the old witch flown by for the rent yet?' When he saw me frown critically, he assumed a sober expression and walked away.

Helen dropped in at noon one dreary day. She had not come for the rent but to leave a case in my room. 'Just for the night,' she said and picked up the telephone. She raised an eyebrow. 'Aren't you writing?'

'I've just been reading a bit,' I said feeling guilty that I hadn't been toiling at the play.

'Oh hello,' she said sweetly into the receiver. 'Geoff darling. Listen dear, just for a moment, call for me at the house. I can't make it home after rehearsal. No, not in time Yes, dear. Bye, love, bye.'

I stared in amazement as Helen replaced the receiver. She saw my bewilderment and frowned questioningly. I was afraid to challenge her lest she kick up a fuss. Above all I could not allow her to see my possessive feelings for nothing irritated her more.

'Are you going somewhere tonight?' I choked.

She nodded and standing smoothed her skirt over her hip. 'An old friend. He's taking me out for dinner.'

Alarmed, I sat forward. 'Is he a producer or director or something?'

Helen laughed. 'No, no, he's a lawyer. He's helping me with legal problems.'

I breathed more easily and must have registered my relief because she smiled coquettishly. 'You didn't think he was another lover, did you. Poor Geoff, he's over fifty, darling. He isn't competing with you. She went to the door. Come and have some sausage and sauerkraut at the pub. I have only an hour for lunch.'

As I followed her, I reasoned that if the man meant anything special to her, she wouldn't have called him in front of me.

'Helen,' I said. 'Let me pay for our lunch.'

She tossed her head back in amusement. 'Thanks dear. I only take from the rich.'

The remainder of the afternoon I spent dreaming of her. We hadn't made love for several days. Surely she needed me as badly as I wanted her. When she came into my room at six, I stormed with impatience.

'Helen! At last!'

'What do you mean?' She stared at me in surprise.

'I've been yearning for you ever since lunch time.'

She laughed. 'We'll have to be more careful what we eat in that pub.'

'No, listen!' I said. 'I'm serious. I need you.'

She pouted a moue. 'That's too bad because I have to be dressed in half an hour.'

Smiling I went to her and put my arms around her, coaxing her, petting her and urging her.

'No! Now leave me alone,' she cried, angrily brushing me away.

I stepped back, hurt and surprised. Sometimes she was contrary but she never refused me when I insisted. I couldn't understand the brusqueness of her attitude and the fierceness of her manner.

As I watched her take off her clothes, I was unable to restrain myself and rushed to hold the firm body in my arms. She walked away, denying me, and I chased her about the room, pleading with her.

'Just for a few minutes. Just for a few minutes, Helen! Please!'

I caught her by the arms and throwing her onto the bed, pinned her down in fun. But she struggled and bit at my hands. She breathed heavily with the effort of fighting free and her face froze into a mask of determination. Alarmed, I let her go immediately, my passion withering like leaves on a limb.

She wiped her hands down over her face and, sighing, stared up at me. 'I wish you had listened.'

'I couldn't help it.'

'Can't you think of anyone but yourself? I'm late. Geoff is coming in...' she held up her wrist and twisted her watch round to see it, 'good Lord! ten minutes.'

'Why is he so important?' I grimaced. 'You've kept me waiting for hours.'

She narrowed her eyes. 'He is a man of business while you are a man of leisure.'

I didn't like the comparison, and I squirmed under it. She would not have said it if she were not furious. I sensed an estrangement growing between us. By forcing Helen to make love, I had stressed the physical over the spiritual, as if allowing the beast in me to run out of control. Perhaps I had earned her dislike.

While she changed into a pink evening dress, I wandered despondently into the kitchen. The light bulb shone nakedly from the centre of the ceiling, leaving no shadows except for the night lurking beyond the window. I heard Helen's high heels click up the stairs to the bathroom. Unfriendliness seemed to creep back down to stand at attention outside the door.

I put two eggs on to boil and went back to the bedroom. Helen's clothes lay scattered about. I picked them up, folded them, and put them in her case, hoping it would please her. I hadn't danced since I had been in England. Helen's evening of dining and dancing channeled like a procession of colourfully swirling pageantry into the lonely night.

A horn blared below the window and Helen's heels swatted the stairs. I picked up her coat in anticipation and held it out as she burst through the door. Her shoulders and arms rounded smoothly out of her dress. A necklace twinkled silverly, and bracelets caught the light as she put back her arms to squirm into her coat. I held her and kissed her cheek.

'Don't,' she said. 'You'll spoil my make-up.' Annoyed, she took out her compact and glanced at her cheek in its mirror.

Hands in pocket, I leaned against the clothes cabinet and watched her gather up her evening bag, close her case, and carry it through the door. She turned to look at me and jammed her case against the door to keep it from swinging closed.

'Have a good time,' I said.

She mellowed. 'Sorry, I couldn't enjoy it, darling. Really, I'm sorry. Ring me at ten tomorrow morning, won't you? I'm a different person when I'm not in a rush.'

'Okay,' I grinned weakly. 'Don't you want to leave the case?'

'I'll take it with me.' She nodded quickly as if she had decided on that course. 'Till tomorrow,' she blew me a kiss and darted for the stairs as the horn blared again. The door swung shut, muffling the sound of her descent. With the feeling of having been deserted, of wretched forlorness, I pushed behind the drapes and stared down at the road. A large black automobile opened a door, and a shape blurred under the misty light passed into it. Helen motored away, taking the pith of my love.

At ten o'clock in the morning, I telephoned Helen. She didn't answer. She must have been sleeping heavily or with cotton in her ears. Rather than wait until she awoke and called me, I decided to go to her apartment. During the night I dreamt of a riotous party in which the guests were falling in love with each other. Only by seeing Helen as soon as possible would I be reassured that she had not fallen for her old friend Geoff.

Although the bus made few stops, it seemed to take longer than usual to reach Helen's apartment house. When I stood outside her door, I listened for any sounds of breakfast dishes. There was silence. I looked through the keyhole directly into the bathroom. Shower curtains hung motionless. The apartment seemed deathly still. I knocked and listened. I knocked again loudly and fiercely. There was no response. The brown envelopes of her morning post peeked out from under the door. I wondered whether she had spent the night out, and whether she had stayed with her friend Geoff. Knocking loudly again, I waited, my ear pressed to the panel, my mind circling about visions of Helen lying with her old friend, her finger to her lips as she waited for me to go.

The door of the neighboring apartment opened and a woman darted a suspicious look at me before ducking back inside.

Suddenly embarrassed, I left the apartment building. I walked in the pale sunshine.

That afternoon, after trying to reach Helen and groaning with heart-sickness each time I failed, the telephone rang.

'Darling?' Helen's voice!

'Helen, where have you been?'

'I slept in Geoff's apartment,' she said simply.

'You what?' I shouted.

'We're shopping now,' she added.

'Helen!' I cried, fury beating at my temples. 'Did you sleep with him?'

'Why yes,' she said. 'But dear, it isn't like us.'

All the producers with their knowing eyes, the actors with their flirty gestures and the old acquaintances stood before me.

'Really, darling, I was too tired to go home,' she insisted. 'Geoff let me sleep in the other twin bed. He was so nice to do it, darling.'

All my old questions which she had resented were stunningly answered. I had been naive, a fool in public places.

'Helen,' I said firmly, 'I don't want to see you again.'

I hung up as she started to protest. I stretched out on my bed and folded my hands over my stomach to press away the ache that had been working in it all day. Helen's betrayal meant nothing compared to the betrayal of an absolute trust which I had believed in. She was versed in the ways of the world and pampered my innocence as an amusing plaything. Clearly she was taking revenge for my behaviour of the previous night by cutting down my romantic ideal with a merciless thrust. I wondered if I could ever stand upright again.

The telephone rang. I let it go on ringing. It stopped and started again. A cool breeze blew through the window and chilled the perspiration on my face. I lurched up and answered. The hoarse voice of an older man asked for me.

'Helen is on her way to you now,' he announced. 'She asked me to let you know.'

It was the mysterious Geoff. I answered gruffly and hung up. Throwing myself on the bed, I cursed him until the strangeness of his call dawned upon me. I had read of women having several lovers. The complacent understanding tone of the man intimated that he was sending our mistress along for my enjoyment - it was my turn. Astounded, I jumped to my feet and tried to think if I could possibly fit into such an arrangement. Could I share Helen? Her figure floated enticingly toward me. I couldn't let her go. But she couldn't have wanted to leave me. Otherwise why would she ask Geoff to telephone me?

Half an hour later Helen was climbing the stairs. I waited listening to her approach my room. She knocked softly and stepped in. She looked distressed, wan, neither as gay nor as young as she had left me. She had lost a certain air of mystery. I felt that I had nothing more to learn about her.

She sensed the change in my manner for she pouted and dropped her case. 'I'm sorry,' she said.

'But why Helen? why?'

She shook her head slowly as if she didn't understand herself. 'I suppose it's because Geoff gives me comfort and affection which an older man has somehow.'

I closed my eyes with shame for my youth. 'I guess I've failed you,' I said glumly.

'It isn't your fault, darling.' She tried to smile. 'Come to me.'

Her arms went out but there was no spontaneity in the movement. It was as if she were acting a role for the 300th performance.

'I don't want you, Helen.' My lips curled in disgust on an impulse to hurt her.

She started as if slapped. Going to the bed she sat down heavily. 'Don't send me away thinking badly of me,' she said.

'I don't want anything to do with you.'

'Darling, please understand.' She drew a hand across her brow and sighed. 'I love you. I haven't left you.'

'But I can't share you,' I said. 'You have to be mine, all mine.' I slammed my fist into my other hand.

'It's impossible,' she protested. 'You can't own a person. You'll discover this one day. You can't have anybody only to yourself.'

The difference in our ages carried its total of experience in her voice. It reminded me that we had met just weeks ago - how could I assume that we belonged together?

'I can't bear to be hurt again, though. I've had enough,' I said.

She looked sadly at me, the rouge like red plasters upon her whitened face. There was a stillness, a deadness. We seemed to be at opposite ends of a raft as if prepared to step off into a watery grave.

Suddenly she fell onto her knees and put her arms about my legs 'Don't leave me thinking ill of me. I never wanted it to end this way.'

I stared down at her. 'But you left me!'

She put her cheek against my kneecap. 'No, I didn't, darling. I hoped you'd understand.'

I tried to break away. 'I don't know who is more of a romanticist, you or me. But I'm not going to be just one of your lovers. Call it false pride if you want but let me go.'

'No, I won't!' She tightened her grip. 'Please understand, please.' She began to cry.

For a moment I stared at the brown wallpaper, its design of criss crosses looking austerely emblematic. Memories of my desire for Helen began to infuse me with warmth. There was no denying that I wanted her. The essence of her pressed against my legs and invaded my groin. I looked at her until I could not restrain from kneeling and caressing her face and throat and then kissing her strongly. She lay back and I came over her. She closed her eyes and I kissed them and her neck. The sadness gave way to a joy. We began to recognize us as a part of one another, or perhaps I saw myself in her, as if traits of my personality underlined the features confronting me. As I sank into her, we clutched each other with sobs of happiness, with gratefulness for the healing power of reunion. Only a shadow of doubt remained like a dark ray across my thoughts.

The ray broadened when Helen claimed she was too busy to see me during the next week; it broadened to cast me into despair. The joy of seeing her had long gone but now the pretense which had taken its place appeared in all its folly. She had imprisoned my emotions yet rejected my being. I returned to her because only through her could I experience the throb of life, the passion of living, Although I yearned to see her and told her so, she put me off until Saturday morning. Fearful of repeating the experience of the past week, I didn't telephone but went directly to her apartment.

She opened the door in her dressing gown, a pattern of green leaves on yellow. The spring sun lit the apartment at her back.

'It's you,' she said. 'I thought you would ring.'

'I was afraid you'd say that you didn't want to see me,' I smiled.

'Well, to be frank,' she pursed her lips, 'I'm busy writing a script and I have housework to do,' she paused as if she expected me to apologize and depart. 'So I'm very busy.'

'A script!' I said, surprised. 'Since when have you been writing?'

'Oh, I've done some but its just for money,' she said. 'I don't write for art like you.'

The sharpness of her tone hurt me. It sounded almost like a reprimand. I owed her many pounds in back rent and while we were waiting for my play to be finished and sold, she had written several for tidy sums.

'But how do you sell them?' I asked in amazement.

'A friend produces for the overseas broadcasting,' she said simply. She was enjoying my reaction and sat on the bed, pulling her gown primly over her knees, to tell me of her success. 'I skim through a biography of a famous person and describe the main events of his life in dialogue and add music or poetry depending on whether he was a musician or a poet. It fills up half an hour and after it is translated into Arabic or Hindustani or some such language, its taped and sent overseas. They pay quite well, really; I mean for the small amount of time it takes me.' She smiled.

I writhed inside. 'Do you think its possible for me to do something like that?'

She shook her head, and gazed in amusement at me. 'He has a lot of script writers, dear. You stick to your play and preserve your talent.'

'But how am I going to pay my debt, Helen? My play might not even be sold. In fact, it probably won't be,' I said desperately.

'Well,' she shrugged, 'you'll have to keep trying like everyone else.'

'I wish I had friends like you do," I mumbled.

She stood. 'I have to tidy up.' She looked at me. 'You'll have to go.'

'But I've been waiting all week,' I cried.

Throwing back her head, she grimaced at the ceiling and then turned to pull up the bed sheets.

'I'm putting the sheets in the wash.'

'Wait until after we make love.'

'Geoff slept here last night. I've had quite enough loving for a while.'

Her words did not startle me. The bland atmosphere of the room and her disinterestedness had forewarned me of disappointment. I felt as if a truth which had been expected were at last announced.

Sensing that I had been forced into a role, I took her by the shoulder and turned her to me. 'I'll go then, Helen, but it'll be for good.'

She nodded and smiled slightly.

I went to the door expecting her to call to me to stop. I fumbled with the knob and turned round in the doorway. She watched me with amusement. She seemed glad that I was going.

'Is it really finished?' I asked.

She nodded.

'Oh Helen!' I ran back to her and held her to me.

Gently she pushed me away. 'I have a lot to do today,' she said.

I whirled, head held high, and plunged along the hallway, feeling defeated, useless, unwanted.

For a week I lay dispirited in my room, only going out to fetch food once a day. Helen's smile and her naked body haunted me. Sexual longing accentuated the emptiness of my soul, the vacant look of my room. Occasionally I heard the doctor's footsteps on the stairs. The sounds of other people, of traffic in the street, used to instill me with poignant loneliness, but I had come to accept being alone as my lot. The blankness around me had invaded the pores of my body so that I was sustained as a mere object in space.

Then I noticed that only one pound remained of my savings. I went into the streets and wandered hopelessly. The thought of buying a big dinner lingered invitingly at the back of my mind. An opposing thought that I would be wasting food that others could eat began to combat it.

A small thin man in a black uniform brushed against me. I turned to watch him hurry towards a taxi. He was carrying suitcases. He looked unhappy, but he was working, he was of some use. I went into the railway station and found the station master's office. I secured work as a porter.

By walking to and from work and scrimping on meals, I was able to save a pound a week. I was always away when Helen called for the rent so I left the money in an envelope and found a receipt when I returned.

I tried to make love to another girl. She was attractive and willing. We ate in the same restaurant and struck up an acquaintance that developed into a walk in the park and a visit to my room.

As we undressed, Helen kept appearing before me, as if taking delight in the performance she was about to witness. The girl had a full, provocative figure and lazily reclined in bed, waiting for me. I climbed in beside her and kissed her and tried to woo some spirit into my lifeless flesh. She glared at me curiously.

'I can't,' I said. 'I can't make love.'

Without a word she left me. I wanted to stop her, apologize, try again, but I watched her dress and go to the door. She wrinkled her nose in disgust. She made no sound descending the stairs. I heard the front door open and slam and then knuckled my fists into my stomach to relieve the pain of failure.

This experience decided me to go back to Helen. Somehow I had to persuade her to make love with me again because it seemed the only way to regain my manhood. I remembered that I had left a book in her apartment and I called her to ask for it.

Her voice carried all the vitality of our love back into me. Just hearing it gave me hope. It was Saturday afternoon.

'Come before six,' she said. 'But be on time because I'm going out.'

I arrived at a quarter to six and tapped apprehensively at her door. She opened it with a bright smile and waved me into the bed-sitting room. She was wearing her dressing gown. The pleasant sensation of seeing her in the flesh made me realize that I had missed her a great deal.

'You look beautiful, Helen.'

'Thank you, but I haven't been feeling well.' She sat carefully on the edge of the bed. 'I can't offer you coffee. I'm going out right away.'

'That's all right,' I said humbly. 'I'm just glad to see you. Can I stay a few minutes?'

Sticking her tongue in her cheek, she transferred her clothes from the chair to the bed. I sat down sensing that she suspected the real reason for my visit.

'The book is on the shelf beside you,' she pointed.

I made no move to take it and she cast a surveying glance over her person as she folded her hands on her lap.

'Is the work heavy?' she asked.

'It's all right,' I said. 'I get enough to eat.'

'Sometimes I think of you, you know.' She crossed her legs so that the gown fell down either side of them, exciting me.

'I miss you, Helen.'

She stood up and patted my shoulder affectionately. Her hip brushed against me as she turned away. 'These things don't last as long as we'd like them to sometimes,' she said softly, and added, 'You can stay awhile but I'll have to begin changing.' She went into the bathroom.

'I can't like another woman,' I confessed. 'I can't get you out of my mind, Helen.'

There was a long pause. Then I heard her sigh and she appeared in the hall. She took off her gown revealing her beautiful nakedness, and hung it in the cupboard behind her. My heart in my throat, I quickly stepped up behind her and buried my lips on her shoulder. She shrugged me away and confronted me with a reproachful look.

'I thought we'd finished with all this.'

'Helen, I need you badly.' A groan came from the pit of my stomach.

She put her hands on her hips and with legs apart as in a stance for trunk-bending exercises, she regarded me. When I tried to clasp her waist she beat my hands away. I stood towering over her, charged with longing passion, but unable to express it.

'You had better go,' she said coldly.

My stomach whirling, I backed away and slumped against the wall. 'Geoff will be here in fifteen minutes,' she announced.

I winced at the name and gritted my teeth in an effort to conquer the weakness rendering me powerless to move.

'Helen, can I kiss you before I go, please, Helen, please?'

With a twinkle in her eye she said, 'If you promise to go right away.'

'Yes,' I swallowed.

She came up to me, her breasts pointing at my chest, her shoulders thrown back, and her head up. 'But don't touch me,' she warned.

As I bent over her, my hands hovered by her flanks, itching to grapple her to me. My lips pressed against hers, which were hard and dry, but before I had tasted the slightest income of my desire, she spun away and stepped back.

'That's all you get. Go away now,' she said.

I hated her. My hate leaped violently into my head, in my hands and along the muscles of my legs. I had an impulse to squeeze her neck until it softened like pulp between my hands.

'Well, go on,' she frowned. 'I have to get ready for Geoff.'

The short body with its painted face became an object of revulsion. I went out the door and quickly along the hall. My one intention was not to meet this man, Geoff, for fear I would want to kill him. With a wad of bills and a pat of his chubby hand, he had transformed my dream of romantic beauty into an obscene joke.

As the spring sun grew warmer and the calendar moved into May, I recovered from the shock of my last meeting with Helen. I took short walks in the park and gazed upon the fountain mermaids who curiously seemed to have endured the same torment and whom I began to regard with sympathy as I would a friend. During the week I worked at a fast pace carrying luggage and slept soundly in the nights. My despondency showed signs of disappearing altogether; for days I was able to forget Helen. There remained, however, the uncertainty of whether I could make love again. Was the rightful inheritance of a young man to be denied me simply because of a fixation complex or whatever psychologists might have termed it? I was not willing to risk a further humiliation by experimenting with another woman. Somehow, to win back my confidence, I had to make love with Helen. I didn't know how to persuade her and rather than cause more disharmony between us, I refrained from seeing her in the hope that providence would arrange that which cunning dare not.

Then on Friday after I came home from work, I found a note from her. She explained that she was relinquishing the house in two weeks' time and coming by on the morrow to make an inventory of the furnishings. Could I give her the money which I owed for back rent?

I counted up the bills I had saved and discovered that they totaled ten shillings over the sum. The knowledge gave me satisfaction when I thought of Helen. I felt as if I had bid my way out from under her paralyzing influence.

On the morrow, Helen knocked and came into the room. She carried a pad and pencil and wore a house smock. A cool breeze wafted the spring fragrance through the window. Morning showers had given way to a sunny afternoon, and so it was in an ambiance of munificent gladness that we greeted each other. I put down my book and stood to the side of my chair so that she could inspect the furniture.

'I suppose you'll be like Eric and complain that I haven't given enough notice,' Helen said.

'There's a house down the road with a room for rent,' I said. 'I can move easily.'

She looked surprised. 'You don't mind?'

'Of course not. I have my rent paid up also.' I gave her an envelope. 'It's all there.'

With raised eyebrows she took it and leafed through the bills. 'You have been working, haven't you! I thought you'd never pay me.'

'You see, you were wrong,' I said.

She smiled sadly, her face drawn and tired-looking. 'I have been cruel to you, haven't I, darling?'

'Not at all,' I laughed. 'I've been cruel to myself.'

'Will you forgive me?' She came to me and worriedly brushed her hand across my forehead.

'I can't forgive you until you release me.'

'Release you?' she puzzled. 'What do you mean?'

'It's easy to understand.' I walked over to sit on the window sill. 'Take back your magic love potion by which you entranced me.'

'Do you still want to make love to me?' she smiled. 'I'd let you if I weren't afraid it would start another romance. And I can't afford it. You wore me out. I was sick for weeks with pleurisy on account of you.'

'Me!' I laughed in surprise. 'You've made me sick for two months.'

She bit her lip in thought. 'Do you think it would do me some good? I've been nervous recently. A rash has come out on my ear.' She drew herself up, inhaled deeply and regarded me with a warm dreaminess. 'You might help my rash, calm my nerves.'

'I guarantee that I will,' I said seriously.

She held out her hands to me. I came to her and took them. There was a look of quiet acceptance in her expression.

She rested her head against my shoulder for seconds, then stood back and smiled broadly.

'Come to the apartment. You can help me carry over some parcels.'

I followed her expectantly yet warily. At the last moment she might turn against me and, like a wicked temptress, keep me thirsting at bay.

'Oh just a moment. I must see the doctor before we go.' She rushed up the stairs.

I was about to call, 'don't be long,' but checked myself on remembering that she took any excuse to be perverse. After about five minutes, during which I fretted and wiped my perspiring palms, I heard the doctor's door open and his voice cheerfully assure Helen that he was moving to the country. She descended, smiling happily at me, like a love goddess preparing to reward this poor mortal for his faithfulness.

We sat without speaking on the bus. She watched the buildings flit by while I regarded the clean-cut lines of her face and looked away if she seemed to become aware of my gaze. I suppose she was musing over memories of a life that had led her "in and out of every bed across Europe," quoting her words, to romantic trysts with handsome sophisticates throughout the Middle East. By a fetching look, by their mere physical presence men had caught this girl's heart and used her body until their passion died; men were her experience, her dreams, and her consolation. Vaguely behind the aura of the male rested a picture of an eighteen-year old actress starring sensationally in the West End and a once-bright hope burning like a lost jewel in the irrevocable past.

When we passed houses fronted by short lawns, she tensed, waiting for her stop. She opened her hand on her lap and slowly brought it over onto my hand and squeezed while she looked piercingly into my eyes. Then she flipped her hand back to her lap and slowly opened the fingers, as if she were releasing a captive spirit to the air.

I wondered then why she was giving herself to me. Was it for pleasure? or was it for the sake of our happy moments together? or was it a sacrificing to expiate the guilt she may have felt? Perhaps it was all three. She entered the apartment breezily and pointed to one corner where I set down the shopping bags.

Her blue eyes danced up at me. 'Well, let's get it over with, shall we?'

The atmosphere of the apartment which I had known for so many nights and mornings and from which I had been exiled for two months entranced me with its perfumes and its disarray. Helen's abode reminded me of a pencil sketch half-completed, which could be said to stand for the very intimate side of Helen also. Sensing almost as if I had returned home, I undressed in the bathroom and waited for Helen to call. Lotions and medicine bottles were pushed together on a glass shelf over the basin and a bath towel sprawled from the tub onto the floor. Strangely, I suffered no misgivings, no fear of impotence. I smelt the breath of spring as it drifted round from the sitting room window. Then I heard Helen's voice and I moved into the room and stopped at the foot of the bed. Helen lay naked, her arms stretched up for me.

As I took her in my arms I made love with a strength that had been conserved for weeks. There was voluptuousness and excitement, but the spirit, which had enkindled our bodies to a translucent unity, was gone. I laboured over her, delighting in her cries of exhaustion, repaying her for the pain she had given me, and rejoicing in the powers of my manhood, miraculously returned to me.

When at last I came away from her, she raised herself weakly on one elbow and glared at me. 'Now that you've fucked me,' she said angrily, 'what else do you want?'

Stunned, hurt, yet grateful, I said nothing, and, dressing quickly, I left her apartment and strode briskly into the late afternoon sun. Invigorated yet not without a faint underlying sadness tinged with regret, I walked for blocks and cut through the park where I saw the fountain mermaids, healthy, passionate creatures, water splashing about them, symbolizing my freedom from Helen. I headed for my room to arrange for my immediate release from the house.

On the Monday I moved to the rooming house down the street, after leaving my address behind so that my post could be forwarded. I settled in at once and put up a writing table as before. The third act of my play read as if it had just come to life. I began working on it in my spare time.

About a week later, the landlady said that a 'Miss Helen Browning' had telephoned. I didn't return her call. Several times afterwards Helen was reported to have telephoned, but I never spoke to her again.

(New York City, 1960)

CARAVETTI

"Une erreur dissipee nous donne un sens de plus."--Proust

I.

Caravetti felt the round form of the shoulders and slipped his hands under the arms and along the clay sides. Deftly his fingers touched the swells and indentations of the male figure. He glanced at the young man standing in front of him, surveyed the near duplicate beside him, and lifted his hands to the face to begin a gentle moulding of its features. The sun waned at seven o'clock, glimmered over the tops of a group of short trees and fell into the garden where the three figures stood, two motionless and the third working silently.

In the lane outside the garden walls some small children were playing with a ragged sandal. It was the type some of their people wore all the year round; a straight sole of woven hemp with black cords to fasten it to the ankles. The children had made up a song about the sandal which was the attractive element in the game, although only the words "*alpargata mas barata*" were distinguishable. The narrow lane led down-hill to the main street of the town. This was the street with the wide sidewalk, which boasted the shopping district.

Although the townspeople of San Bernardino found everything they needed in the dozen stores of the town, the few tourists who happened to sojourn there preferred to shop in Izina, the cosmopolitan centre of the island. There the houses fell together over narrow streets cut into the side of the hill where the old town descended from behind its Roman wall to mix with the shops, banks, pensions, and white squatty houses of a newer age.

San Bernardino attracted a smaller number of tourists because of its parochial dullness. Retired people who preferred a quiet atmosphere, like the Spanish artist whose bald head had been licked dry of ideas by the flaming sun and who enjoyed taking admirers about his garden plots before allowing them to see work he had done thirty years before, were fixtures of the town. The fishermen were content with the catches surrendered by the waters off the coast there. And the farmers knew their land was more fertile than on mainland Spain. Nature painters liked San Bernardino for its flowers which bloomed mani-colored near the little river that trickled coolly on hot summer days under the old Moorish bridge before sliding into the salt blue of the Mediterranean, warm and sloppy against the low rocky shore.

Caravetti preferred San Bernardino to any other spot he had known. That was the impression he gave to those who found him wandering along the shore or on the hillside. He was a painter, it was said, who could achieve fame and perhaps fortune in one of the large cities of the world, yet he remained in little

San Bernardino selling his canvases at small prices to tourists and friends. Artists, who visited the town and quickly fell under its spell of lethargy, waited for the rainy season so that they could throw off summer stupor and leave the island to do some work. They thought Caravetti mad to live there the year round; when they saw him painting they went so far as to call him a masochist.

"Almost finished, Pedro. Patience."

From where he had sat down on a stone garden stool Pedro smiled handsomely. "It'll soon be too dark to see."

"Only five minutes more of your charms," laughed Caravetti.

"You know a lot of American songs, Caravetti. How'd you learn them all?"

"One cannot live in Paris without being subjected to juke boxes a l'Americain. I studied there two years ago and I haven't recovered yet."

Pedro laughed loud and easily. It was easy to make him laugh because he was amused at everything he did not understand. "But you must have learned something."

"Yes, you see what I'm doing to your nose now. I'm giving it the Rodin slant. If I were doing a group of figures your nose would carry the rhythm on to your fellow." When he saw the credulous expression on his model's face, Caravetti shook his head and laughed. "I'm joking. As most people were crazy over Rodin's sculptoring, I was against it. I suppose an artist must always train himself to hate the mode of the moment if only in self-defence. Unless he wants to be dragged away from developing his own expression, only to reproduce the art of another force because it happens to be momentarily stronger."

"But why not? What's wrong with that?"

"Because for me 'momentarily' is a killer. It can last from a second to a century and then it is completely forgotten. There is no way of labelling it with time. If it lasts a century, it has controlled two or three generations, and sometimes, if it lasts for a second, it has enough force to influence the same number of people and the same number of years. So you see it really doesn't matter how long it lasts according to man. The main idea is to stay away from any momentary thing altogether."

"How do you expect to learn about a thing if you don't give yourself momentarily to it?" asked Pedro.

"When you run away from something you're giving a part of your energy to it in defending yourself, and a part is enough. If you give your whole you only become confused because you lack comparisons. Besides, you always learn more about a thing when you're running away from it than when attracted to it, because you're more aware of it."

Pedro swore he would not get into any more discussions with Caravetti. His head was beginning to ache so that he shifted uneasily on his stool.

"All right. We're finished for today. We have only a few more touches to make before we advise your senora to buy it," Caravetti grinned.

Pedro stretched his muscled limbs and followed Caravetti into the house. For sheer beauty of male physique Caravetti could not have found a better model than Pedro, save perhaps himself. But then Caravetti was slightly more angular and his features spoke of individuiality while Pedro had the roundness of youth and a face that had been ascribed to so many Hermes and Mercurys that it was more or less classic.

Pedro stretched his legs into a close-fitting pair of blue trousers and pulled a sweater over his head. The sleeves had been cut off at the shoulders to show off his arms, and the sweater was a brilliant yellow to offset the clear complexion of his face and his dark brown hair. They were standing in Caravetti's studio, a large room with two large windows looking east. The best time to work according to Caravetti was between sun-rise and breakfast; and the breakfast hour depended on how interested he was in working. He valued the light in the morning. In the afternoons he used the garden as his workshop until twilight. Then in the studio he would switch on the electric light he was fortunate to have and either talk to a visitor or read from one of the books heaped untidily in a corner of the room. Tonight he turned on the lamp beside the one comfortable chair in the room, chose a volume about an Italian architect, and sat down to read.

But Pedro seemed loath to go. He sat on a wooden chair opposite Caravetti to watch the artist who was immediately engrossed in his book. The light fell on Caravetti's head like a speaking trumpet of transparent gold. It bounced off his curly black hair, fell on his cheek bones, missed the rest of his face until it ticked at his chin, and then enframed his shoulders. His nose was long and sharp, a throw-back to Roman ancestory. His eyes looked intelligent and were always alive, conscious under dark finely-cut brows. His sharp features had a fierceness about them that became attractive when added to the quick movements of his lithe, athletic body. There was no doubt that Caravetti was good-looking. Age could merely carve a few thoughtful lines on the beautiful bone structure of his face. And his body seemed chiselled from rock, undiminishable once formed.

A few of the painters who visited the island would ask if they might portray him. But Caravetti would laugh and shake his head. "Why waste your time trying to paint me when you have all these beautiful hills and rocky coasts around you?" Once, when an Italian friend he had known in Paris visited him, he almost let himself be persuaded. But then recovering from the joking mood of acquiescence in which he found himself, he shook his head violently and fell into silence.

"But you're not only depriving the world of a pleasant representation of this age, you're depriving me of what will perhaps be my best portrait," admonished his friend.

"A face of this age will be no different from a face of another; as for you, I'm truly sorry," he smiled. "But I remember Paris too vividly." His voice betrayed a grief that terminated the subject.

"Well, Pedro, what's on your mind?" he asked without looking away from his book.

"I'm wondering how much money we can get from Senora Cosmos for that statue of me. I know if I talk to her the right way you can get a fair amount."

"Why do you care? I'm paying you for sitting and I want only a little for myself. I don't suppose it's worth much anyway."

"I'm hard up for money at the moment, that's all. She won't be giving me any till the end of the month. I know that from experience. But if you could ask a little more and then give it to me, I would do the persuading."

Caravetti laughed. "All right. We'll see what we can do. Come out and we'll find a drink."

As Caravetti put on a blue pullover, a comfortable addition against the cool night air, Pedro asked. "Why don't you want more for yourself, Caravetti? That's a lot of work."

"The finished statue has no value to me. I'm only happy to get it out of the way for the price of a few meals," he said.

"Not complimentary to me," laughed Pedro.

"Oh you can stay as long as you want. It's just your statue that I can't stand," Caravetti smiled. "But come along and I'll buy you a drink in town," he added as he went out.

The path leading from Caravetti's room to the town ran down the side of the mountain for a short distance before breaking into the main street. A few electric lights shone from some of the open Bars. Caravetti and Pedro entered the first one. Several fishermen were sprawled on chairs about two small tables. They nodded as the two men passed them to reach the bar. Weak lights in the ceiling glowed hazily. The owner rose from one of the tables to pour the drinks Caravetti asked for. The atmosphere was quiet and poor like the town, like the people.

Presently some young farmers came to stand near them. They lived about twenty minutes walk from the town and found the time to come for a drink only in the hour before dinner. The men were tall for Spaniards. They looked ragged in cotton shirts and soiled trousers. Their faces betrayed a hard life with plenty of determination. Pedro joined in their conversation. The men were careful to exclude Caravetti, but Pedro was a favorite with them. One of them suggested that they move on to another Bar. As Pedro was enjoying himself, he agreed to go with them.

"Thanks for the drink, Caravetti. I'll see you tomorrow afternoon again."

A feeling of detachment, as if pushing a piece of lumber away from the shore into the current of mid-stream, and then a sense of regret, as if wishing that the lumber would float back to shore, touched Caravetti. He smiled and held himself back; the pride that came from somewhere in an unknown past masked his face with rigidity. His aloofness could rebuff any slights the townsmen might make to him. Pedro, he knew, was unconscious of his part in the ostracization.

Caravetti finished his drink while he faced the backs of the fishermen. Ignored, he walked into the street. A half-moon gave him light to see his way back to his house and his books.

2.

The sun leapt through the east window and shone off Caravetti where he lay in bed. As the studio brightened he stirred slightly and opened his eyes to the landscape he had left on the easel the day before.

"Distorted piece of lunacy," he growled.

His disgust came more from despondency than from anger. The last time he had been happy about one of his paintings seemed long ago. Too long ago. By selling the odd drawing he managed to make enough to live. If he couldn't sell something, Juan would always take it for the price of a few meals. Caravetti owed much to the short, chubby-cheeked chef who ran the best restaurant on the island. Juan hung Caravetti's work on the walls of his Casa with other paintings left by grateful artists who had found that the value of their pictures depended on how many meals their pride would let them take in return for them. The more the artist esteemed his work, the more free meals he took from Juan. Caravetti, commissioned by Senora Cosmos to do Pedro's statue, now felt liberated from further obligations to Juan. It was a state of pleasant independence to be able to lie in bed and contemplate walking into Juan's Casa order a coffee and rolls and know the bill would be paid with cash and not an oil canvas. To breakfast at Juan's Casa was an excellent idea. There was a freshness about it. He would wear a clean white shirt and eat soft brown rolls. His cluttered studio would pass into temporary oblivion.

With a conscientious effort he swung his legs out of bed and stubbed his toes on the cover of the book he had been reading the night before. But he knew he could not escape from his schedule of work without a twinge of conscience. Even as he walked down the path toward the main street, he allotted himself the number of minutes he would stay before returning.

"*Buenas dias*!" Juan sang out in a happy tone from behind the long bar of his cooking shed. His brown eyes laughed at Caravetti 's unexpected arrival.

Of the very few people to whom Caravetti could speak or at least who would answer when Caravetti spoke, Juan was the most cheering. The little man used a variety of comic expressions. He could adapt himself to the humour of a wealthy guest so that the bill was always a pleasant offering. And he had the dignity of a great comedian - an endearing manner with the approach of an artist. But the real character of his restaurant was the preparation of the food. His artistry was renowned throughout the islands.

"L'artist!" he cried.

Caravetti grinned at him. "Sold anything of mine?"

"An Englishman took the small landscape."

Caravetti laughed. "You mean San Bernardino from the shore line?"

"Of course, he was slightly inebriated at the time. The money's inside. I'll give it to you."

"No. Keep it. It's yours, my friend."

Caravetti took the black coffee and stirred it until it clouded a muddy brown.

"And Pedro's statue? Is it finished?" asked Juan. "Senora Cosmos talks about nothing else. She's mad about this boy. You should get a good price for it."

"Is Pedro still playing about as much as always?"

"Of course. Last night he met a German tourist here. Within half an hour she couldn't say no to him."

Caravetti took a final swallow and smiled good-bye. He left through the courtyard and strolled into the alley which took him up the hillside.

Pedro was as cavalier as they came, he thought. Every woman attracted him. It was merely a chase, and the conquest was followed by someone new. In a way Caravetti wished he were like him. Pedro was never tied down because his spirit carried him away to greener fields. If Caravetti were like that, he would not be in the mess he was in now. He would have no Maria to worry about; no obligations; no torment; only release. "Oh hail, blithe spirit." That was it! If he could be another Byron scattering women as Shelley's west wind scattered leaves.

"Grotesque, Monsieur! Grotesque!" That's what Monsieur Turnier would have said. That old, bald-headed sensible art teacher. The Monsieur could make anyone and anything look silly. Disdain had been one of his constant and most successful attitudes. If Caravetti could have been as cynical about life as was his venerable Parisian mentor, he would be secure now; perhaps even happy. He supposed disdain of life brought content within the mind; one would begin to value so highly whatever one had that outside occurrences would look pitifully insignificant. But then in matters of love, life was certainly special. A man cannot be practical, ruthless, hard-hearted, he argued. Love had no meaning if it were stopped as soon as it began. The pleasure of eating a fine meal did not stop with the first mouthful; one savored it long after one had finished. He winced at the comparision: his love to a fine meal. He shook his head. Sentimentalist. Some men's brains are linked too strongly to their hearts. He imagined that was the difference between Pedro and himself. Pedro did not need to rationalize his actions and could fearlessly engulf himself in dangerous circumstances. Man was helpless against circumstance; it little mattered if the heart was there or not. It was only that some people did not worry about it like others. Again he wished he were like Pedro.

"Hi, Caravetti!"

A yellow sweater detached itself from a group of fishermen sauntering towards him. Pedro's bright smile contrasted with the sullen glances shot at him by the men. "Why don't you come fishing with us?"

One of the fishermen growled and the group passed by.

Caravetti smiled cynically. But his smile was a front. He wanted to be one of them; he wanted to row with them, to pull up the nets, to swap stories under the hot sun, to see the skies crimson as they toiled for home.

"I've got work to do."

"Oh, come on, you're always working. You're like a hermit."

"It's discipline, Pedro. I'd never get anyting done if I went out with you all day."

Pedro laughed good naturedly. He respected hard work as long as he could stay away from it.

"I know. I've been telling the senora what hard work that sculptoring is. She got talking to some Englishman about a painting of yours. He told her you were the greatest living Spanish artist. She'll pay anything you ask now."

"Don't be too sure. She's not a business woman for nothing." Caravetti mistrusted optimism. He could see no reason for being optimistic about anything.

"Well, hold out for good money. I need it." Pedro slapped him on the shoulder.

"You'd better catch up with your friends," Caravetti suggested. "They're leaving you behind."

He watched Pedro run quickly after the fishermen until the yellow sweater disappeared behind a white wall. He wondered whether the time were right to wait for Maria. She would probably be sending her maid to market again, but there was a chance she would come herself. He remembered the days when she would take the market basket and announce they were going to have something special for dinner. Her cupid face would smile like a Michelangelo cherub, blissful with traces of knowing peeping from the eyes. Long black hair accentuated her youth. Her slim body wrapped sveltly in printed silk brought summer to him and with it vapors that emerged from the past and reached him now in nostalgic scents. He could almost cup her soft brown cheek within the palm of his hand. He could see her brown arms swing gracefully in the sun.

Maria had fulfilled the promise of a bride to her husband. She had given him contentment; that is, until he left for Paris. One of Maria's relations in Barcelona was responsible for winning him an art scholarship to study a year at the Beaux-Arts, and so he had left Maria with their son and baby daughter. He had not the money to take his family with him, but the opportunity was too wonderful to miss. Art called louder than paternal duties. He was deaf to any objections Maria tried to raise. "What is a year?" he had asked as if it were a week. When he left her, the bliss had faded from her Michelangelo smile.

Caravetti stopped beside a short wall, perched himself upon it, and, turning his sharp features, he squinted under the brightness of the sun at the gate to his wife's house. He had not long to wait. The gate opened and a woman carrying a basket stepped into the lane. It was Maria. He watched her descend the path with her head down watching her footing. When she was close to him, he jumped to confront her in the middle of the path.

"Maria!"

Surprised she stopped and stared at him. Then, sullenly, she looked in his eyes. Her face would blacken the sun, he thought.

"I want to talk to you." Caravetti's voice sounded incredibly humble coming from his proud visage.

Maria began to walk again but he would not let her pass.

"We've said all we can," she retorted flatly.

"I want to know about the children," he said as if it were an excuse for stopping her.

"Well?"

"I want to know how they are feeling. They aren't sick?"

"No." Maria's tone was heavy with sarcasm. "I didn't know you could be concerned about them."

"Maria, believe me, I want to come back to you. You must take me."

"Let me pass."

"I want you; more than I ever have."

"That is not enough." She pushed by him.

"Don't make me plead after you. I've suffered enough humiliation in the eyes of the people of this town."

The note of nobility abasing itself stopped her. Fixing her eyes on him again but backing away when he tried to approach, she waited for him to speak.

"Give me a chance to prove my good faith. I promise you everything."

"Did you give me a chance?"

"But, for God's sake, give me some hope?"

"How much hope did you give me for two years? How much thought did you give me? How much money?" Embittered she mouthed the words as if she had repeated and repeated them until they were recorded in her brain. She turned away and walked quickly downhill.

Caravetti felt the sharpness of her tongue. Slowly he closed his eyes on her retreating back. The hopelessness of his situation hung about him like a large black question mark.

Turning, he walked up the hill. As he passed her house, the home that was once his, where he had seen his parents die, he strained to catch some movement, to see a sign of his children, but the front was as quietly impersonal as a Parisian monument, and he felt the barrier of time that had come between himself and the front gate.

A hill woman, clothed in black shawls, glanced up from under a humped back and then quickly studied the ground again as she walked by him toward the town. Caravetti recognized her as a distant relative. Because the island people had been cut off from mainland Spain for centuries the families had intermarried so that almost everyone was related to everyone else. It was a happy union. There were no family feuds. The land was fertile enough to keep everyone satisfied, and the Church had been responsible for keeping everyone together as "brothers". But it was the Church that had turned everyone against him, Caravetti reflected. No relative ever spoke to him now. He was a sinner; a breaker of orthodoxy. Yet he had wanted to be one of them; he had not looked intentionally for an outlet; he was no rebel. He had merely seen the futility of it all.

Whenever he tried to approach Maria it was this sense of futility that opposed him. Nor would she listen to reason. The question seemed beyond that; or above it. Yet he had to win her love again or at least her confidence. Some force within drove him to seek her forgiveness and his repentence.

She had been a mainland girl and a stranger on the island when he had brought her there to live. Yet within the two years he was away she had so won the affection of the islanders that she was able to turn them against him. Though it was not really her fault. That was why he could not hate her; that was why he had to love her.

As he pushed through the door of his studio from the sun-baked dirt to the cool tiled floor, he sought relief from the tragic emotions that had embittered his past and resolved his present. When he returned from Paris he thought he would find that relief on the island, that piece of land which was a piece of himself, surrounded by invincible fate. Soon he discovered that his sorrow became more unbearable, for often in his solitude memories of his love in Paris swept over him without mercy, driving him in upon himself until his soul threatened to break, and he yearned to end his life, to become as cold and unfeeling as the tiles under his feet. If he had fled to live elsewhere he would most certainly have killed himself. What kept him alive was the succour the island gave him and the hope that he might live in the comfort of his family again.

Life left an unsavoury taste in his mouth when he woke in the mornings. In the afternoon his body felt bloated with the excess of living, and night opened before him like a grave-pit. His art and his dreams offered temporary refuge from this feeling of satiety; the open countryside helped even more. But most of all, his memories, by torturing him, forced him onward to make his peace with Maria, thus giving him a reason for living.

His memories acted like a paradox. They told of the destruction of one life at the same time that they provided the force to create another. Caravetti's torture was the combining of both these lives in one passionate body.

The dampness of his room struck at him like a wet cloth, bringing him to his knees before his bed. Hopelessness swam dizzily down from his head to his stomach. A bridal gown flashed in his eyes, and the distant sound of churchbells brought a swelling to his throat. Abruptly, he pushed himself up, stood away from the bed and shook his shoulders as if he wished to throw off his thoughts like heavy coils about him. The room seemed as sombre as a tomb. He stepped into the garden to a chair in the shade of a tree. The chant of a church processional reached his ears, and he frowned angrily. When he rented his room, he had taken the crucifix off the wall and hurled it into the sea. In the same manner he had gotten rid of his religious beliefs several years before.

A fixed set of rules needed constant testing, which belief did not permit, he thought. And as an artist he had been obliged to do the testing. The crucifix and the processional no longer belonged to his world, except in one way, as a compelling reminder of the black vacuum of the past, which, since Paris, he had been sinking into gradually, just as he was being drawn into the black eyes of Maria's soul.

The statue of Pedro, with its classical lines formed through generations of experiment, stood up against Caravetti as a representative of this past. Caravetti would have smashed it if he could have forgotten that it provided him with bread. He would have liked to destroy the supernatural hold that Maria had over him too. But she was as necessary for his spirit as bread was for his hunger.

He slumped in the chair in the shade and covered his face with his hands. The core of his being still lay in Paris and perhaps always would remain there. His pursuit of Maria was meaningless when his experience in Paris was overlooked. Yet by making his peace with Maria he felt he would be justifying somehow those two years of bright warmth, of treasured freedom from the drab, conventional little island, freedom which he found through love along the banks of the Seine. He never questioned the need for its justification – that was implied with implacable force all throughout those years and all throughout his very being.

The voices in the Processional chanted loudly as they passed along the alleyway outside the wall. The top of the cross appeared above the stone for a moment while the clang of cymbals spelled solemnity. Caravetti covered his ears with his hands and wished only to be allowed to forget. Maria seemed so impossibly out of reach. He yearned to be able to drift until he came to lodge at some bend in the stream where the gentle splash of the water might heal his wounds and count off the days remaining to him. This struggle upstream was too much for one man alone. If at times that phantom of a girl did not appear to help him, he would have drifted into downstream oblivion, for he won his strength from knowing that he was not alone.

3.

The island bus, its gray tin speckled like a lake trout by the sun shining through the branches of the trees in front of the café, waited with doors open like pectoral fins, swallowing black-shawled women with bundles and boxes. Caravetti stopped by the front of the bus and made an impatient gesture at Pedro who extricated his arm from the fat grasp of Senora Cosmos and sauntered to him. The Senora flicked her pony tail so that it swished capriciously across her bull neck.

"Bring him safely back to me," she shouted. She smiled knowingly at Caravetti and shifted her heavy body into a chair so that she sat squarely facing the bus. Several fishermen sat down at her table. They knew that when the bus had gone, they were assured of free drinks.

Pedro directed Caravetti to a long bench on the bus where two senoritas had seated themselves. As the bus was a series of extended partitions from the hood of a Model T, there were four doors along the side, one for each segment. Pedro could sit beside the girls and know that they could not move elsewhere unless they stepped from the bus and entered into another partition. It was not until the bus was ready to leave that he squeezed against them while apologizing for the bus being so crowded. Cranked, the motor sputtered to life, and the bus moved slowly over the road. Caravetti glanced behind to see Senora Cosmos sadly pouting at Pedro's fraternization.

"Tourists eh! Caravetti, they're tourists." Pedro turned happily to him. "From Valencia."

"Valencia, huh!" Caravetti was not interested. He had retired from that game of youth. He did not want to shout above the rattling of the bus to keep up a conversation, to pretend interest in superficialities in the hope of striking at the one basic interest. But he could enjoy watching Pedro, he thought.

"So you are going to Izina just for the day. My friend and I are too; just for the day." Pedro had pivoted himself to a key position so that he demanded the attention of the women.

Looking from the window on his side, Caravetti counted the telegraph poles. Ploughed fields stretched out from squat farmhouses. Bamboo thickets and fir trees sometimes lined the road. A mediterranean breeze seemed to sweep the clouds in the morning sky. Occasionally the bus passed a woman carrying washing or a farmer leading a mule. All of the tourists in the world could not change the serene, complacent life of the island, Caravetti thought. A crowd of tourists were like butterflies hovering about a flower-bed. Strong, autumnal winds blew them away, while the natives, rooted to the soil, lived in their traditions unaffected by their summer visitors.

He looked at the other women in the bus. They were swathed in the black gowns that the Moors had decreed for their women and although they might have envied the cool, colorful sundresses of the girls, they kept to their tradition. Not to do so would have been unthinkable.

Caravetti glanced at the pretty, bare-armed tourists. He wondered how much the native women envied them for Pedro's attention. He sympathised with the Izina women and yet he was glad they remained unchanged. They gave him a feeling of permanency, where time could bring no outward changes. He had once fled from that feeling into the new world of the individual, but now he began to admire what he had left. The harbor of Izina bent like an archer's bow before him. The town tumbled in white-walled houses down the hill sitting massively across the water.

Pedro turned to speak to him. He glowed with animation. "The senoritas have agreed to let us show them the more interesting parts of the town," he winked.

"I thought we were going to get some oils and canvases."

"Oh... I mean after that," Pedro said.

"And then drink at Peppino's with some of the boys."

"The girls can come with us," Pedro urged.

Caravetti shrugged his shoulders.

The bus stopped squeakily at the square amidst swarms of market-goers. Heavy carts wound awkwardly up the street as drivers tried to miss hitting bearded artists strolling aimlessly with market baskets amongst the traffic.

"Look out!" Caravetti warned as he grabbed the wrist of one of the girls and pulled her from under a horse's nose. "Those wheels are big." A two-wheeled cart, looking like its Roman progenitor, crushed the road beside them.

The girl leaned against him, caught her breath, and smiled. She was extremely good-looking; a dark-skinned Andalusian whose passion lay almost visible under the skin.

He took her hand. "Come. Let's catch up with Pedro and your friend."

As he guided her, unexpected happiness surged within him. His head swam with the emotion. Bubbling mirth rose to his ears with the delight at being able to pull a woman by the hand and to have her docilely, willingly follow him; it was as if he were a boy with his first love ready to burst into freedom, positive he would conquer inhibition. Momentarily, for the first time, he was happy.

"Pedro, turn right," he called.

As they entered the Art Shop he slapped her playfully on the behind and followed her exaggerated wiggle through the doorway.

Pedro was delighted to see the sudden change in his friend. He urged him to make a quick purchase so that they could be on their way.

"Leave that stuff here; you can collect it on your way back."

"That, my dear Pedro, was what I intended to do," Caravetti smiled.

The senoritas were delighted to find that Caravetti was an artist. They exclaimed shrilly with wide open eyes. Although Caravetti was slightly scornful towards them, he was, nevertheless, attracted to their femaleness.

By the time they climbed the hill where they overlooked the flat roofs of the houses and the glancing blue of the Mediterranean, the sun hung at its zenith. They retreated into the dark cathedral with its Gothic dome, and they stared through the inner blackness at the dimly-lit figure of the crucified Christ suitably wearing a white skirt out of respect for Spanish chastity.

Caravetti disliked the atmosphere of the place which he considered superficially mystical. He had been away from the Church too long to succumb to its spell. The others with serious faces knelt before the altar and when they returned to the heat of the mid-day, they laughed unconsciously as if they had been delivered of a burden. Caravetti was a sober figure by their side. Not long ago he would have enjoyed the simplicity of their happiness, but since his tragedy, he almost wished that he could have been made happy with them. Anything to obliterate the past, to revel in the present.

They ate lunch in a pension that overlooked the sea. Slight breezes lifted light strands of the women's black hair. When the woman that was with him, for he had ceased to look on them as girls, leaned over her plate, he glimpsed the naked lines of her breasts over the top of her dress. She was no more than twenty, he imagined. It seemed so long since he had been with a woman.

The red wine energized their talk and encouraged their sympathy. Presently Pedro suggested to his girl that they siesta in an alcove. Caravetti did not notice their departure. He had his forehead pressed in the neck of the Andalusian and the two of them had fallen asleep in the merciful shade of a vine-covered trellis.

"Hey, wake up! It's after three." Pedro shook Caravetti.

Handsome Pedro and his smiling senorita stood behind transparent curtains which opened as Caravetti awoke.

"We'll have only a couple of hours at Peppino's," Pedro added.

The Andalusian leaned her back against Caravetti's shoulder and stretched her bare arms symmetrically towards the intruders. Caravetti tried to picture her in a painting by one of the Impressionists, but he could think only of movie posters in front of Parisian cinemas. He thought it was a healthy image.

They woke a waiter, paid him for the meal, and descended to the lower section of the town. Here, in the narrow streets, people began to appear in doorways, dogs sat up sleepily against the houses while their masters were going through the same movements on the other side of the wall. Groups of bohemians had already gathered in Peppino's Bar. Unshaven northerners, siesta time was drinking time to them. A pale young man greeted Caravetti. He was sitting alone and so they joined him.

"Buenos, Enrico," Caravetti smiled. He noticed that the young man was much thinner than when he had last seen him. His tuberculosis had ravaged him.

"What are you all drinking?" Enrico asked. He was very generous. Caravetti guessed that he knew he did not have long to live.

Three painters came to their table; a Swede, a German, and an American. They wore trousers cut short below the knee. That was their way of getting round the Spanish prohibition of shorts. They began quarelling about the merits of a painter who had lately gained public recognition. That he had gone commercial they all agreed. Caravetti loved this sort of talk. It was his only connection with that part of the outside world he cared about. They spoke in English except when Pedro and Enrico came into the conversation when the foreigners had to make themselves understood with a mixture of broken Spanish, groans, and pliable faces.

Caravetti glanced at the women. They seemed to be enjoying the excited talk and the anarchic atmosphere. He gazed at his Andalusian, sitting curvaciously next to him, and she returned his look. He knew he would take her home; that she would come with him. When he smiled at her and nodded about the room as if asking her what she thought of it, she laughed at him and reached out affectionately for his hand.

Pedro's girl was trying to look disagreeably unresponsive to a barrel-chested male who had fixed his eye on her form half-way across the room. Pedro glared at the intruder with no effect. Both Pedro and the girl stirred uneasily in their seats until Pedro could stand it no longer. He called out defiantly to the man. The anger in his voice cut through the midst of the talkers, stopping them.

The other man rose from his chair. Young and bearded he looked tall and powerfully-built. He was an American who lived in the bohemian fashion yet he made no pretensions at being artistic. "I don't need you to tell me where I can look and where I can't."

Pedro stood to answer him. "Don't you?" He smiled lazily which implied that he did.

The beachcomber took a step forward but Peppino, quietly determined, detained him by one arm. With the thumb of his other hand cocked the man motioned for Pedro to join him outside. He was bigger than Pedro and his savage looks gave him a psychological advantage over Pedro's handsomeness in the eyes of the on-lookers.

"Beauty is about to be bashed by the Beast," an Englishman remarked loudly enough for the room to hear.

The two men took no notice of the laughter. They demanded an outlet for their anger and walked quickly from the Bar. No one followed them. The conversation recommenced and the room was lost in it as before. Only the slight quivering of Pedro's senorita was an indication that they were fighting outside.

A quarter of an hour later Caravetti saw the beachcomber approaching. The man's beard was spotted with blood. His face, which glistened from a fresh wash, was cut and bruised. As he walked toward the girl Caravetti stood to face him.

The American attempted to push Caravetti aside but the painter grabbed the man's arm and twisted it behind his back. So quick was the motion, so intense was the pain that the man could utter only a small cry before he found that he was stumbling into the sunlight. Caravetti walked back from the doorway and told the senoritas that it was time for them to leave or they would miss the bus. He shook hands with Enrico who prolonged the grasp as if he feared it might be for the last time.

"Come soon again, Caravetti. We all like your company." Enrico wisely had not mentioned Maria in front of the senoritas, but now he added, "They're all a lot of dumb bastards in San Bernardino!"

When they were in the street the senoritas insisted on looking for Pedro. They were afraid he had been badly hurt, perhaps killed. But Caravetti, smiling at their fears, led them through the market place where the cries of the vendors made them look round expecting to see Pedro hailing them. When he stopped off at the Art Shop, they paced impatiently while he picked up his parcel. He took them finally to the town square where they found Pedro reclining on a bench while he ate a bunch of grapes.

Probably, Caravetti mused, Pedro, remaining true to character, forgot his anger after suffering the first blows of the fight, and having shown a face of bravery before the women, he retreated to a safe place. Now he awaited his reward with confidence for he knew the heart of a woman. He waved cheerily at them. Although his clothes were torn and his forehead wore a band-aid, he seemed otherwise unhurt.

"Sorry, I didn't go back to the Bar to pick you up," he apologized, "but I didn't 'come to' until a little while ago."

His senorita put her arms around him. So as not to hear the confession which followed, Caravetti and the Andalusian boarded the bus which had drawn up near-by.

"Thanks for taking care of that fellow, Caravetti." Pedro and his girl climbed into the seat behind.

If Pedro was acting true to his character, Caravetti had forsaken his. To pick up women and brawl over them had never been a part of his life. The day seemed like light phantasy through which he tap-danced in unfamiliar steps, yet he was thoroughly enjoying it. Every moment carried a deep sense of drama, heightened in tempo by his strong attraction for the woman beside him. He wanted to love her but a blade-cold restraint began to whittle at his zeal as the bus started along the San Bernardino road. The grace of her figure, the smooth, warm feel of her skin, the beauty of her features attracted him as strongly as ever, yet the intimacy they had enjoyed seemed to be over-shadowed instead of increased. Caravetti felt he was losing his love for the Andalusian, that what had promised to be an affair was simply a brief encounter. He pressed her hand and she, sensing that he was troubled, held his hand in both of hers.

Strange how his mood had altered, he thought. Surely he was insane if he parted company with this beauty, yet a subconscious warning urged him to be rid of her. His mood had sailed along in harmony with her charms until the beachcomber stepped forward to challenge their peacefulness. He fixed the moment of change upon the incident with the beachcomber. The man seemed to symbolize the intervention of fate forcing him back into his regular way of life, as if reminding him of a duty that he owed to others as well as to himself.

He had sidestepped the intervention and easily propelled the intruder away, yet he could not so easily rid himself of the impact upon his conscience. Where would his attraction for this girl lead him? An affair with her was aimless because he had set a different course long ago and now it was too late to turn aside from it. The beachcomber may not have struck his skull but he had well succeeded in making an impression upon his thinking.

Pedro clapped him upon the shoulder and leaned forward to whisper in his ear. “Let’s arrange to meet them tonight out of sight of the townspeople.”

“Why?”

“Aren’t you afraid of Maria? And think of my position.”

Caravetti laughed. “Your position?” He shook his head. “You arrange what you want.”

His senorita stared at him with lustrous brown eyes. He felt guilty. He should not have encouraged her, he thought. Frowning in anger, he reflected upon the grueling task he had set himself. Beauty of the flesh could not save him from it, but rather make it harder for him after his pleasure was past. In this senorita he might drown his troubles for a few days but he could not anchor them in her. Soon they would be sorely conspicuous again and he would suffer for attempting to escape them. The intrusion of the drunken stranger upon his idyll proved how suddenly the blissful mood could be destroyed. Reaching to the side, he cupped the girl’s long dark hair in his hand and sadly let it slip through his fingers.

When the bus drew up under the trees in front of the café, Pedro saw Senora Cosmos walking jauntily, swaying her huge hind parts, toward it. Whispering to his senorita that he would see her that night, he jumped from the vehicle to run to the Senora who gasped with concern at his ragged appearance.

Caravetti took the tourists back to their hotel. Pedro’s senorita, smiling, went straight inside to leave her friend alone with Caravetti. Several farmers passed near where they were standing and spat. Caravetti knew that he could never see the girl again. He tried to explain to her. But she did not understand, and, turning contemptuously, she strode away.

He watched her slim body disappear into the hotel with regret and frustration. Strangely the image coincided through dark shades of emotion with the retreating figure of the girl he had known in Paris.

4.

Caravetti pushed the brush into others lying on a shelf and, stepping back, looked at his painting. Disgusted, he grunted. He was attempting to paint a view of the narrow lane from his window but the work looked out of proportion to him. One house seemed too large for the scene although he had repainted it several times. Often he wished he could paint the wide open stretches of land, the fields, the mountainside, or the shore of the sea as he once had done. But he had no heart for it. He seemed to be anchored to the job of doing little streets with their little secrets; the poverties of those back lanes where mothers nursed children, where teen-age girls scrubbed over boards, where blind men sat in doorways, and the miseries that had lived in the lanes since their construction. With this feeling heavy upon him he was forced to paint them, yet he could not.

"Like a third rate Utrillo," he cursed. He thought of the painted scenes that sold for a couple of hundred francs at the stalls in the Montmartre. Tourists would buy them to take home and show friends. He imagined them saying, "See. This is Parisian. That's real art!" He looked at his attempt and repeated, "See, that's real art," and sadly shook his head.

On an impulse he walked to where his canvases were piled against the wall, thumbed through several of them, lifted one out and set it up on his easel. Then taking a high stool to a distance he sat down and gazed at the portrait of a woman.

The sun streaming in the window lit sparks in her brown hair. Her face was turned so that she seemed to be looking at someone who was standing to her left. She wore a man's shirt open at the collar. Its blue stripes were the colour of her eyes. Her hair was cut short so that it curled up before reaching the collar. The haircut accentuated the curve of her cheeks, held firm by high cheek bones. Her face was more oval than square, but her chin, delicate in its lines, tended to firmness. "Mother says when I'm middle-aged I'll look terribly determined." Her small nose and the nobility of her brows were distinctly northern. But her mouth with high arches of the upper lip and the fullness of the lower could only have come from the Mediterranean. "And do you know what they used to say to me in High School? 'You slay me with those lips, you do'."

"If I could only paint like that now," Caravetti muttered aloud.

"Gee. If I could only draw like that." He turned to see her standing behind her own easel but leaning sideways from the hips so that she was looking at his.

He laughed. "You're joking. Mine's not very good."

"What are you? Italian?"

"No. Spanish."

"El Greco was Spanish. Or was he a Greek turned Spanish?"

"Picasso is Spanish. Is that a help?"

"That depends on you. Is it?"

Caravetti looked at his drawing. "Not much."

She laughed. "You speak English well. How'd you learn?"

"I've been in Paris over six months."

"But this is France."

"I speak with more American G. I.'s than French because it's so easy to make friends with them. And, there are so many."

"I know what you mean. I've met more G. I. Billers on painting scholarships than I thought there were soldiers in the World War."

"But you are American?"

"Yes. How'd you guess? Did my lil' ol' south'n accen' give m' way?"

"No. It's not your accent," he smiled.

"Say! We only have five minutes left and it's the last time we get this girl. Excuse me."

He watched her sketch. Her hand played easily on the paper. Firm, bold strokes. Her tongue tucked itself in the hollow of her check, then slowly licked round the arch of her upper lip. She used no lip-stick which made her more beautiful and more desirable in his eyes.

After class as she was gathering her papers together, he tapped her on the shoulder. “Would you like a coffee with me?”

“Love to, but not now.”

“Why not?”

“Because there’s a very handsome man waiting to take me out to dinner and I must hurry home to dress up and make him think that the money he’ll spend was worth it.” She smiled. “Awfully sophisticated aren’t I? But you’ll be here tomorrow?”

“Yes.” Caravetti felt his answer was a compensation, but he did not know why. “Yes. I’ll be here tomorrow.”

“I’ve just started the class and I like it. What’s your name?” she asked as she started to walk away from him.

“Caravetti. And yours?”

“Barbara.” And she was gone.

“Come in, Barbara, and bring the snow with you.” Caravetti opened wide the door of his room.

“I can’t bring in any snow. You live so high up that it all melted by the time I got here.” She breathed her words in small gasps.

“Don’t let it worry you,” he laughed.

“Your American slang is getting better,” she frowned. "I’m beginning to forget that you’re Spanish. I almost asked your concierge where the American painter lived!”

“Did she give you the right directions?”

“Well, she said she didn’t know anything about a painter but she said that an awfully cute Spaniard lived on the top floor, fifth door on the left.”

“I’m glad you thought it was me.” Caravetti put his arm about her. It was the first time. He felt the curves of her figure, the pliability of her back, float before his eyes. He wanted to hold her close to him, but he took his arm away.

“Where are the paintings you were going to show me. I want to know just how good you really are.” She walked to some canvases leaning against the wall and pointed at them. “Are these the ones?”

Caravetti walked over to them and began to place them about the room wherever he could find a support. “I’m sorry the room is so small, but it just fits me and no more. I have a shelf for my books and a big window to paint by. That’s all I need.”

“Is your bed soft?” she asked. She looked mischievous.

“Soft enough for me. Would you like to try it?” he grinned.

“No thankyou. If I lie down after climbing those stairs I’d never get up again. But that’s good. Where is it?”

"The island where I grew up in the Mediterranean. You can see a palm tree at the side."

“It looks beautiful. I’d like to visit it.” Her eyes were bright with sincerity.

“Perhaps you will.” Caravetti stared at her back but she did not turn round.

“And what are these paintings? They look surrealistic. I especially like this one.” She centered herself in front of it. A Roman acquaduct was depicted carrying a stream of skeletons from a background of caves and stunted trees to the same scene except that the ground was paved with gold coins. Some skeletons had fallen off the acquaduct and were praying to it. Others, having arrived safely, were watching them from the edge of the gold pavement. "What does it all mean?" Barbara frowned.

"It's just an idea I have. I'm trying to say that the past is with us in the present. No matter how hard we try, we cannot escape the past. The acquaduct carrying the skeletons along the stream of life is really a bridge of hope spanning past and future. Essentially the ground on both sides is the same except that the future glitters superficially in wealth. The new land is fashioned after the old. Those skeletons you see below have lost hope and are praying for themselves. Those others who have already arrived in the future are wondering why the ones at the bottom are praying when they could climb the hill and get back on the acquaduct. There is nothing more deceptive than progress and nothing which disheartens people quite so much. Perhaps you can see what I'm getting at."

"Well, a bit." She bit her lip. "But I think you should leave it alone."

"Why?" he asked surprised.

"Because if you become too intellectual you forget how to paint. Or painting forgets you."

Slowly Caravetti reached forward and took her chin between his thumb and forefinger. "You know too much." Then he noticed the rougeless lips and brought his to them.

Willingly she embraced him. It was as if it has been intended. Caravetti firmly believed in fate.

"Do you want to go to bed?" He gently whispered it in her ear.

She reared back and smiled at him. "Certainly, silly. You don't think I'd come to a man's room if I didn't, do you?"

And in everything she did, it was as simple as that. There was no pretence, no false pride, no egotism; and yet she was practical. "I believe in looking things in the face and calling them by their right names," she said.

"But how do you know that the names you are giving them are the right ones?" Caravetti loved to tease her.

"Intuition, I guess. Anyway I'm standing by what I feel is right – with my own eyes, my own ears and my own brains. I know it sounds D. H. Lawrencey but still!"

"Who is D. H. Lawrence?" Caravetti had seen the name on a book prominent on Paris bookstands, 'L'Amant de Lady Chatterly!'

"Don't you know him? He's the man who put the life back into English literature; and probably into some English people."

"He sounds like a medicine man."

"Oh you!" she expostulated as she shoved her coffee cup away from her.

The sun, like a half tomato, floated in the winter mists over the Luxembourg Gardens. From the window of the café she saw the agent's white stick flash. The movement was heavy; small cars and Vespas scooted through the larger traffic; their engines roared in imitation of speed. Pedestrians walked quickly; their forms appeared suddenly large against the glass and then receded to be followed by others.

Turning to Caravetti and laying her hand on his, she looked into his eyes. Her voice was intimate. "I've been your mistress for a month now, and, do you know, I just discovered that I love you."

Caravetti took her hand in both of his. "That's nice to hear," he said.

It was then that Caravetti started the portrait of Barbara. They had pooled their resources and rented a furnished apartment on Rue de la Seine. The apartment house was not fashionable. One had to pass from the street through a grassless court yard where the one distinguishable monument, as Caravetti remembered, was an empty oil drum. The stairs were wide but rickety; they were hardly ever cleaned, and on entering the hallway the aspect was of dust and cobwebs. They lived on the first floor overlooking the street. It was not the quietest spot they could have found, but it was the cheapest.

Barbara had received money from an international scholarship organisation, which was to last one year; she had spent it in ten months. She received small sums from home and gave the odd lesson in English. Occasionally she sold a painting but it was never for very much. She made only enough money from her sales to buy more oils. But she found she was attractive enough to be taken out for meals several times a week. That is until she met Caravetti. When she lived with him she was expected to keep up her own end of the partnership without any outside help. Caravetti was poor, and he was jealous.

Once, when she had stayed out one evening without warning him and then did not return until early morning, he was furious. He heard her get into bed, but he did not trust himself to speak to her. In the morning he said nothing and that evening when they had both returned from classes, he acted sullenly.

Barbara had spent over the budget to buy the essential to cook a good dinner. She was using the old recipe of attacking a man through his stomach. But Caravetti had little appetite and could eat only small portions of what she gave him.

"What's wrong?" she asked, although she knew.

"I don't think we ought to live together any longer."

His statement frightened her because this was the first argument she had had with him and she did not know how to react. Impulsively, she took the cue. Live dangerously, she thought. "Perhaps you're right."

Caravetti was surprised. He had expected a different answer. Perhaps she really did not love him. He wondered if the other man were a fatal rival.

"Who were you with last night?" He was angry.

"A man. He took me to dinner and then to a night club." She dug her fork into a roasted potato.

"And then?"

"And then he brought me here and said good-night."

"It sounds very platonic." Caravetti spoke sarcastically but it did not become him and he knew it.

"You don't mind my getting a free meal and saving us expense at the same time do you? Besides I like some fun." Her accentuation of 'some' was peculiarly feminine and particularly irking.

Caravetti was hurt. He felt his heart sink; and a large bubble of air filled in his throat. Barbara noticed his look with horror. She had not realised how ruthlessly common forms of speech could sound when they fell on ears that were not accustomed to hearing them.

Jumping up from the table she ran to his side. The awkwardness of having to round the table filled her with a dragging sense of time. It seemed as if Caravetti could get up and walk away while she was still running to him. But then she had her arms about him and she kissed him until the man of stone turned into the man of emotion and strongly held her to him.

"I didn't mean it; you know I didn't mean it. I never want to go out again with anyone but you."

Taking her head in his hands, he looked into her face lined with concern. Slowly he rubbed at the lines with his long strong fingers until they disappeared. Then sliding his hands down so that they clasped her throat and his thumbs propped up her chin, he placed a kiss across her lips.

"Will you be a good girl if I paint your portrait?" he asked.

"But I am a good girl." Her blue eyes became round.

"Then I'll start your portrait tonight. Will you sit for me?"

"Yes, if you say you're sorry for getting angry with me."

"I'm sorry. I was jealous," he smiled.

"That's funny," she laughed. "When I refused to kiss the guy, he said he would never see me again."

"So, I guess you are doomed to Caravetti," he added whimsically.

"So, I guess I am doomed," she smiled.

That first spring they took long walks together. Paris is made for long walks but especially so in the springtime. The new leaves on the trees along the boulevards shiver in the breezes that are still tainted with the freshness of winter. The sun beats warmly on wide sidewalks and along the avenues. The parks bloom with tulips, daffodils, narcissi, and magnolia blossoms. Cafes break down their partitions of glass and the world is sitting *sur le trottoir*.

They would stroll by the Seine and stop to sketch a scene that interested them; an old man with pigeons; a bookseller and a customer; a fisherman, a long pole, and Notre Dame. On Sundays, Barbara fixed a lunch, and they spent the day in one of the woods; across La Pace de la Concorde, along the Champs-Elysees, L'Avenue Foch, to the Bois de Boulogne they journeyed in search of a spot where no one encroached on their privacy, where a picnic was a paradise.

They walked a good distance into the wood when Caravetti pointed to a small clearing just visible from the path. There was no one very near it; the last couple they had passed were sprawled in oblivion twenty yards away; they approached it on tip-toe expecting to find it occupied.

"No. We're in luck. It's ours for to-day." Caravetti was happy. He set the sketch books by the base of a tree and helped Barbara spread the rug. They had everything in the basket; sandwiches, coffee, fruit, paints, brushes, pencils, books.

"Darling, you should have let me pack this. It's in a mess. Come and help me find the food." Barbara was parting the goods on top to the side and peering into the basket. "Never mind. I see it." She pulled out a thermos and a paper bag that contained their lunch and put them to the side. The time was mid-morning so that they had a while to wait before eating. Caravetti wanted something to eat then, but she would not let him.

"You're like a child, a great big child in long pants. How old are you, Caravetti?"

"Twenty-eight. How old are you?"

"Twenty."

"You're very young to be wandering about the continent by yourself." He chucked her under the chin, and she, smiling mischievously, let him do it.

Taking a sketch book, he sat down and propped his back against a tree. Caravetti was always in good humour when beginning a sketch. Barbara knew this from experience so that she started to question him about things that had not interested her before.

"What town were you born in, darling?"

"Oh, a little place called San Bernardino. It's not very big."

"What was there to do on the island? Did you have many sports when you were young?"

"The town's on the water. I swam a lot; deep-sea fishing, sailing, the usual things."

"I bet the girls were pretty."

"Some were."

"Ah, those beautiful Spanish girls with their dark and flashing eyes. Did you ever like one especially?"

"Yes," he said. He looked up from his sketch at Barbara. "I married one."

Barbara paused half-way between embarrassment and curiosity. "Are you still married?"

"Yes, and I have two children." His voice was calm.

"But..." she stammered. "Caravetti, you should have told me."

"Why? I don't see that it makes any difference."

"But what about me?"

"What about you?" he frowned.

Her disappointment sought and found his sympathy. He wished then that he had not told her. He took her by the shoulders and looked straight into her teary eyes. "Barbara, don't cry. It's you whom I love."

"Do you? But how could you?"

"How could you love me?" he asked calmly.

"But it's different. You're married."

"That other woman is my wife in name only."

His obvious sincerity made her eyes brighten in wonder. She threw back her head and laughed. "This is a completely new idea to me. What does your wife say about it?"

"She can't say much about what she doesn't know. Besides the role of a Spanish wife is to do what her husband tells her. I know that the roles are often reversed in America."

"That must be it." Laughing she bent forward and kissed his cheek. "We American women are spoiled." Suddenly she sat back. "What does she do about money?"

"She has enough money of her own to keep her, I think. We agreed that she support the family on what she had while I was in Paris." Caravetti was getting bored with the subject and he began to sketch again.

"But you don't seem to write her. I haven't seen you receive any letters from her."

"I didn't give her my address. Occasionally she writes care of the American Express where I can always pick up the letter. Why don't you just sit still where you are now. I want to try sketching your mouth for the portrait."

One night every week or every two weeks would be devoted to Barbara's portrait. Caravetti liked to paint it slowly because he said the painting was important to him. Barbara was amused at the pains he was taking.

"My mouth today and my soul tomorrow," she philosophized.

Caravetti took the painting down and placed it back among the other canvases. She had not lost her soul to him; he had lost his to her.

He had no desire to start again at the street scene. The morning was half-gone. He decided to walk. The path by the shore would serve his mood. He loved to see the waves lap the rocks. Perhaps the water would be rough. He hoped so.

5.

Pedro waved to him as he was crossing over the main street. Caravetti waited for him. The youth's face swam with good humour.

"How did it go with you?" he asked. "Mine was as sweet and fresh as a melon."

Caravetti shrugged his shoulders. "Mine didn't go anywhere." And in reply to Pedro's raised eyebrow, he added. "Naturally it couldn't. Not when I'm trying to patch things up with Maria."

"She's hopeless! Why do you want to go back to her when there are so many other women around?"

"I'd like to know the answer to that. Probably because I want to see my children and I feel it's where I should be."

Pedro parodied the sad tone. "Let's all drown our tears in buckets of beer. Come on, I'll buy you a pernod; the senora's been getting generous lately."

They crossed through Juan's dining room where Caravetti noticed that no more of his paintings were sold, and entered the small bar to the side. Pedro called out and immediately Juan, his cheeks like peaches, pushed through the coloured chains in the doorway from the courtyard. A fly found its way in with him, but Juan seizing a swatter killed it on its first landing.

"Oh me! It's always the bar-top," the little man groaned as he felt under the counter for a cloth.

"Aw, leave it there," Pedro said. "I've never seen anybody so clean."

Juan scooped the fly into a basket and polished the bar-top. He was proud of his reputation for running the best restaurant on the islands. He knew that cleanliness attracted the tourists, those Germanic tribes from the north.

"You want flies in your wine?" he asked Pedro. "Like you get in some country grocery?"

The pernod stood greenish-yellow in two tall glasses, the colour of small elm in autumn. Caravetti remembered the tree-lined boulevards of Paris.

"Senora Cosmos said she'd come round to see the statue," Pedro smiled. "I told her it was finished."

"I'll be home tomorrow morning."

Juan looked up at Caravetti under dark eye-brows. He polished glasses as he spoke. "Maria was here today," he said. "She brought some wine."

Caravetti looked closely at him. "And…?"

Juan placed a glass on the shelf above him. "She said she heard that you had taken up with a tourist staying at the hotel."

Caravetti shrugged his shoulders. "In this place you're liable to hear anything."

"I told her it wasn't true," Juan said.

"He was crazy not to," Pedro added. "Weren't you?"

Women's faces surged through the painter's thoughts, but they were all superimposed over the head of Maria whose steady gaze rebuked him through them.

Pedro could not see why Caravetti had had no luck in winning back his wife. He himself had little trouble with women. He suddenly felt generous. "Maybe you're using the wrong approach," he suggested. "Why not let me talk to Maria? I'll explain to her exactly the way you feel about it."

Automatically Caravetti shook his head. Maria was his problem and only he could find a solution. Even if Pedro had managed to persuade her of his sincerity it would have meant nothing. He had to clear his own conscience.

"Let him try," Juan encouraged.

Caravetti smiled. "Okay. Tell me what happens." He was certain Pedro would fail.

Pedro swallowed the last of his Pernod. "I'll see her tomorrow for you." He brushed his hand through his hair letting the dark brown strands weigh against his fingers. "It's getting late," he said, "and I've got some work to do."

"Don't overwork," Caravetti warned. "Mama might catch you one of these days."

Juan and he watched the confident stride and the brown arms part the hanging tinsel in the doorway as Pedro disappeared into the waning light of the day.

"I'd better leave you too," Caravetti said. "So you can cook your dinner."

"Your dinner, you mean," laughed Juan.

Caravetti turned at the door to watch the little chef walk behind the cooking bar in the courtyard where he began to lift down huge frying pans from heavy hooks. Juan had donned his chef's cap; he looked officially comic.

Caravetti pushed through the hangings and stepped into the street. A quarter moon made a crest in the sky. Senoritas were walking and chatting; their arms were linked comfortably; their skirts rustled against their limbs. He smelt faint traces of perfume and he watched the full bodies sway in soft curves and the slight gestures of feminine hands. Walking at the side of the road, he found a lone table outside a Bar where he sat clothed in the semi-darkness. People walked by not seeing him. Some strode quickly, in contrast to the slow pace of the senoritas. An old woman, gowned in black, a stick across her shoulder, shadowed three goats as she did at the same hour every night. The high-pitched lisping voice of a small boy chanted a popular song from one of the houses across the street. "Ro, Ro, Ri, Rola," the refrain hung in the night air. All sound had a peculiar resonance. It was as if the night were made of small hollows. Caught in one hollow, a sound quivered there until released into the next. Caravetti sensed the solitude of the night fall on him, leaving him isolated from the movement and the sounds about him. The crest made by the moon might have been a peeking hole through which someone could watch the turnings of the world for all time.

Two old men walked slowly down the centre of the road. Caravetti distinguished the black robe and the round tummy of the priest who had returned from South America. Born in the town, he had left it when a boy. And now he was back, walking with a boyhood chum, a tall, pleasant-faced man who carried a cane.

A fisherman lumbered along the pavement. He approached the chair opposite Caravetti's table and lowered himself heavily into it. Leaning on the table he peered through the dark at Caravetti. He was about to speak but he stopped when he recognized the painter. Grunting in disgust he got to his feet and strode into the Bar.

No one had come out to serve him. He sensed that he was being deliberately overlooked. He smiled bitterly. He despised these people who were forcing solitude on him, who were hurting him. As far as he was concerned the affair was personal to his wife and himself. Society had no right to intrude and appoint itself judge and warder over him, he argued. The sympathy of the townspeople for Maria was reflected in their faces. He had seen it so often that he had been tempted to accept their point of view and hate himself.

Yet he did not remain in San Bernardino to win his redemption, he told himself. He had no respect for society and its set of rules. It was a very personal emotion that kept him there. It lay twisted unrecognizably on the floor of his stomach.

Maria was a part of that emotion; perhaps she was the core of it. Her resolute stand against all his advances had frustrated him so that at times he hated her, and he would burst into short tempers that were succeeded quickly by remorse and understanding. She had no other lovers; of that he was sure; although she may have had when he was in Paris. He had thought that he would woo her back and regain his status as the father of the family. But she was not so easily won over. It was as if she kept a militant force drilled inside her to move against him. Her eyes that were once so tender were now so fierce. Her mouth that used to repeat his words like an obedient schoolgirl now flung them back at him with demoniacal force.

He stood up suddenly with the thought of how she insulted his attempts to conciliate her. Anger and humiliation made the muscles of his face twitch. Yet, although he feared her rebuffs, he realized that at times he derived a pleasure from them, for the intensity of her feelings reflected the depth of her acknowledgment of him.

The path to the shore ran past a low bungalow with villa pretensions; a marquessa lived there, quietly. And then the shore path wound over rock and grass through spots of bamboo trees and finally up a hill where sat a formation of boulders which from out at sea looked like an old man brooding. Caravetti sat on a rock and looked at the sea lapping below him and at the moon, now yellow in the night with its troops of stars. He listened to the soft noises of the night. A shooting star slipped round the black bowl of the sky that covered him.

"Did you make a wish?"

Barbara's face came over his and blotted out the sky. Starlight touched faintly at the side of her face and he saw her features come down to meet his. They were lying on the roof in the tepid heat of a July evening.

Friends had lent them their sky-lighted studio while they were in Italy for six months. Because of the housing shortage, the government ruled that flats had to be sub-let if unoccupied. These people preferred to have Caravetti and Barbara living there. It had saved Caravetti from the worry of rent; he and Barbara had more room in which to work; and they had escaped the summer heat in that unbearable little room on Rue de la Seine.

"I don't bother making wishes," Caravetti sighed. "They never come true."

"But you don't make a wish just to have it come true. That might even spoil it if it did."

"Then what do you make a wish for," he smiled.

She snuggled closer to him. "For the wish itself. It means so much more if the heavens are in on it."

"Can you tell me?" he asked.

"Yes," she whispered, "because you are a part of it, and I feel you are a part of me."

He put his arms about her and brought his hands to press lightly on her shoulder blades.

"I wished that our life together would never stop."

"Oh, Barbara," he groaned, "don't tell me you're thinking that it might."

She moved slightly, and he saw another star plummet past its fellows to blink out in the blackness.

The next morning Barbara made them breakfast early. She was in a hurry to get to a life class, as she had been assigned to a new model and she wanted to find a good position before most of the class arrived.

"What is it this time?" asked Caravetti as he slipped on his sandals and began to wind the laces about his ankles.

"An old man," she grimaced, "as if the last one I did wasn't good enough."

"You did over-gloss it a bit, Barbara. Try and tone it down. After all, Marquet was passé long ago."

"You pay attention to your art and I'll look after mine," she retorted.

Professor Turnier had dropped by to see some of Caravetti's paintings several nights earlier, and he had agreed to purchase a small landscape looking from the roof of their house over Montparnasse. Caravetti was delivering it to him that morning. Although the professor was not a painter he knew a great deal about art and its history. Caravetti had learned much about composition from him.

As he began to wrap the painting, Barbara chose a canvas and painting materials. He watched her take tubes of colour from the drawer where they kept them.

"Don't take all the yellow," he warned.

"I'm sorry, I have to," she said not looking at him. "There's only a half-tube here."

"I haven't any money to get more," he shouted.

"You will have this morning, I presume, unless you've started giving away your stuff."

As she went out the door Caravetti glowered at her. Getting up early in the morning was an unhappy experience, he reflected. The cobwebs had to be broken through and then he was disillusioned with the dirty breakfast dishes he found after all his effort. Swallowing the last of his coffee, he sat still, letting the caffeine creep above his eyes and clear the objects of the room as well as his outlook on life. After a moment, he was in a better humour and ready to set about his own business. Singing, he took up his painting and walked out of the building to seek rejuvenation in the sunshine. Before he had gone far he remembered that he had intended to show the professor another painting he had done recently. As the style was surrealistic, he had refrained from introducing it to the art-lover who had not broken really free from the willowy trammels of the romantic tradition. But this morning he wanted to express his philosophy to someone, and the professor would understand it, if anyone could. As he turned back for the painting, he remembered the dirty breakfast dishes and sighed with the onus of washing them.

Monsieur Turnier lived in an apartment block near the Bois de Boulogne. When he answered the ring of his doorbell, he was wearing a red robe as a lounging coat. He liked to feel Faustian when he read, he said. It helped give him the illusion that he was learning something.

Caravetti smiled at the bespectacled, bemused face and entered into the living room. A small Boudin beach scene was hanging like a gray moth on the wall facing him. M. Turnier explained that he had already made wall space for Caravetti's painting. "We will place it right there, *mon cher*," he said, pointing to the space beside the beach scene.

"Won't it put Boudin in the shade?" queried Caravetti.

"Never!" The old man rounded his eyes in a show of being aesthetically offended. "Never!"

Caravetti tried to look amused.

"Don't you worry," M. Turnier smiled. "I shall rearrange it. But I see you have two paintings, mon cher. Did you make another sale?"

"No, I'm going to try to interest you in this." Caravetti unlashed both canvases.

As he placed his surrealistic creation against the back of a chair for the professor to see, the art-lover slapped at his pockets and held out empty palms.

"I'm not asking you to buy it; I just want to hear what you think of it."

The colours in the painting were light and clear yet there was an illusion of haze as if the foreground were fading into the background. A wind-swept desert melted into a greying sky. There was no demarcation between the two. In the desert small white shapes, some looking like pieces of machinery, others like sea-shells, settled themselves in various attitudes. They would have been amusing if it had not been for the oppressing greyness of the atmosphere. They looked delicately mechanical.

M. Turnier touched his chin with his finger tips. "What do the figures mean, if anything?" he asked. He did not know if the painting was merely atmospheric.

Caravetti smiled. "You're right. They're symbolic. Some oriental religions have odd shapes like those as their symbols. Take the sea shell. When you put it to your ear you seem to hear another world captured in the shell, yet the shell is dead to the world you are living in. In the same way, the study of religions is fascinating from an artistic point of view."

"Illustrating a philosophy are you?"

"That's right," he laughed. "I'm illustrating that philosophy is a kind of art. It is the artistic form that is the attraction in philosophy. Unfortunately, when you begin to live the philosophy, the art form falls away and the same old human nature takes over. In other words, philosophy may change a few things but the fundamentals of life remain and their permanency renders anything new seem unnecessary."

"Do you mean, Caravetti, that if we were made to adopt a new way of life by government decree, our lives would not differ essentially from what they were?"

"Yes, because our new mode of life is dependent upon the mode that went before it. I have always believed that the past insidiously and inconspicuously takes control of the present. When people begin to realize that government decree has not altered their lives for the better, then the new rules become tiresome. Rules have to be lax enough to be eventually disregarded, or sooner or later they will be swept away, rather violently."

"My dear friend," the professor sadly shook his head, "I can hardly believe that anyone could talk with such a revolutionary tongue and yet feel with such a conservative heart."

Caravetti laughed. "No, you misunderstand me, sir. My belief in the ubiquity of the past seems conservative, I suppose, but I am not opposed to change."

The professor raised his finger and screwing up his eyes said, "You would like to be a revolutionary."

The painter regarded him questioningly. "Perhaps."

"Yet you never will be. You are not the crusading kind, thank God," continued M. Turnier. "Like most artists you cannot be excited by political ideas because you know that those ideas must become generally accepted, or shall we say vulgar, before they can be turned to any practical use. By that time they will have lost their novelty and your interest. You will sit and swear at conditions but that is as revolutionary as you'll ever get." The professor's eyes twinkled. "I don't suppose that slogan 'working for the public good' has ever appealed to any painter."

"But a painter can truthfully show up the evils of the time."

"And if he is not truthful it shows in his work."

"Right," Caravetti nodded. "Artists never attach themselves to a slogan. They are too interested in maintaining their individulaity. By being one of a mass you lose the romantic touch so necessary to imaginative minds."

"I can see the romantic touch in this painting," smiled M. Turnier, "but I don't see why you bother wasting your imagination in surrealistic design when the movement died over twenty years ago as far as most people are concerned."

"I'm not trying to sell it to you," Caravetti replied. "It's merely of interest to me and I hoped you might understand."

Taking Caravetti by the arm the professor led him into his study where two leather chairs and a heavy broad desk took up most of the room. "*Mon cher*, it is indeed personal and because it has so much of you in it, I consider the painting quite as valuable as the one I have bought. May I write double the amount we had agreed on or would you ask more for both paintings?"

Caravetti saw the professor don his glasses and bend his bald pate hemmed with sleek gray hair over a cheque book and pen. He resisted the temptation to call out the highest price he could think of, and he suppressed the desire to offer the canvases free so that he might walk disdainfully away. M. Turnier had no intention of looking bourgeois; the old man was playing the cheque book role from force of habit, Caravetti realized.

"The paintings are worth about the same," he drawled.

As the professor's pen scratched across the paper, Caravetti saw tubes of yellow pigment rain over Barbara's sulking face.

Caravetti sat outside at the corner café across from St. Germain de las Pres. The cathedral looked rusty cold in the warm sun so he squirmed in his seat for a different view. He was waiting for Barbara to tell her their good luck and to take her out to lunch. He expected her to pass that way within an hour or two.

Action in the streets was slow. Pedestrians seemed uninterested in going anywhere. The workers were closeted in their office buildings. Caravetti looked about the café with his sketch book settled on his lap. At a table near him sat a girl he had known slightly in the quarter. She was one of the dying species of atheistic existentialists. Although she still wore the black trousers, the black sweater, and let her blonde hair fall long and dirty about her white face, she had changed her make-up. She and her lover had plastered their handsome faces with shining white cream, gruesome blood marks, and green, yellow and purple tints in an effort to shock and repel others. Caravetti had heard that they had become repellant to each other and their relationship had dissolved into the "neant", nothingness. Although their philosphy preached that result, it was small compensation to be practising it.

He walked to her table when she shot a smile of recognition across to him.

"Good-day, Gina. This is early for you, isn't it?"

It was obvious he would have to pay for her drinks if he sat down, but he sat beside her.

She looked at him mournfully. Her smile was quickly replaced with a pout. “I have nothing to stay in bed for now.”

The painter noticed she was wearing uplifts which accentuated the slimness of her body. She was like a black narcissus ready to break into blossom.

“There are plenty more fish in the sea,” he said.

“Not like him. They’re all mackerels.”

“Am I a mackerel?” he asked.

She drank gin with precocious eyes. She made Caravetti want to prove to her that he was not a mackerel.

“Well, am I?” he insisted.

“How should I know.” She turned slightly so that he might benefit from a different angle. “I'd have to ask your American girl friend, wouldn’t I?”

Her smile needed exploring.

"You’re better looking without all those colours on your face. I have never realized you could be so attractive.” He spoke seriously.

She returned the compliment by lowering her eyes over him. They were large black eyes that could magnetize.

When they had had their third gin he paid the bill and took her to lunch at a small restaurant behind the Quai D’Orsay. Gina’s choice of menu was immodest and Caravetti equalled hers on the reasoning that his recent sales were an indication of his imminent popular success. Half-way through the meal, he thought he glimpsed Barbara with two male friends as they retreated out the door. Had she seen him joking with Gina over what must have looked like an expensive meal? His spirits faded with misgiving. He had seen only the girl’s red-sweatered back, yet for a moment he was sure it was Barbara. Gina, however, sparkled in such high spirits that what had seemed a certainty slipped into phantasy; he passed it off as an imagined fear.

It was not until that evening when he left Gina’s flat that the red sweater he had seen took on a new fear. Inevitability sunk in his throat like a dry swallow. Barbara had seen him with Gina. He hurried his steps. He wondered if she would be waiting for him.

She was. Barbara sat darning his socks under one light that shone forlornly in the large studio. She had put his dinner in the warming oven.

Quietly he went to take it, but she called out to him.

“If you’ve already eaten, don’t bother to be kind.”

He went to her and kissed her cheek. “Sweetheart, that wasn’t me you saw in the restaurant. That was just a wine drunken excuse for a painter who let a small sale go to his head.”

“It looks as if he let more than that go to his head. Gina probably needed a good meal anyway,” she sighed.

“Oh darling, I had planned to take you so we could celebrate together. Turnier took two.”

“It’s all right,” she said.

Barbara and he knew that he was not going to see Gina again, but the knowledge saddened them. They were so linked that one of them could not stay away from the other for long. Together they had made a hearth that burnt like the eternal flame. It seemed unlikely to ever go out, and as long as they had it they had always to come home to it. Although at first this attachment was beautiful in its simple certainty, later the feeling became disconcerting, sometimes oppressive, because of the unhappy natures of their positions. It was as if they were predestined to live together as a unit of society, yet fate was unkind by offering them no social sanction.

"Perhaps you can take me out for lunch tomorrow," Barbara said.

When he answered, his tone suggested resentment at the inevitability. "Of course."

He walked disconsolately to a distant chair, and he sat brooding in the dark. As he watched Barbara's fingers twitch nervously at the wool, the air in the room became loud with uneasiness. Then, as if to spite the malevolence that hung over them, Barbara threw away her mending and turned off the light. Her slippers scraped softly over the floor. When she whispered, it was with the lisp of feminine intimacy.

The summer slipped into August, and Paris, like the rest of the continent, was blessed with fine warm days. Barbara and Caravetti painted together in the woods about Versailles and on the grounds of Fontainebleau. Caravetti became interested in sculpture and often Barbara sat watching him chip from rock a form that pushed itself like some powerful monster from an earthly imprisonment. And when the pale light of evening grew fuzzy, they left the monster rooted in his rock and passed through the courtyard between the ancient gates of the Beaux-Arts into the streets where gaiety laughed at adventure, and where night life made one forget creation and think only of the created.

They spent many evenings with friends in small cabarets where they made a costly drink last all evening or in cafes drinking beer and joking with strangers. Sometimes they went to the theatre or the opera on student tickets which cost a quarter of the ordinary price. Paris seen through the eyes of a student was slightly cheaper and happier than the same city seen by a worker who earned barely enough to feed and house his family poorly. The grimness in the streets and on the back stairs of one-time aristocratic houses, the threadbare lost look of those who rented the front rooms of those houses as they poured cheap wine in meagre glasses; these scenes the young had to forget in wild, uninhibited parties. Occasionally Barbara and Caravetti would find themselves dragged by friends to a jazz-frenzied jumble of sexes where freedom of expression was unlimited and neurosis the basis of behaviour.

They managed, however, to find enjoyment wherever they went. Where sordidness may have saddened them individually, together they made light of it and felt remote from it as if the bitter side of life could never tarnish the sacredness of their togetherness. And, for the most part, they managed to suppress any fears about their future together. Any tendency to sally into a hedonistic attitude was promptly tempered by the look in the eyes of the other. They knew that a pretence of love would be a travesty beside the reality they shared. They had to value the present and shun all thoughts of past and future.

"The silly fool put gin in the wine," Caravetti remarked as he tottered to a chair which had just been vacated by a damsel in distress.

"We can't get out the front door." Barbara was standing beside him. "The concierge has locked it from the outside."

Several people were climbing out a window and dropping to the street, but Caravetti did not feel like attempting it just then. "Let's wait a while," he said. "The party might get interesting."

A Dutchman, who had brooded in a corner for half the evening, seized Barbara by the wrist in a paroxysm of joy and reeled her amongst dancing couples in the next room.

"We're unhappy because everybody has forsaken us," said a gloomy voice.

Caravetti listened because he needed an area of concentration until the circle stopped swimming in his vision.

The face spoke on the necessity for independence, on the uselessness of governments, and on practically every social illusion, in short, on the merits of anarchy. Then as he nodded his head sympathetically in time with the theoretic cadences sounding behind him, Caravetti rose and walked into the next room.

Barbara was dancing with a neat-looking young man who looked soberly out of place at the party. The Dutchman had forsaken her for someone else in a wild spin. Caravetti noticed that he was still swinging about as if at Reuben's Bacchanale, a contrast from the quiet movements of Barbara and her partner. He stood half-deciding to turn back when Barbara called to him.

The man with her was an Americanized Frenchman. He had spent the latter part of his school days and his college years in Arizona.

"Let's go now," Caravetti suggested as he approached her. The party seemed to go suddenly flat. He endured his introduction to Barbara's friend and suggested again that they leave.

"Not so soon, surely!" The man's polite surprise made Caravetti smile. The over-eagerness of the rival crept naively in his tone. "Let us finish this dance, at least."

He watched Barbara laugh and agree with an irritation that must have appeared on his features, he thought, because he saw the sudden humour on the Frenchman's face.

"I'll wait for you in the other room," he said sternly.

At the door he stopped to watch Barbara take the fellow's card and smilingly glance at it before putting it in her purse.

He studied pictures on the wall without any interest while the record sent sweet music sickeningly through his bones. He thought of leaving Barbara at the party and returning home. Someone would see her safely back. Yet her partner's unwholesome personality worried him and kept him lingering on. The record ended and he looked expectantly at the doorway. Two girls came from the room but Barbara did not appear. Again a sentimental song invoked a romantic mood, and with disgust he turned to leave. Then, unexpectedly, the sentimental strains caught at his heart conjuring up the irreplaceable loveliness he was relinquishing so easily to another man. But if she preferred to remain with the stranger why should he interfere, he reasoned. He tried to laugh at the thought that Barbara might prefer the Frenchman to him. Still, women acted strangely sometimes. He walked to the window and was on the point of lowering himself to the pavement, when he felt that he might be leaving Barbara for good. The dark channel of the street ran lonesomely before him. Fear touched lightly at his heart. Calling it curiosity, he stepped back into the room. He touched his forehead to find it wet with perspiration. This torment was humiliating and unnecessary, he thought. He walked up to Barbara who was still dancing and without a word he led her by the wrist out of the room.

When they were in the street they kept a bitter silence until Caravetti asked, "Who was he?"

"An agent for a firm of dress designers." Her answer sounded like a retort, as if it was his profession alone which had warranted her attention.

"So what?"

"He said I would make a wonderful model."

Caravetti gaped at her. Could it have been only her vanity that had kept her from coming? "Didn't he say you'd make a wonderful anything else?"

"Oh no, darling!" Surprise and delight shone in an open smile.

The short-armed street lamps with their souless white lights became funny old men in the spontaneous laughter of two happy young people.

A week later the subject of modeling came up suddenly and forcibly. Caravetti had taken a few minutes from his painting to read in the lethargy of the mid-afternoon when Barbara burst into the room.

"Hi!" Caravetti echoed her happy greeting. "Where have you been all day?"

She stood still and posed with her hands on her hips until she saw the awed expression creep into his face. There she stood; a smartly-cut summer suit clasping her body in blue pastel; her long legs sheened in nylon; a chic hat peeked over a new hair-do; lipstick smiled brightly.

"I'm modeling," she laughed as if that was all the explanation he needed.

"But..." he stuttered. "Why?"

"Do you remember that fellow we met at the party last week?" 'We' was irritatingly redundant. "He arranged for me to be interviewed, and I started this morning."

She spoke lightly, happily, but Caravetti sensed her uneasiness. He knew she was afraid of how he would react to the news, especially to the author of it: that pseudo-Frenchman.

"This is rather unexpected." He tried to smile. "I wish you'd told me."

"I wanted to surprise you, darling. You'll never guess how much money I'm making. And these super clothes! I took a taxi home to show you."

"What about your painting?" he asked.

"Oh that," she sighed. "I decided I needed a rest."

Caravetti's brows rose suspiciously. "Why the quick change? You know you may never get back to art again."

Her eyes took on a false sorry look that seemed to be part of the costume. "But sweetheart, I want some fun once in a while, instead of being cooped up here all the time." She squared her jaw. "We don't go to any of the smart places because we don't have the money. And now, when I can get the money, you don't want it." She paused to watch Caravetti's angry stare. Her chin began to tremble.

"Take those rags back and tell them you don't want the work. I'm not living off the money you make." Caravetti had a fear of the life she would drag them into. Bright lights and lipstick.

Barbara looked furiously at him. She stamped her foot and shouted something unintelligible.

Caravetti jumped to his feet and strode to the door. Looking straight ahead he shouted, "If you like your dress designer so much, why don't you go and live with him."

He returned drunk late that night. Barbara's belongings and suitcases were gone. There was a drawing propped on her empty bureau. Unoriginally, a note said, "Something to remember me by." Caravetti looked closely at the drawing. A weighing machine was illustrated with many arms. In the hand of each arm there was a section of a woman. The arm which weighed the most carried the only organ pictured: a heart. Behind the machine and glowering at it stood a sharp-featured chemist wearing glasses; he could have been Caravetti. Stupid with alcohol, Caravetti yawned and walked abruptly to his bed where, flopping heavily, he decided to decipher all symbolical meaning in the morning.

There was a lull in shooting stars. The heavens were sparkling with tiny gems and the slit of a moon sat like a religious soul in its aureole of yellow light hallowing only the sky immediately surrounding it. He got up from the rock and looked down into the sea, black below him. He sympathized with that swirling mass, enslaved helplessly to the will of the moon. It was a passionate, unreasonable serf and its master as coldly irreproachable. Turning toward home, he thought of the cold hate that lay in Maria's eyes and of how it drew him helplessly to her.

6.

When Caravetti returned from breakfasting at Juan's, he found Senora Cosmos regarding a painting she had carried from the wall to his easel.

"Some of your paintings are sadly meaningless." She spoke in monotonous low tones and raised her chin to the top of the picture. "Others I like. And a few I like very much." Her chin dropped into three rows above her grand stentorian figure like the balcony tiers of an opera house.

Caravetti laughed. He was not intimidated by the senora and thereby remained on good terms with her. "You have not been amusing yourself at the expense of my paintings, have you?"

"I was seriously considering that I might hang them in my pension, which would benefit you, for I have guests with money, you know. It also would benefit me, although not nearly as much as you, as I would not demand a high per cent of the take."

Caravetti looked at the broad white forehead that fronted her heavy features. It was like a shield hiding the opponent who plotted cunningly behind it. He thought of the statue of Pedro and guessed that she was preparing to pay a low price.

"Perhaps, but let's see how much are you willing to pay for the statue, first," he grinned.

"You scoundrel," she laughed gutterally and her eyes beamed a playful allusion at him. "Where is it?"

He took her into the garden where the clay Pedro red-tinted in the sun gazed loftily from his stand in the centre of the green.

"Oh... he's marvelous!" Her body moved animatedly forward.

Caravetti stood by the door while he watched her run her hands over the immobile muscles and then pinch the unfeeling nose.

"It took a lot of work," he commented.

She named a figure. He shook his head. Frowning she named a higher one. "That is, if you let me hang some of your work where my guests can see it."

He shrugged his shoulders and agreed. He was getting more than he had hoped, but then he knew that she was in love with Pedro.

"I'll even put this in my sitting room with a plaque, 'By the local artist, Caravetti'," she joked. She came to stand beside him while they admired the statue from a distance. "You can catch a likeness," she remarked with an emphasis that was unusual with her. "Would you do a bust of me? Just a bust," she added when he smiled. "I know you would need too much clay for the whole me."

Sweet big woman, he thought. How easy it would be to catch those bulwark features in clay. "We'll talk about it," he said.

When she left she offered to send a couple of boys in a taxi to pick up the statue that afternoon. "I should send Pedro with a wheelbarrow for it. That good for nothing never does any work. Do you know where he is now?" she sighed.

Caravetti shook his head and tried to look sympathetic.

"Yes, poor me. He's probably doing something against the law."

As he watched her backside swing down the path like a hippopotamus ambling into the water, he imagined with apprehension the rigid law she would enforce.

Five minutes later Pedro opened his door. The youth's face rued happiness and justice in life. "She is not a woman, Caravetti. She's a rock."

"Come now," he cried. "You should be celebrating. She paid enough for your likeness to leave a fair amount over for you."

He brightened. "Did she? But I don't mean her." His face fell. "I mean Maria."

Caravetti bowed his head and motioned for him to sit down. "So you saw my wife."

"Wife! I wouldn't be married to her for all the money in the world!"

Caravetti smirked. "You wouldn't be married period."

"Oh yes, in fact I'm thinking of taking a senorita from Valencia, but I'll tell you about that later."

Lying back on his bed and propping his head high on pillows Caravetti affected patience in waiting to hear about Maria. He had known nothing would come from Pedro's visit to her. If he, himself, had not managed to persuade her, how could an emissary?

"She received me very well, although I guess she was a bit surprised to see me paying a social visit."

"And a bit frightened too, I imagine," smiled Caravetti.

"Then when we were sitting and I mentioned you, her attitude changed. I don't know how to describe it, but it was as if the mention of your name made her go all stiff and unfriendly. I tried the indirect method. I talked about you as if I was merely interested in you as a friend and an artist, and I wanted to get her opinon about you."

"And she told you I was black sheep."

"No, she said nothing. She changed the subject and I could see she was waiting for me to leave so I praised you to the skies. She didn't respond to that either. Finally, I told her that you were very unhappy and all that stuff. I went sentimental, but she didn't go for that."

"Not even a crocodile's tear?" Caravetti spoke bitterly. "Did she agree to let me see the children?"

"No. She said that you knew the rules of the separation. There was little use pestering her about it."

Caravetti looked glumly about the room. "Since when," he said, "have I been a bad influence on children? I don't see how I could influence them if I merely saw them once a month."

"In the end she got mad and showed me the door."

"You didn't try anything, did you?" Caravetti asked suspiciously.

Pedro shifted uneasily. "Well, when she didn't respond to you, I thought she might to me and when I'd won her sympathy I could sort of transfer it to you. But I couldn't even get started."

"You idiot!" Caravetti laughed. "When will you ever learn?"

"I've usually been successful," Pedro pouted.

Caravetti saw Pedro as the boy with the thorn in his foot. It would have been terribly funny if he had succeeded with Maria and to know she had dropped that stoic veil for once. Although he would have had a harder task eventually to win her, a setback was better than the monotony of no progress at all.

"But I'm ready to settle down," Pedro added. "There's a girl in Valencia with a big dowry and I've heard that she's beautiful. Her father was a friend of my father before the civil war, before my family lost its money."

"So you're thinking of marrying her," Caravetti concluded.

"My mother wrote to them but there's a catch in it, as always. There's something about my taking a partnership in their manufacturing business."

"Good work!" Caravetti cried.

"That's the trouble! I may have to work at first, but after a while I think I can find a way out."

Caravetti admired confidence and now he found Pedro intriguing. "What about Senora Cosmos?"

Pedro shrugged. "She'll manage. Though she'll probably be lucky to find another like me." He laughed and left as abruptly as he had come.

Caravetti watched the young man swinging his brown arms glistening from the yellow shoulders of his sleeveless sweater. In the room lingered a sadness that was connected vaguely to Pedro's cheerful optimism. True,

Caravetti was going to miss his friendship but there was more to it than that. Pedro's antics with women, all under the senora's nose, had helped Caravetti to see the irony of his own position. As long as Pedro was about town he was a living reminder that Caravetti too might be successful. Yet his sadness was rooted deeper than the gigolo's departure. Maria was the bottom of it as she was the basis for everything then. She could keep him in perpetual gloom or allow him to break into bright daylight. Everything depended on her, he decided. All he could do was to wait, and he knew how terrible that was. He had done it before.

7.

For a long time after Barbara had left him, Caravetti suffered a grief that did not let him work for long stretches of time and that did not allow him to concentrate with purpose. He gave up painting and contented himself with small sketches of street life that a friend who ran a stall in Montmartre sold to tourists. He wandered the streets every day in search of interesting scenes which might amuse him to sketch, though often he day-dreamed of Barbara as he walked and came to himself hours later in some unrecognizable district with no recollection of the city scenes he passed. Usually then he had to find the nearest metro and plot his position from the map posted outside.

Throughout Paris he found much diversion in sketching the changing atmospheres and classes of people and took satisfaction in concentrating on human nature in the raw, which afforded him a respite from a driving necessity to be always on the move. He liked the Latin Quarter. The narrow streets wedged between ancient tiny hotels, as on Rue de la Harpe, had an impoverished character about it that was more valuable than wealth. He sketched the front of a cheap restaurant where through the open doors a stone-faced Arab with grey beard and white robes sat with an impeccably-dressed Jewish friend who did most of the talking, where truck drivers clamoured for more bread, and where a student tried to study a book over steaming chunks of beef. He visited the street markets of Paris, the Arab quarter behind Notre Dame in the early morning when respectability slept. He saw tables of colourful cloths, stands of baggy suits, old men selling mechanical toys cluttering the sidewalks of La Rue de Rivoli. Most of all, he depicted the market of Rue de Levis where women behind fruit stalls raucously hailed passers-by, their breasts round as the fruit they sold, bulging in their ragged sweaters, where a white-mustached confectioner cornered what remained of the narrow sidewalk, where butcher stalls gaped like white caves, where flower stalls spilt colour into crowds of women ambling in the street, and where huge honking lorries scraped past wooden stands and tracked down unwary individuals amongst the milling shoppers. He sketched the rail-thin woman shouting desperately at the crowds with a burlap bag at her feet, her thin face raised in supplication, her tiny eyes darting to see who was watching while she held out yellow apples in bony hands, apples from the nearly empty burlap bag selling at ten francs cheaper than those in the legitimate stand hidden from view on the other side of a parked white van.

In the parks, he perched inconspicuously on benches, his pencil catching the stoic forms of nursemaids pushing baby carriages along predetermined walks, the school-boys jocosely rough-housing for the admiration of a pretty girl smiling encouragement, and mischievously, he drew caricatures of student artists painting columns about the pool in Parc Monceau or of little boys launching sail boats under the eyes of Sunday strollers in the Jardin des Tuileries.

The streets of Montmartre enclosed the raw mixture of the lower classes of many races, slaves to the bright lights and the pleasures of the flesh, and servants to the tourists whom they robbed with high prices as if everyting under the name of business had no conscience. There he found the tourists sitting at café tables or mis-directed into staring at grotesque representations of modern painting in a brightly lit gallery. And here he did minute portraits which he sold immediately to the sitter. It was a source of income not to be overlooked.

During all of this time, he wondered why Barbara had left him. He had been sure that she loved him, and he loved her as much in return. The break was so sudden that he thought he would never recover from the shock. There had been no apparent change in her attitude to him. She had had no other man that he knew of; she did not have the time, perhaps during the day, but it was unlikely because the only times they were separate were during classes and at odd hours.

Three months passed before he saw her again. It was October. The leaves were falling from the trees and in the Jardin du Luxembourg, the winds blew them rasping along the ground like bands of scurrying brown beetles. He was sitting on a wooden bench just off the main pathway through the Jardin. The afternoon was grey. Brisk autumn air tickled the cheeks and drew clearly through one's nostrils. There was a lull in the people passing through the park. The benches were almost all vacant. He alone watched the world bleakly fall into decay. And then he saw her.

She was smartly dressed in a fawn coat which might have been the Fath special for women's fall wear. Gayly she was conversing with an older man who appeared to be enjoying her company. When they were almost upon Caravetti, her eyes met his. The suddenness made her stumble over a few words and try to smile, but she could not in the face of Caravetti's icy exterior. Dismayed, she walked on with the man who sensed that something was wrong but did not know what.

Caravetti watched her walk on. He felt as if his stomach had suddenly leaped into his mouth. The muscles of his chest ached and when he tried to taste his saliva he had none. When he first saw her, his mind had told him to hate her, and his facial muscles betrayed no sign of recognition, but, now that she was disappearing, a panic whispered to him to run after her, to twist her about by the shoulders, to shout at her, and he felt he would have done so were she not with another man.

When they reached the steps leading to the middle section where the fountain climbs up in front of the palace, Barbara turned. The man, wearing a neatly-pressssed blue suit, politely tipped his homburg to her and walked down the steps. She was almost running when she got to Caravetti.

She sat on the bench beside him and then their arms were about one another. Her tears felt like drops of fresh soda water on the tops of his ears. He held her until his body returned to normal and was rejoicing in the warmth of his hold.

"How are you?" he asked. It was almost a joke.

She sat back and smilingly wiped the tear stains from her cheeks with a corner of her hankie. Her looks had not changed. The lipstick and the odd superficial touching that beauty shops had given her had not destroyed her naturalness. Caravetti loved her.

"How are you?" she smiled. "You looked so sad I had to come back to say hello."

"I'm glad you did. I almost ran after you."

Impulsively she kissed him on the cheek. "But I must go," she said.

Caravetti's brow rumpled in thick folds. "Why are you in such a hurry? Is that fellow waiting for you?"

Barbara pried at his fingers to soften his grip. Caravetti realised how firmly he held her; he brought his fingers together so that they pressed lightly along the top of her arm.

"No. I told him to go on. That I'd forgotten something." She turned her arm under his hand and her fingers encircled his wrist. "Caravetti!" She bowed her head. "We can't live together. You know why. When you go back to Spain, back to your family, what would become of me?" She looked up, her clear blue eyes reflecting the torment she was passing through. "A break now, over a misunderstanding, is a hundred times better than a break then. Don't you see?"

He feared she would leave him before he could answer. Already shc tended to pull away when every extra second meant a year to him. "But darling, don't cross our bridges before we get to them. Wait and see what happens. Wait! Don't go. Why did you take the modelling job? To break us up because you knew I'd object?"

"No! Of course not, silly," she laughed almost successfully. "I needed something different, something not connected with you. It softened the blow weighing over me then.When you made a fuss, it seemed that fate was... well, fate was giving me a helping hand. But leaving you wasn't easy."

"But I'm not going for another year or more," Caravetti said in a surprised voice.

"I know. I didn't plan it then. It just happened."

"But now you can come back." His fingers pressed harder against her arm.

"No. I won't come back. I'm all right now. I can stay away." The words fell like the last sentence of a funeral oration on Caravetti's ears.

He stared in her eyes. They were steady in returning his gaze. She knew what she was doing. She was sure of herself.

As she pulled away from him he said, "Don't you love me anymore?"

"I do."

"Come back." He stood with her.

"I can't."

He seized her before she could turn and he kissed her mouth until it parted and he pressed his tongue against the roof of her mouth. When he thought that he had won her back, he relaxed his grip. But she turned and left him. After she had disappeared down the steps, he noticed the faces of the women glancing furtively at him as they hurried by, the smiling men, and the little boys, drama-struck.

In the days following, Caravetti watched for Barbara in the streets and parks. The chance meeting buoyed his hopes of seeing her again, but as the days dragged by, his fruitless search humbled his spirit. He visited all the salons near the Champs-Elysees because he did not know to which salon she belonged, if indeed she worked with a salon instead of a fashion magazine or a special agency. She seemed so near, perhaps in one of the buildings he stared at, like a sparrow that might alight in his hands yet kept far out of reach. He held to a purpose; if he met her often enough he might persuade her to return to him. Unfortunately, the failure of the stipulated 'if' brought failure upon the whole, and his purpose gradually weakened to a vain aim, spasmodically throbbing like a weak pulse in a dying animal.

He tried to find some of her acquaintances, but any of the Americans she had known had left Paris during the summer. Her French friends had seen her occasionally on the street, but they did not know where she lived; her life had altered from what it was before.

Caravetti finished her portrait by memory. Now that he understood why she had left him and that she loved him, he returned to his painting and he began working seriously again. He still did sketches when he took long walks. He did many in the Jardin du Luxembourg.

Paris seemed like a world in itself. He had wandered about the main districts until he knew the streets. Then Paris seemed small to him. But when he was looking for someone, and he knew she was not far away, the city seemed immense. He worried lest he never see her again. If he did, he was determined to persuade her to come back at all costs. He would make all the sacrifices, he thought. He would promise her never to go back to Spain.

Maria and his children were like possessions to him. He liked them as people, but as emotional connections they had no meaning. Maria had been a good girl, she had obeyed him, the children had come as a matter of course, but he had not got to know them; the boy was just over a year and the girl newly born when he left. When the chance to study in Paris came he did not think twice about leaving the family. He had always expected to return to them, that life would go on as usual, but now he was prepared never to see them again. How they were going to look after themselves without him he did not know. He did not think about it. It all seemed far away and unimportant.

In the month of December, he thought he saw Barbara walking ahead of him on Boulevard St-Michel, down from St. Germain in the direction of the Seine. He started. Then he quickened his steps. The girl went among a crowd of people coming up the street. He dashed through them in time to see her cross over to look in a shop window. As he rushed to tap her on the shoulder, he saw the reflection of the girl's face in the window. In the background of women's white slips and sweaters he saw pretty features. But they were not Barbara's. He swerved and kept on walking quickly until he reached the Seine. He stood looking over the cement side at the flowing water. It began to rain. Drops lightly patted the backs of his hands and the top of his head. The book sellers began to close up their stalls. There were only a few of them who sold books this late in the year and they did not stay long at the job. December brought cold winds and fog and piercing wet. The sides of the Seine looked bleak. The grey walls of the cement rose coldly from the greyness of the waters. Caravetti sensed the heaviness of the afternoon. He felt that he had nowhere to go and that he had nothing to do.

The walls of his room reminded him of the inside of a tomb, and his bed might have been a funeral bier. In the evenings when it grew too cold to walk the streets, when he had no money to sit in a café, he huddled fully clothed under the bed covers and listened to the sounds of the building, the stealthy tread along his ceiling, the mordant giggle behind the wall, the monotonous step of traffic on the stairs. Tired of painting, drawing, and reading, his mind felt like a chunk of iron set into his head. Occasionally at night he jumped from bed to gaze out the window at the vacant courtyard where one light glimmered over the passageway to the street. He waited to see someone pass through the light and derived enjoyment when some stranger finally did. Unable to sleep, he spent hours in this lonely game with rarely more than five or six persons to his credit at dawn.

He visited galleries on Sundays when admission was free. If he met acquaintances or painter friends, he eluded them. He refused to return greetings and gradually he received less until he remained on speaking terms with only a few of his best friends. He never visited friends, and he never opened his door to them. Chance meetings in the street were his only human contact. When he did encounter friends he hated to relate what he was doing. His personal life became excessively private to him, as if he were ashamed of its emptiness, although he associated it so thoroughly with himself that he accepted it as part of his nature.

The more he kept to himself, the closer he felt to Barbara. It intensified his awareness of her in his solitude. His avoidance of well-meaning friends who wanted to 'drag him from his shell' arose from this perverse longing for solitude. He reached a point where he dreaded having to speak to anyone. A question asked by a passer-by in the street startled him so violently that he passed the next blocks in a state of nervous tension. A distaste and sometimes a fear of his fellow humans developed in him. Unaware of the subtle changes in his personality, he kept restricting his area of interest until he began to think that he was useless in everything, including painting, and useless to everybody, which explained why Barbara left him.

One evening when he returned with groceries, he met a Spanish friend sitting on his stairs waiting for him. He had to invite him into the apartment for coffee. At first he was stiff and unfriendly, but, in the course of conversation, he forgot himself. The evening flew by and it was midnight when he bade his friend adieu and promised to come to a Christmas reveillon the following week.

As he watched the river water smack against the cement of the bridge, he thought of the coming reveillon with unquiet. His first impulse had been to avoid the party yet the hours of comradeship the other evening had awakened a response in him to human society. He remembered the laughter and the happy chatter of throngs of people. Perhaps, he thought, he might drop by for a few minutes, long enough for a glass of wine. A young woman, plain-looking, walked toward him by the side of the bridge. He saw her look at him and then stop to gaze meditatively over the side in imitation. He knew that she was waiting for him. He began walking towards her. Quickly he passed her, crossed over to the metro, descended the steps and took the train in the direction at which he chanced on. He preferred to be alone.

On Christmas Eve, he kept his promise to his friend and arrived at the reveillon. He brought a bottle of wine and shyly surrendered it to one of the girls who greeted him at the door. Over thirty guests arrived before him so that he found the party in full swing. As he wandered about the rooms the high spirits thawed his stiffness. He descended to the cellar where a large table had been set up to accommodate the guests in the middle of the recreation room which boasted a small bar and a kitchen at the side. Some of the girls were in the kitchen roasting turkeys, cooking food, preparing plates, and pouring drinks for themselves. Others were pouring drinks for those who had wandered down from the floor above where couples were dancing. One of the wanderers complained to Caravetti.

"Here it is almost eight o'clock and we haven't had a thing to eat yet." His French suffered from an American accent.

"Hold your horses, Eddie," a girl looking through from the kitchen broke into the American language. "How'd you like to be here 'stead of us?"

"I bet I could do a damn sight faster job."

"Oh," she snorted and turned away.

Eddie picked a glass of gin and tonic from a tray, glared at it, and put half of it down his throat. "Great stuff," he said, "Is it made here?"

"In France?" smiled Caravetti. "There's the bottle. Look on the label."

"Aw, it doesn't matter," Eddie made a face and waved his hand. "I was just wonderin'. Where do you come from?"

"From an island off the coast of Spain."

"Really!" He swallowed the last of his gin. "It must get awful lonely living on an island. Ever read Robinson Crusoe?"

"It's not as bad as that," laughed Caravetti. "There are a few women around."

Eddie laughed loudly and clapped Caravetti on the shoulder. "Say, you're all right man! Come on up stairs and I'll show you some women." When they were climbing the stairs, he said: "Out of the whole bunch, there're about five worth considering. 'Course the trouble is the best lookin' ones always come with other guys, and boy! Those guys stick to 'em like candy to paper. It's tough on stags like you and me."

A record was playing an American popular song. A young voiced crooner was singing. "She had a dark and flashin' eye, and her hair hung down in ringlets."

"There's the girl for you." Eddie indicated with a nod a well-proportioned red-head who was having a wonderful time with her dancing partner. "Why don't you cut in?"

"Not now," Caravetti answered. "She seems to be enjoying herself."

"Nonsense." He began to shove Caravetti by the shoulder toward the couple. "Don't miss your big chance."

Caravetti stepped away from him. "No, not now," he laughed. "Later, when she's alone."

"Jeez, you'll never get any women like that. You'd better go back to your island."

The host saved Caravetti from further implications. He was a Spanish architect who obtained a good salary from a Parisian firm. He led him to a corner of the room. "I'm glad you could come to-night. It's nice to be able to speak your native tongue on Christmas eve."

While they were talking, Caravetti observed Eddie dancing with the red-head. Although he was talking excitedly, she was looking about the room as if she had lost something.

A girl signalled to the architect, who, detaching himself from Caravetti, announced dinner in French over the noise of the music. Someone stopped the record player and a general movement aimed for the doorway; Eddie was well out in front. Caravetti found himself sitting between two French girls who chattered across him about politics. He put his hands on their shoulders as if to calm them. "But," he said, "I think Mendes-France is the best man for the job."

They, surprised, looked at him and emphatically agreed. The girl on his right hand was wearing a strapless dress. He felt the flesh of her shoulder tingle under the warmth of his palm.

"Oh! *Vous etes Espagnol! Un bel Espagnol!"*

"Tell me," he smiled, "Why are the French intellectual?"

The girl in the strapless raised her eye-brows and said in the chicest French manner: "Someone has to make up for thc rest of the world. Didn't you know? It's we who are the chosen race."

They all laughed, and Caravetti entered into the conversation so whole-heartedly that, during the dinner, he forgot about himself and about Barbara and about everything outside of the people at the table and the feast in front of him. The gay French mood, the gay French wine, the gay mixture of nationalities spun like dancing joy about him. Laughter was in his ears; he saw it with his eyes; he joined in it with his soul. "Hey, there, Caravetti, you need more of this red liquid." Where does time go? Where did it start and where did it end? How long does it last? There's no such thing as time.

Caravetti had a second helping of turkey, two more slices of ham, a pile of peas and mashed potatoes, a tablespoonful of Cranberry jelly. Someone passed him the carrots and the sauce; someone filled his glass with red wine, and he kissed the girl in the strapless.

"As an artist, what do you think of Picasso?" The man across the table posing this question considered himself an authority on the subject. He made a wry face to discourage a favourable reply.

"Wonderful," sang out Caravetti. "Marvelous. Great sense of humour. Great artist."

"What?" The young man had a long face edged with a strip of black beard as was the fashion with some students so that when he was surprised his face fell oblong. "Do you think painting women with two noses, three breasts, and four eyes is amusing?"

"Yes. It's a matter of sensing these things. He's not painting a surface picture; he's painting the character of the person," Caravetti explained. "We've had all the Van Dongen's we want; now let's see what really makes women tick."

The student shrugged his shoulders as if passing Caravetti off as another Communist and reflecting how completely a rigid social concept could bias the mind of its judgement on all matters.

"If you're an artist," said the girl in the strapless, "what do you paint? I mean, are you a portrait painter or a landscape painter or what?"

"Everything," said Caravetti. "I could even paint you," he smiled. He was feeling whimsical.

"Oh good! What would that include? A visit to the studio of the artist?"

Caravetti noticed her firm round breast pushing at the material of her dress. Her shoulder rounded with the smoothness of curves in a pear. He sensed a well, deep and langorous, in her eyes. Soft and inviting like webbing in a rose, her lips smiled at him. He had desire but something inside him forbade him to express it. He looked longingly at her, and then smiled.

"My studio isn't much to see. It's a room with a few canvases, that's all." Then he could not stop from adding, "But you might find it interesting."

As his invitation sounded hesitant, the girl pretended intimate approval, yet she guarded herself with a half-smile in order to pretend that she was joking if he were not serious.

"I'm sure I would. When would you suggest that I come? Early in the morning? I understand most artists paint better then."

"No, late at night when I do my best work," he smiled. He was getting interested in the game. His desire was beginning to overflood that sore spot in his chest which had warned him against it earlier.

A girl interrupted them to place a portion of Christmas pudding in front of both of them. The rich smell of raisins and hot brown sauce distracted him slightly, but, when the arm withdrew, he saw his companion's strapless figure again, and desire surged from his loins. He seized the girl's hand in his own and strongly held it under the table.

"I work in the mornings." His eyes blazed the answer. He felt the muscles of his face straining from his temples to his jaw. "When the party is over."

All humour ran from the girl's face. She swallowed hard and pushed her hand that he held onto his knee. As she squeezed his leg, her eye-lids drooped half-closed. He and she swooned in a rapture of passion, then parted. Caravetti felt instantly happy. The joy of expectation stirred in him as if he were a general riding triumphantly home from a glorious victory. "Would you like some more sauce for your pudding?" he laughed. His hand shot for the bowl in front of them.

The host patted him on the shoulder from behind. He spoke in Spanish. "Caravetti, I've got a surprise for you. Some people said they would drop by after dinner and Barbara's one of them. She's upstairs now. I happened to run into her last week. She asked me first if you were going to be here. I said no, and that I thought you'd gone to Italy." Ecstatically he winked and pushed his tongue into his cheek. "I know how you feel, old man." And he dashed away to talk to someone who was calling him.

"Thanks, old man," Caravetti called after him with difficulty for his wits had been scattered like grapeshot and weakly he collected them to form a thought: Barbara was upstairs. Impossible! A picture of her smiling at him as in old times slowly crystallized in his consciousness, and he squirmed nervously with thoughts of leaving the party immediately. He felt embarrassed that Barbara should catch him enjoying himself with other women. At least he intended to stay clear of her. But then they were free of each other. And he had as much right to be there as did she. He smiled at the girl beside him and noticed with relief that she had not understood,

"What was that?" she asked.

"He just gave me an address where I can get good picture frames."

A sense of hopelessness swept over Caravetti. Barbara's shadow seemed to be suspended over him whatever he did. Now, when he had managed to forget her for an instant, she came back to haunt him. He knew that although this time she was with him in the flesh, it would be her shadow that he would be talking to. He would not be able to get close to her. It all seemed so futile. And when he should be overjoyed to see her, when these moments had seemed as if they would never come, he felt lethargic and turgid. Although sentimentally his emotions were for Barbara, sexually, for the present, for the here and now of things, he was in love with the French girl. The mixture depressed him. Temporarily he was angry with Barbara for making an appearance at a time he was enjoying himself. But gradually, as he looked at the girl beside him and as he thought of Barbara in the room upstairs, his desire began to flow from the one to the other. He could see Barbara as he had seen her many times. But he checked himself. Barbara was probably with another man; she did not want him; he felt as if the girl in the strapless were his salvation from Barbara; and, after all, she was desirable. If he and the girl appeared together, Barbara would see that he could find someone also; that he had not missed her.

"Come on," he cried. "Lucille, isn't it? Let's get our coffee upstairs."

Barbara was there. She was seated on the arm of an easy chair while she talked to three other people. She was wearing red. It was stunningly becoming. She could wear anything, reflected Caravetti. She did not see him enter. Ignoring her, he took Lucille directly across the room to the coffee table. As he poured out the cups, he knew Barbara's eyes were on him. He joked with Lucille and he made a special effort to charm her. Lucille was quite animated. She clung to his arm and chanced a kiss on his cheek. They walked away from the table to sit down and it was then that he pretended to see Barbara for the first time. He smiled and bowed slightly to her. She smiled back, rather anxiously, he thought. He led Lucille to some chairs where others from the dinner party were gathering. Purposely, he sat with his back to Barbara, but he could not resist a glance at her as he sat down. She had not seen him look. She was looking at the fellow talking to her.

"Yes, we've changed our address. We're living at …."

"Why don't you come with us, we've…."

The conversation about him ducked in and around phrases and intonations like the harmony of a choral group. A woman's voice would go up and a man's would go down and then they would interchange. Caravetti was not listening to the words. To him, it was as abstract as music. Lucille was talking to the woman beside her. Caravetti added a few words here and there to show that he was interested.

The dinner lasted over three hours so that as the guests were drinking their coffee, midnight sounded. A voice shouted "Joyeux Noel" and the men kissed the women standing next to them. Balloons and ribbons floated down from the ceiling. A box filled with toy horns, clatter-sticks, and paper hats appeared in the centre of the room. Everyone was on his or her feet singing, joining hands, kissing. Caravetti kissed Lucille. She was taken over by a friend and passed to another so that he felt momentarily free to see where Barbara was.

She held a balloon the colour of her dress. He saw her blue eyes when they turned to him. Caravetti walked toward her and they embraced. He did not let go of her until a couple budged him from behind. People were dancing; the lights had been dimmed. As they started to dance he felt romantic.

"My Latin blood is coming out in me," he said.

"Who hasn't got Latin blood?" she answered and snuggled closer to him.

He forgot about all else but their movement together; the gentle swaying in the shadows; the placing of their hands, up on his chest and then down at their sides. He brushed his lips along her cheek, and she parted hers and rubbed them over his.

"It feels good after so long," whispered Caravetti.

"Too long," she said

"Have you been drinking," he said

She laughed and put both her arms about his neck. "Yes, and on top of that I'm madly in love."

He kissed her. "Are you going to leave me again?" His heart paused.

"No," she said.

He could not believe what he heard. He thought she meant no, she was not coming back.

"No?" His voice went way high.

"Don't you want me?" she smiled.

"Darling." He pressed his lips hard against the corner of her eye. "Let's go. Let's get out of this party."

"But," she said "What about the girl you're with?"

Caravetti looked at her. His eyes narrowed in amusement. "What about the man you're with?"

"I think they'd go well together," she laughed.

They grasped hands and hurried to get their coats. In the hallway they encountered the architect. He was beaming at them.

"Thanks, old man. Tell Lucille I'm sorry not to see her before I had to leave."

As he opened the door he caught sight of Eddie standing with a tray of drinks, hailing him. "Golly!" Eddie said, "I didn't think you'd ever do it."

They hurried along the dark streets until they came to a taxi stand.

"Come to my place," she said. She leaned forward to speak to the driver.

Caravetti could sense the long lines of her body under her coat. She leaned back beside him. For now it seemed to be an agreement to just hold hands.

"Have you been living with anyone?" he asked moodily.

"No," she smiled quietly. "I've been able to afford independence." She lightly kissed him.

"Who were you with tonight?" he asked slightly relieved.

"I wasn't with anyone in particular. There was a group of us who went from one house to another."

"What made you want to come back?" he said in squeezing her hand, "so suddenly?"

"I couldn't hold out any longer." She pushed her head on his shoulder. Inside she wished he would stop asking questions. But she was so peaceful with him that she would have answered him forever, she felt.

Caravetti was glad he had talked to Lucille in front of Barbara. Jealousy is still a potent weapon, he mused.

Her apartment was located in the swanky Etoile district. A self-run elevator took them up a few floors. The door of her apartment was a light-grained wood, polished to look first class. Inside, the atmosphere was first class, a dramatic change from their old apartment on Rue de la Seine. Large, comfortable chairs, low tables of dark mahogany, indirect lighting, a radio-phonograph.

"Did you buy all this yourself?" he gasped.

"Most of it. At sales and bargain prices." She had wanted him to see the elegance of her apartment, but suddenly the atmosphere meant nothing to her. When contrasted to him, it meant nothing.

"You must be a top model," he said.

"I've been lucky, darling, but I've been at it quite a while now, and we work for our money." Her understatement sounded modest.

"You said 'most of it'; who helped you?"

"Admirers," she smiled. "One always has them in this game."

Admirers! Caravetti wondered how people could show admiration by giving presents. If it was desire, why not call it by its right name and express it as such, he thought. And yet, he smiled, how much could be done under the veil of hypocrisy. Women accepted the presents on the basis of admiration yet they knew it was desire. And if they let the man realize his desire they still pretended it was admiration.

"Did you have many?" he asked.

"Several," she said. "And you. How many did you have?"

"None."

"I'm sorry," she said.

Perhaps she was sorry, he thought. He could not help but feel irritated. "I suppose it was too much to hope for," he said.

"They didn't last long. They couldn't replace you."

He looked in her eyes. She meant what she said. He took her in his arms.

They compromised. While he agreed that she keep her modelling job, she agreed to give up her apartment. They settled in the Iena district so that he was not far from classes, and she was close to her place of work. She kept most of her furniture; the furniture that she had bought. The money she received for the rest, she put into a savings account. It was for the future, she said. With money deposited for it, she promised not to worry about it.

"At least, I'll have a consolation."

Caravetti worked harder than he had ever done before. Her success had stimulated him. He enjoyed the added comforts, and he found that they did not hinder his thinking as he had feared they might. He regarded luxury skeptically. It was a possession not to be admired but to be ridiculed. He knew that as long as he could keep it from becoming a necessity, he could enjoy it. As for the odd nights each week when he took Barbara dancing, or to the theatre, or to the parties of her friends, he enjoyed them. Life was different, so gay, so superficial, so sophisticated that the change relaxed his mind. The mornings after when he returned to his painting, it was with an added zeal. He felt that it added to his experience.

"You know, I like our apartment. It has an air of being lived in with a sense of loving the living. Our other one was so drab that it was like an unmade bed, that had a sense of loving, yet the loving seemed to have been over with long ago. But here one feels as if he were in someone's neat little library where the classical books are kept on the shelves near the floor and at eye-height all you can see are modern titles. And one feels so much at home; the sort of feeling you get when you rest your arms along the leather arms of a big easy chair. And you're all alone in the room, but you know other people are somewhere around outside. And if you put your nose next to the leather arms of the chair you can smell it."

Barbara laughed and then quietly said: "That's sweet, dear."

"No, I mean it. Really, how I thought I'd hate any change from Latin Quarter life. I thought my art would go to pieces. But here I am selling more than I have before, and I haven't commercialised it at all. I've stuck to the same ideas. It seems as if I've been lifted on a platform to a high level. It's like taking the elevator and bringing your luggage with you. And I've got you to thank for the ride. I think you must be Lady Luck."

She curtsied. "Your metaphors are in good form to-day."

"Well," he joked. "I almost called you the elevator boy to stay in the same metaphor. But then I saw you dressed like that, in a smart brown suit with round lapels, and I thought you looked more like a lady."

She walked behind his chair and ruffled his hair with a sweep of her hand. When he tried to grab at her, she stepped away.

"What's the matter?" he asked. "Here I'm being complimentary and you attack me. And from behind, like all women."

"Compliments," she grunted.

"Wait a moment and I'll show you what I really think of you." He left his chair and disappeared into the next room which he used as a workshop. He returned with a painting wrapped in green paper. He gave it to her.

"Open it. I'm sorry this isn't your birthday or mother's day or something, but open it."

It was the finished portrait of her. He had framed it. The colour of the frame was the colour of her hair.

"Darling! I love it!"

"Where can we hang it?" He began looking at the walls of the room.

She put the painting on the chair, and, standing beside him, she turned him by the shoulder until he was facing her. He saw that her eyes were wet.

"I never thought you'd finish it." She spoke in a low voice. "When did you do it?"

"When do you think?" he said.

"Oh Caravetti!" Her arms encircled his waist and she pressed her face against his chest. "And the frame is so pretty."

8.

The two men slowly paced the shore path. Pedro had his hands pushed in his pockets; Caravetti had crossed his arms in front of him. They looked worried.

"Didn't the doctor try to guess what was wrong?"

Pedro shook his head.

"Did Maria ask for another doctor?"

"A specialist is coming from the mainland the day after tomorrow."

They paced in silence. A full moon broke out from behind a cloud. Rays of tinsel shattered the darkness turning a deep purple about the planet. The sea wallowed beneath it. Pedro had found Caravetti in Juan's to tell him about the sickness of his boy. The doctor had sent him, after he chanced on him while coming from Maria's house.

"A specialist in what?" Caravetti asked suddenly. "If they don't know what it is, how can they get a specialist?"

"He thinks it has something to do with the liver," Pedro said.

"Who? Our doctor? He's getting too old to be a doctor if he thinks instead of knows."

"He knows what he's doing. Don't worry," Pedro advised.

Caravetti kicked a rock over the edge of the bank and they listened to it being gulped in the water. "Did he say that I could see him?" he asked as if he expected a denial.

"He didn't mention that to me. You'll have to ask him yourself."

Caravetti brooded. "Are they sure it isn't turberculosis? This year's worse than most."

He thought of the boys he had known on the island when he was growing. They would get thin, cough continually, and die. His father died from T. B. when Caravetti was nine years old. He did not want his son to suffer the same way.

"No, it's not tuberculosis," Pedro said. "The doctor's done enough cases in forty years here to be able to recognize that by now."

Caravetti smiled. He had even lost faith in doctors. "I hope they let me see him." His voice sounded distantly.

"They will," Pedro said confidently. "But the doctor wants you to come to his office tomorrow morning. You can ask him when you can visit."

"Do you know that my little boy doesn't know I'm his father?" Caravetti looked fiercely at Pedro. "Since I've been back on the island over a year now, I've seen him twice. Once with Maria and once with the maid. I've seen the little girl once."

Caravetti was not asking for pity. He did not think of his circumstance as an injustice. It all appeared as part of an overwhelming obstacle. He had to climb over the ramp and while he was climbing it, he had to keep reminding himself of it or he would give up.

Pedro smiled. He clapped Caravetti on the shoulder. "Don't worry about it. Your son will be all right."

Caravetti jerked his head up to smile at him. "How are your home problems?"

"Settled. I'm leaving by ship for Valencia tomorrow morning."

"No!" Caravetti ejaculated. "How is Senora Cosmos taking it?"

Pedro swung his foot at the bamboo clustered by the side of the path. "I haven't told her."

"You're sure of marrying this girl?"

"Yes. Her father wrote me and the marriage has been arranged. You know, I'll be quite rich. You must come and visit me in all my elegance." Pedro took a foppish stance.

"Perhaps you'll patronize my art," Caravetti joked.

"You bet. I can hardly wait until I can offer the senora a good price for my statue. She won't be wanting it when I'm gone."

He was right, Caravetti reflected. Most people valued art only as far as they were personally connected to it. The work of art itself, its beauty, or its truth, was only prized by the small minority.

"It's funny the way life goes," he said as they began walking back to the town. "You seem to walk deliberately into trouble and everything turns out just fine. Myself, I'm struggling like hell to keep out of trouble but everything turns out just rotten."

At that moment the moon, which had been riding the sky in the poetic tradition, dipped behind a dense cloud from which it seemed it would never reappear.

9.

Caravetti rose early. The first rays of the sun beamed from a hilltop through his studio as he made his coffee. At that time he was still painting street scenes, but the picture on the easel was a street scene of Paris he was recalling from memory. The scene from his window was having a rest in a half-produced condition. He could not understand why he painted it so much more cramped than it really was. After he had practised with familiar Parisian scenes, he wanted to return to it.

Hefty prostitutes leaned against the dirty brick walls in the painting on the easel. A big-bosomed woman was posted the most prominently. About her were the tall, thin and timid, the quietly pretty, the leg-stretching roues, the bucksome blondes, and old Bessie. They were lined along the street watching and waiting. The hefty ones were sporting in a wide stretch of the sidewalk formed by a turn in the street. He had given them the look of caged cats. Several years ago, he thought, he would have made them sultry.

He painted until he decided it was time to see the doctor before he left on his morning calls. The walk to the man's office was short. There was no one in the streets. He was afraid he was too early. The doctor's daughter answered the door and ushered him to her father's sitting room. He had to wait until the doctor finished his breakfast. The room looked out on the street. Across the road was the hotel. A chamber maid was mopping the lobby. She was the only movement. The atmosphere of the room rested uncomfortably on old furniture. Caravetti favoured the smooth low lines of modern furniture so that his eye remarked the straight upholstering with distaste. A chair of the oval-shaped back variety spread out two delicately carved arms to receive him. Sensing the discomfort before he sat down, he sat on the edge of it. The paintings on the wall were small landscapes of communal picnics and wandering sheep.

The doctor walked slowly into the room, greeted Caravetti with a handshake, and eased himself into a chair. Caravetti remembered that the town doctor could not make enough money to buy the latest furniture. Nor would he have the time to care about it. These chairs were probably heirlooms, treasured as personal memoirs for each part of the past they represented.

"The condition of your boy is not dangerous," the doctor intoned. "But it is serious." He paused to wipe his mouth with his handkerchief. "A specialist in liver ailments will be coming from the mainland tomorrow. I thought I should inform you because I know how anxious you are about your children, even if others do not." He smiled with his eyes.

"Thank you doctor," Caravetti liked the old man really. "But do you have any idea what's wrong yourself?"

The doctor looked grave. "Frankly, no."

Shrugging his shoulders, Caravetti looked out the window. "I hope the delay before the other doctor arrives won't hurt at all."

The doctor rose and went over to pat him lightly on the shoulder. "No, no. In these cases it will take some time to diagnose correctly. Time heals in many other ways too. A boy living near Izina was paralysed in both legs owing to an accident, but he'll regain the use of all his muscles after a long and patient therapy. So, don't worry too much about it, Caravetti."

Caravetti walked with the doctor to the front door. The doctor had that professional manner of ushering people politely out of the room that irritated him. "May I see him," he asked hopefully.

"Well now, I don't know," the doctor replied slowly. "It depends on what Maria says, I suppose."

"She'll say 'no'," Caravetti's jaw hardened.

"Then I'm afraid you cannot." The doctor looked professionally sorry.

"Can't you tell her that I must see my children when they are seriously ill? Doesn't it seem proper to you, doctor?"

"Yes. Of course you should." He paused. "Tell Maria that I gave you permission to see him. But if she still refuses, there is nothing I can do about it." He waved his hand helplessly to the side and drew in his lips.

After leaving him, Caravetti walked toward the cathedral on the hill-top. Women were opening shutters as he passed them. The town was stretching its limbs in the bright morning sun. Like a person it went through the same motions every morning. Caravetti wondered how far into the past the town had acted the same way. People's habits were dictated by the climate. He could not believe that the Romans got out of bed any sooner than the Spaniards. Through the centuries of inhabitants in this small town the surficial actions were the same. Fisherman had fished off the coast years ago as they fished then. Even the melon rind design of the boats had been retained from Phoenician times. He smiled. The Phoenicians were probably as lazy too. A cloud in the sky was bad weather unless they were in sore need of fish.

When he reached the crest of the hill, he walked to the cathedral steps from which there was a view of the town and the sea beyond it. He climbed half-way to the church door and sat down to watch the actions below him. Tiny peg-like figures moved from out of one house into another further along the street. A cart rolled through the main street and stopped in front of the general store. The driver unloaded cantaloupes and left them on the sidewalk and drove on. Caravetti recognized the red skirt of the girl who delivered the bread to the cafes and the restaurant and to some of the houses of the wealthier people. From across the street she had a striking figure. From his present perch, she was disappointingly another peg.

Viewing the town, as he was now, from a distant height, Caravetti was fond of it. He found a joy in remembering things about it and in picking people out in the street by the clothes they were wearing. But when he walked through the streets, when he was snubbed by the very people he could pick out from a distance, his home town became a prison. A symbol of penitence seemed to stand at the end of every street. If it was not the stare of an aged relative, it was the averted look of a fisherman's wife. The townspeople had infected the town with a hostile attitude, and although he did not dislike them as people, he resented the pernicious influence they had as a group over hearts both young and old. He yearned for the day they would accept him freely amongst them, but he refused stubbornly to ask their forgiveness.

This unwholesome hositility influenced his style of painting as well. When he tried to paint directly from nature, the finished object turned out grotesquely different from what he had intended. The town streets enclosed a disturbing mystery that he determined to reveal through his painting, but he could not project on canvas the strange essence that he sensed in them. His continuous failure led him to the conclusion that he had to endure this penitence before he could recreate on canvas. Meanwhile this mournful longing to wrap himself in the mystery of the town through painting the streets drove him onward in his work, and led him from one disappointing canvas to another. Caravetti was suffering the pangs of artistic frustration.

As he contemplated the scene before him, the bell in the cathedral tower pealed an early morning ring down into the town. Caravetti looked round to see a priest come from the door of the church. He was the one who had lived in South America for most his life. Caravetti had noticed him in the town. He looked happy. He waved and smiled at the townspeople he knew and seemed ready to meet any stranger. He approached Caravetti with this demeanor of good will. A tall man, his stomach bulged like that of an expectant mother. A chubby face smiled under a wide-brimmed black hat which concealed his white hair and his bald spots.

"Good morning!"

"Good morning, Father."

"Lovely view from here, isn't it?"

"Wonderful view, Father."

"Would I disturb your contemplation if I sat down for a few minutes to enjoy it with you?"

"I'd like you to sit down, Father."

The priest put his hand on the step two above that which he intended to sit on and lowered himself onto the stone. He took off his hat and hooked it over his knee. The sun illumined the wrinkles in his forehead.

"The town doesn't seem to change much over the years, does it? When I was a boy I climbed here to sit on these steps and to watch people walking in the streets. Of all the views I know, it is perhaps the most peaceful. You can feel a slight breeze on the side of your face and you think you're somewhere up in the sky. Then looking down on the world below, you feel so far removed from all earthly traffic that it seems separate from you as if you were no longer dependent on it. Then you realize that it's time you were going down, and you climb off your cloud ready to be dependent on others again. But it was a good rest while it lasted," he laughed.

"That's what I feel it is," Caravetti agreed, "a good rest."

"One needs it after climbing that hill," the priest laughed again.

"Do you come up here every morning, Father?"

"Yes, regularly," he smiled. "Do you come here often yourself?"

"No. Just when I'm feeling I need a rest."

"You don't go any further up the steps?" the priest said.

"I'm afraid I don't any more," Caravetti smiled. He disliked a religious discussion, especially with a priest. There was such a thing as logic and there was such a thing as faith. For Caravetti the two did not mix.

"You were born after I left the town, weren't you, Caravetti?"

"How do you know my name?"

The priest chuckled. "You're a familiar figure in town. Everyone knows your story, and I, for one, am not behind the times."

"I suppose I've been pointed out as an outcast."

"Not an outcast," the priest smiled, "merely a deserter."

"One is as bad as the other it seems."

The priest fingered the brim of his hat. "Well no. One is an outcast because he has committed an irredeemable crime against society and refuses to acknowledge his guilt. A deserter is a man who recognizes the harm he has caused in the society and who refuses to continue living in it because he senses his own guilt in conflict with it."

"Very good, Father." Caravetti was listening intently. The priest's words had found a crack in his armour against religious discussion.

"It is understood that you have repented your mistakes in the past and now want to be rejoined with your wife."

"That's more difficult than it sounds," Caravetti said.

"Nothing's easy, Caravetti. You can't expect your wife to bend like plastercine."

Caravetti laughed. "She doesn't bend at all. In a year on the island I've not had one long conversation with her. She won't listen to me."

"Meanwhile the townspeople are making you suffer for forsaking her. It's rather ironic isn't it?"

"But it's serious now, Father." Caravetti turned eagerly to him. "My boy is sick and I'm afraid she won't permit me to see him. By the terms of our separation she has the right to do that."

"Do you love your son?"

"I don't know, I haven't really known him. I think so."

"You're worried about him?"

"Yes."

"Then I think you should be allowed to see him. If Maria denies you the right, I'll speak to her."

"With the doctor and the priest on my side I should be allowed to see him," Caravetti spoke wistfully. "Yet I wish I could accomplish it alone. Somehow it doesn't mean much when I have to depend on the advocation of others. The importance of seeing him loses its value. But thanks just the same."

Turning to look Caravetti in the eyes, the priest paused before replying. He remarked the determination in the artist. "I see what you mean. You're right, of course. If you want to regard your son as your son you must do it with your own will. Help from others makes it all superficial and therefore worthless. I like you, Caravetti. You're a man." The priest looked admirably at him. "If I can ever be of any help, you can count on me."

"Thank you, Father. You've been a help already."

The priest put on his hat and placing his hands on his knees he lurched forward onto his feet. He wished Caravetti luck and waved to him before disappearing round a bend in the path.

Caravetti was glad that they had met. He felt comfortably secure with the good will of the priest behind him. He did not know why. He had never expected to feel secure with a priest. It is amazing what a right personality can do, he thought.

When the sun had risen a quarter of the way in the sky, when the town was alive as a bargaining agent, when the shops were open, and when the women were in the streets with their market baskets, Caravetti went down the side of the hill to Maria's Casa. The servant girl answered the door. She asked him to wait outside. Then Maria came to speak to him. Her countenance sternly rebuked him for coming.

"How is the boy?" Caravetti asked.

"He'll be fine," she answered. Maria disliked the role she had to play with Caravetti. A need for revenge had induced her to adopt it, but after a year of it, the revenge had become tiresome. When she saw Caravetti, however, she spurred herself to support the façade.

"May I see him now?"

"No."

"But why not? If he's sick I should be allowed to see him."

"We've been through this before," she said. "You cannot regard the children as yours. You know that." She wanted to remind him of how he once had felt.

"But they are my children and I don't care what law says I can't see them, I'm going to see them."

"I won't let you through the door." Maria blocked the movement he had made to walk in the house.

Caravetti was angry. He grabbed her arm to push her out of the way, but she flew at him in a temper. She clawed at his face so that he had to hold both her wrists.

"Both the doctor and the priest said I could see him," he shouted helplessly.

Maria sobbed with anger. She pitted all her energy against allowing him to enter the house. The servant girl, who had run to the door, beat at him with the handle of a broom. Bewildered by Maria's obstinacy, he walked from the porch and stumbled into the lane. His scenes with Maria had always been short but none was as brutal. He groaned in despair as he thought of all the ground he had lost in the battle of winning back her sympathy.

Presently he found himself at the foot of the hill on the turn-off to the shore road. He could not face his studio; he did not want to wander about the town where he would suffer the slights that would remind him of Maria; Pedro either had left or he was having a terrifying scene with Senora Cosmos in trying to leave. The country opened expansively to him. And so he chose the shore road as the most comforting direction in which to walk.

As he walked he thought of his son. The little boy had good-looking features, he thought. He looked more like Maria than himself. Perhaps he would be practical like her. Perhaps he would look into the future and plan as Maria had done. As a result of her prudence, she enjoyed the children and the little support he gave them, while he had nothing save himself, his boring self. If he could be reinstated as the head of the family, he would lose himself in the enjoyment it would give him. His boy would be diverting. Even now the sickness had given Caravetti a strong interest in him. He had been even ready to quarrel with Maria for the sake of seeing him. No. Perhaps he was wrong. He was not sure if he battled for the sake of the boy or for Maria's sake. At any rate it was diverting.

A shrill shout startled him. He turned to see Juan speeding up from behind on a bicycle. The little chef had food supplies stuffed in his carrier. He smiled hugely as he skidded the cycle to a stop. "Come out to the beach," he said. "We'll have a big lunch. You see what I've got?" He lifted the cover to the carrier and stared comically in at a collection of greens and meats.

There was a pension that Juan owned near the beach at the end of the island. Its only business was the taxi-going tourists and the people who lived in the few houses scattered about that part. Juan was proud of the tiny white house. He referred to it as "my popular beach villa."

"Well, I might," Caravetti drawled thoughtfully. He remembered the long stretch of sand shiny like sandalwood when he used to hike there as a boy. There was a tranquility about the spot. The peaceful playground of his boyhood might temporarily usurp his mood of depression with memories of irresponsible bliss.

"You must come! It will give you inspiration." Juan minced the words as if he were tasting a spicy dish.

"Then I will," Caravetti smiled. "But I warn you, I'm not feeling happy."

"Aha, we shall make you that very thing." Juan twirled a carving knife from his carrier in the air. "Come, I'll ride you on the cross-bar."

"Oh no!" Caravetti protested. The suggestion was far too jolly for his present mood. "You go ahead and start the cooking. I'll be there in a hour."

Juan called back through the dust he left in his wake. "My sister and her children will be there."

The family life of other people always sounded like a celebration. As he continued walking he recalled the glow of children's smiles. He missed being the father of his family. In one way Barbara had been right, he remembered. Obstinately she had insisted that she knew what was best for him. Even though she didn't always know what was best for herself as when, for instance, she stayed late at nerve-wearing night clubs.

The legs swung from both sides, and the girls touched toes at the top of the swing. The short blue skirts flapped revealingly causing the spectators near the stage to strain their necks. Two lines of tall girls wearing bird feathers swayed through the gauntlet of swinging legs.

Caravetti watched the other couple at the table. They were enjoying themselves. He signalled the waiter to replenish their glasses with champagne. The other man turned a wide, happy face to wink at Caravetti. Middle-aged, the man and his wife were guests of the model agency at whose expense Barbara and Caravetti were entertaining them.

"What do you think of that?" The visitor spoke with a Californian accent.

"It's really something, isn't it?" Caravetti said. He knew the lingo well enough to make the fellow comfortable by employing it.

"So, this is really Paris." The man held up his glass. "I never thought it'd be as good as this." He gulped a mouthful of champagne and turned back to watch the show.

Caravetti looked at Barbara and smiled. She was tired, he knew, but she did not show it. He liked her hair the way it licked up in front of her ear. Her profile was illumined by the lights up-stage. He caressed the delicate curves with his eyes.

She turned in time to catch his smile. In her look they were alone. All the nudes jumping on the stage in front of him, all the champagne in the world could not divert him from Barbara's eyes.

"Say, Caravetti, when do we get the comedian? He's supposed to be good."

"Uh...he's coming on pretty soon. Yes, he's really good. Top stuff," he added.

The comedian was very popular. He did take-offs on feminine singers by miming to the accompaniment of their hit records. When he had finished his encores, there would be one more spectacle and then they could go home.

As they were leaving the night-club, the Californian whispered to Caravetti. "I hear those girls have their breasts packed in ice for half an hour before they go on stage. To keep them firm, you know"

Caravetti looked as if he doubted it. "I think they'd catch cold."

They dropped the couple off at their hotel and fell together in the back seat of the taxi.

"Nice evening." He kissed her. "But I'm getting bored with them. How about you?"

"They do get tiring. It's lucky we had pleasant people tonight or I'd have pleaded illness and left early," she sighed.

"Next time why not suggest someone else to do the honours," Caravetti suggested. "You can afford a little rest once in a while, dear."

Barbara nestled her head on his shoulder where she kept it until the cab stopped in front of their apartment house. She leaned on him as they climbed the stairs.

"Tired phew! I'm done for." She fell on the bed.

"Well, damn it. They make you work too hard at that job. You get there at some ridiculous hour in the morning when even the birds are still sleeping. You stand all day in various poses which a circus strong man would find difficult to hold. You get back just in time to cook a late dinner. And then they expect you to revel half the night with somebody they're too tired to revel with themselves. What are they trying to do? Kill you?" He worked himself into a temper.

"Darling!" she protested. "I get paid for it."

"Okay. We'll all kneel down with arms outstretched towards any spot with a golden sparkle. Oh, come on, Barbara! Let's forget all this big money business."

"But darling, I can't. I told you I'm saving money for when you leave me. I'll need it then. I'll want to go back to the States." She propped herself on an elbow.

Caravetti frowned. "Will you please stop talking like that. I'm not going to leave you. Ever, ever, ever. Now that's final."

"Yes you will," she said sadly. "You'll have to."

"What do you mean?"

"I know you," she said.

"You crazy goof," he sat down beside her and took her in his arms. "Why would I ever want to leave a sleepy old goof like you. I don't know what I'd do without you," he added soberly.

Barbara put her face in the nape of his neck.

June. The slim trees along the sides of the boulevards fluttered their leaves in the warm breeze. Buildings cut deep shadows in the streets as the sun sparkled on roof tops and windows and beat hotly on pedestrians who had walked in its rays for more than a block. Sacre Coeur pillared Babylonically in the distance. The Seine moved serenely below its bridges. The Bateau-moux pushed from shore and idled into mid-stream. A smaller boat, loaded with passengers, scooted about the park on the end of L'Isle de la Cite. From the aft deck red-coated buglers tooted a hunting air of times past. People swarmed in the Latin Quarter. Police and stoplight had given up on the corner of St. Michel and St. Germain. Traffic thickened the boulevards as automobiles pushed their way across intersections. The blowing of car horns was forbidden by law. Pedestrians were thankful for small mercies.

On the right bank of the Seine, the traffic squeezed through narrow streets. On Rue St. Denis, the owner of a chevrefils began to brawl with the driver of a large truck. Gleefully, the crowd watched the young man hurl the bulky truck driver to the ground. An Agent, his cape furling behind him, separated them and waved the traffic on. At other intersections more Agents frantically blew whistles and waved white batons while they stood in the hot sun, their woolen capes sprawled over a hydrant on the sidewalk. Metro cars moved ceaselessly under the ground. Men and women pressed themselves through the open doors into the over-crowded cars. The doors slid shut. The station attendant ran from car to car to batter in the rear-end, the arm, or the brief case of an occupant. The oval-shaped sign poked up yellow and the cars ran forward. Passengers on the Nation-Etoile line looked interestedly out of the windows as the train rose above the ground to travel scenically over the Seine. The Eiffel Tower stood at ease as it watched them.

Caravetti sauntered through the streets of the Latin Quarter. He hiked his arm to settle his sketch book in a more comfortable position. Book stores displayed attractive titles in their windows, and low price marks peaked from the paper covers of the second-hand copies boxed in stands on the sidewalks. Students were coming from the Sorbonne. The marks of failure showed clearly on the faces of some. Pretty girls cast colourful reflections in store windows. Caravetti looked into the street several times to see the thing in the flesh. As his head began to gyrate with the interest they caused, he gave up the stores and contented himself with striding athletically down the boulevard. He walked by the Seine and prided himself for not stopping at any of the book sellers. By the time he had reached the Iena district, he wished he had taken a bus. When he opened the door of the apartment, Barbara waved to him from the living room.

"What are you doing home so early? Did the boss give you a holiday?" he laughed.

"Sort of," she laughed with him. "I've been so nice to him lately that he just had to let me go on this wonderful day."

Caravetti took her hand and placing it on her head he said, "Say, 'If I'm fibbing, may all the inside turn into sawdust!'"

"I'm fibbing."

"What happened?"

"I just fainted." Barbara let her hands fall in the air. "Like that. And my partner on the set caught me."

"Why darling, what's wrong?"

"I've been working too hard, Caravetti. I'm glad tomorrow's Sunday."

"Sunday! Wonderful Sunday! We haven't had any picnics this year. How'd you like to go on a picnic tomorrow, sweetheart? It'll be fun."

She smiled. Caravetti seemed so much younger than when she had met him. Woman-like, she wondered if it were she who had drawn out the youth in him.

"Love to, darling. But let's go and come back by taxi. We can afford it now more than we could last year."

"Lazy bones," Caravetti joked. "Don't worry. If you faint, I'll be around to catch you."

Barbara packed a lunch basket. They took a taxi to the boat house on the tiny lake in the Bois de Boulogne.

"I haven't rowed since I left Spain," Caravetti said as he dipped the oars in the water.

The days were all the same. Sunny and clear. Other couples rowed by them. Caravetti aimed for the loneliest part of the lake.

Barbara reached into the lunch basket and took out a pencil and some drawing paper.

"I haven't sketched for ages either. I think I'll do a memento of you in a row-boat."

"How are you going to do me? Forward like this? Or backward like this? When I'm forward I look puffed out. When I'm backward I grit my teeth."

"You've rowed enough now," she said. "Just rest on your oars and let the boat glide. Yes, like that. Now just hold yourself a little straighter. That's just dandy!"

Caravetti sat straight to please her although he knew that she was being amusing. Intuitively he felt that he would not have many more opportunites to please her. But the feeling passed making only an unhappy impression on his consciousness.

"At least, look happy," she pouted. "I don't want to draw an ugly old bear."

Caravetti mimicked her pout and then looked happily at her. A moment later, she handed him the paper. He recognized himself. She had captured his personality, but she had not finished the features. That was the way she sketched. Her drawings had personality but they lacked character. She left out the detail.

"It's good, Barbara. Is it for me?"

"Of course not. I'm going to keep it," she smiled.

They rowed until they were hungry. Then Caravetti took the boat back and they strolled into the woods to find a secluded spot to eat their lunch. They did not go far before they found a place that suited them.

As Caravetti watched Barbara spread out the rug and then sit on it with the basket, his eyes were saturated with the movements she made. He loved her tenderly. Oh how tenderly! he thought. And when she was near him, he was optimistic. Although he had not thought of the future, it appeared to him as a rosy glow when he was with Barbara. The future to him before he had met her was harsh and ugly. The years ahead of him had stretched out like so many gray markings until he would hit the last one, his grave-stone.

Maria and his children were a part of the past he had forgotton. He wrote to her occasionally, but he could give her no sympathy. She was the millstone that was dragging him down into the gray sea of the future. But when he was with

Barbara the millstone was cut from off his neck. He floated half-way between paradise and reality.

In the last letter he had received from Maria, she mentioned that the family expected him home soon. He did not want to go. He wanted to live on indefinitely in Paris with Barbara. If his family needed money, he could send it to them. He hoped that his paintings would become better known so that he could afford to support them. If he could not help them, then Maria would have to support herself. It was life, he thought, the gray life of Maria's future.

As the time approached for him to return to San Bernardino he thought more about asking Maria for a separation. After that was achieved, he could work on the subject of divorce. Although Maria, living in Spain, could not remarry, he could marry Barbara. But he did not think much about it; he took it for granted.

Barbara had settled her back against a tree and Caravetti lay on his back with his head in her lap. He put his cheek against her tummy and looked up into blue eyes and finely-arched eye-brows. She broke a piece off her sandwich and popped it in his mouth.

"Caravetti," she said. "I was thinking about your family."

"Telepathy," he said to himself.

"Have you heard any news from your wife lately?"

"Yes. She's fine."

"How are your children?"

"Fine too, I guess. She doesn't say much about them."

"Do they talk about you?"

"I don't know. I suppose they do."

"Don't you have any interest in them at all, darling?" She looked dismayed.

"How can I when I have you to interest me?" he said.

She bit her underlip. "But I don't want you to feel that way. After all, you have to go back to them."

"Are you still harping on that subject." He looked crossly at her. "I told you that I'm staying with you."

"Oh no, you are not! When your summer term is over, I'm leaving you to go to the States and you, my dear boy, are going straight back to your family in Spain."

Caravetti blinked at the surety of her words. While on the surface she appeared to speak light-heartedly, underneath he knew she meant what she said.

"Barbara!" he called her sharply. She frightened him. "Don't Barbara." He spoke softly. "Don't leave me."

"I'm sorry," she whispered. "We'll have to start new lives again."

"What do you mean?"

"When you leave here, you'll have to forget all about me. And I shall forget all about you." She brushed her fingers through his hair. "You won't find it hard."

"Why do you want to do this?" he asked suspiciously.

"Because we must. You have your duty to your wife and children to fulfill."

"But what will you do?"

"If I'm lucky I'll find someone I can love. Then we can be married and have children. You have your children and I'll have mine. We'll send snapshots of them to each other." She grappled his head playfully in her arms.

Caravetti thought the scene too pitiful to continue it. Holding her by the shoulders he pulled himself up so that his lips were opposite hers. "Forget about it now. Let's enjoy every moment we've got."

Caravetti undid the bow at his back and then knotted the sleeves tighter about his waist. He was using Barbara's smock as an apron. When she was late getting home, he prepared the dinner. As she was often late, he was becoming expert at cooking. He opened the oven door and pulled out the pan to look at the roasting potatoes. Smacking his lips, he pushed the pan back, closed the oven and picked the lid from a pot of green beans. With a fork he poked the beans to find they were not soft enough. He looked at the clock. Barbara was later than late. He wondered if she had had an accident. But then he decided it was no use to wonder. Either one knew those things or one did not. He turned over the steak in the frying pan. Suddenly he remembered to set the table. The cutlery, the napkins, and something else? He paused to think. Ah yes, milk. He poured two glasses of milk. The American idea of drinking milk at meals had revolted him at first, especially when he could drink French wine. But he was so accustomed to seeing Barbara drink it, that presently it became a habit with him too. Insidious American innovations, he thought.

Finally, as he was heating the meal to keep it warm, the door opened and Barbara appeared. She was flushed and excited.

"Sorry I'm late, darling."

"Phooee!" he said. "Were you posing this late?"

She came into the kitchen to watch him put the vegetables on the plates.

"No, I wasn't modelling. When are you supposed to be leaving for Spain, Caravetti?"

"In four months. But I'm not, you know."

"Well, I'm one month gone."

Caravetti put the roast potatoes on the plates. They looked rich brown and crispy. "Gone where?" he asked.

She laughed. "I'm one month gone with chld."

Caravetti gaped at her. "Ouch," he said hoarsely. And then he added after pausing to look at her. "Are you happy about it?"

"Deliriously happy." She threw her arms about his neck.

"Oh, Barbara! That means you really do want me. You won't leave me after all." He clasped her and kissed her neck strongly.

Groaning she brought her hand to his neck and reached her fingers up to direct his head against hers. "Darling, I still have to leave you. This doesn't change things."

"But it must. I can't let you have my child without being married to me. I want to marry you." He stopped to look at her as if struck by a chilling thought. "It is my child?"

"Of course," she laughed. "But you don't have to marry me, darling. I'm just as glad it happened. This way I'm not really leaving you because I'll be taking some of you with me."

"But you're crazy!" he cried. "The child will be a bastard. It needs a father."

Barbara shook her head vigorously. "Do you remember what you said to me once. 'Only the laws of society produce bastards.' Your children that are yours legally need your attention more than the child with me who will be born illegally. Without you, your children are bastards because they will never be able to know another father. Being born after a wedding is of little consequence in their case. As for this child, he has a chance to know a father because when he needs one, I'll provide him with one."

Caravetti noticed a vein in her forehead pushing with the effort of her sacrifice.

Holding her tenderly, he whispered. "Everything will be all right. Calm down now."

She sat in her place at the table. Her smile radiated a happiness that he had not seen in her before.

"It's lucky," he said, "that I've written Maria for a separation. That might help me to get a divorce sooner."

Barbara held her head in her hands. "Don't do that," she spoke through her fingers. "It'll hurt us all. You mostly."

The dinner steamed on their plates. Caravetti pressed his fork through a potato while Barbara went to wash her hands. When she returned to the table they sat in silence, both of them wondering what the other was thinking.

"I still don't understand why you're being so obstinate." His voice sounded subdued. "Nor do I understand why you want a child of mine without me."

Barbara pushed her hand across the table to fondle his fingers. "Because I love you. And as I can't have you, God, or Fate, or whatever it is that makes the world turn, has given me a part of you to take with me. I'm glad it happened. But I'm glad too that you won't be here when it's born. Our parting will be easier if you don't see the child." Soothingly her voice caressed his ears with the light touch of her fingers caressing his hand.

"I love you too much to leave you," he said slowly. He spoke as if he were thinking of something else, but his mind was a blank.

"If you really love me, you'll do what I ask.'

He smiled fondly at her. "I didn't think children could be this important."

"You silly," she said.

Three houses stood with short distances between them. The last was Juan's pension. Caravetti walked by it to see the beach. He looked across the long stretch of white sand, sable smooth, bordered on one side with pine, young-looking, green-smelling, and on the other with the crystal blue water, lapping quietly. The beach was bare of movement, exuding tranquillity. Trodding far onto it, he fell into the sand and stretched his limbs comfortably in the warmth.

A depth marker plumbed the darkness and Caravetti rolled over with a weight on his shoulder to open his eyes in the sun.

"Wake up." Pedro laughed taking his hand away. "This is no place for my saviour."

"Your saviour?'" Caravetti blinked at him.

"Well, I'm still here on the island," Pedro said, feeling uncomfortable under Caravetti's perturbed stare. "Only you can deliver me from it."

"Go away," Caravetti turned back on his stomach.

"No listen." Pedro squatted beside him. "The old dame found my boat ticket and locked me in my room this morning. I didn't get out until half an hour ago."

"And you came directly to me."

"You're the only person I can trust."

Caravetti sat up. "Say that again. You trust me? What do you want, Pedro?'"

"To get away." Pedro's sunny smile cracked into jagged lines of petulant misery. "She's keeping me a prisoner. She says that I owe her so much money she'll throw me into jail if I try to leave. Back rent and everything."

"And do you?'"

"Of course not. She didn't ask for any money. Good God! I wouldn't have stayed if she did."

Caravetti saw the taxi driver pacing impatiently in front of his model A. He knew Pedro would ask him for the fare eventually, and he felt in his pocket for the note that was to have brought him food for the day.

"Thanks, Caravetti. You're a sport," Pedro smiled again as he took the money. "I'll be right back."

Caravetti watched the light-footed Hermes speed across the sand, and he got to his feet slowly, feeling the weight of an extra problem.

Pedro caught up to him a short distance from Juan's Casa. "If you row me out from a point of land this side of San Bernardino tomorrow morning, I can arrange for the captain to take me on board. It's the last ship leaving this week. I've got to get to Valencia soon."

"Why don't you ask your fishermen pals to do it?"

Pedro squinted at him. "Do you know how much Senora Cosmos would reward someone to tell her my plans? I wouldn't trust anyone but you. I wouldn't even blame you if you told her. It's a lot of money."

"But there's something else, isn't there?" Caravetti looked askance at Pedro.

Pedro laughed and threw his arm about Caravetti's shoulders. "Only that you send flowers to my bride. She's beautiful. I've seen her picture."

"Why is her father willing to spend her dowry on you?'" Caravetti asked sharply.

Pedro looked hurt. "My family was rich too before the war. My father was his best friend. I guess he thinks it's a way to take care of his dead friend's poor young son. I couldn't think of a better way, could you?"

Caravetti moved away. "And how will you treat this young girl you don't know?"

Pedro frowned with amusement. "No different from how you treated Maria."

His words struck Caravetti, stopping him.

"Though, believe me," Pedro enunciated, "I will not let her treat me as Maria treats you."

"You know nothing about it," Caravetti murmured laconically.

"Ah now, don't quarrel. Don't be jealous of my good luck when you have all the bad. I am sorry for you, but I cannot refrain from being happy for myself."

"You would be happy wherever there was money," Caravetti said.

"And pretty women," Pedro smiled. "That's very important."

Caravetti was not amused. Pedro's remark about Maria rankled in him. It was true that he had not really loved Maria, but that was because he had not known what love was at the time. He married because society demanded it, and Maria had been just another property piece to add to his social status, although she gave him more pleasure than anything else he owned. He could not accuse Pedro of selfishness, materialistic motives and so forth. Pedro would laugh at his moral outlook, as if he were either mad or facetious, and no one would be persuaded of his seriousness. It was his Paris experience which had changed him, made him unrecognizable to those human cogs like Pedro, superfically turning with society's wheel.

"Juan!" Pedro called when the chef appeared in the doorway. "Tell Caravetti to put down his cross for a while, at least for the afternoon."

The small children of Juan's sister ran happily to them. Caravetti took the little girl in his arms and rocked her as he approached the house. "I've just traded my cross for something more human," he said.

How much more human was this bouncing, happy little animal, only Caravetti knew. He loved this moment of complete escape from worry, of enjoyment for the instant, of a certain intuitive contact with the thing called life, which, although transient, filled him with an eternal feeling. He walked through the house to the shaded courtyard at the back, and, when he saw the scene of the mother with her children around her, tears came to his eyes. He was thinking of Barbara and of how happy she would have been with these children.

He heard Pedro tell Juan that he could not stay to eat because he had a previous appointment with a senorita who lived in the hills behind the beach.

"Remember," Pedro came toward Caravetti with hand outstretched, "tomorrow morning."

Caravetti gripped his hand warmly, and he thought that he envied Pedro more than any one on earth. The light-heartedness of the handsome young man seemed utopian to him then, but he knew that it could not last. Pedro would be made to care, or he would die resisting the solemn impact of living.

Resistance was difficult for Pedro in all ways. He could not resist telling the senora that night before his departure that he loved her so that she would give him two weeks of his allowance in advance. He waved the money at Caravetti as he hurried along the shore path to where the painter waited with a small boat.

"I'm late but it couldn't be helped. She was home and I had to creep out the back way." He leaped into the boat as Caravetti was pushing off from shore and they stood rocking with the shock. "Look, I can pay you back what I owe you."

"Keep it," Caravetti said and watched Pedro happily pocket the notes. He wanted to touch only honest money, and he knew that Pedro was incapable of coming by it honestly as yet.

The water was calm and they glided over the blue until a white passenger ship rounded a point of land. Pedro pointed at it gleefully and waved his arms above his head. Their boat lay directly in the ship's path, and, presently, Pedro clambered up a rope ladder and waved to Caravetti while the ship moved away.

As Caravetti pulled on the oars for shore, he thought of Senora Cosmos and felt guilty. If she knew that he had helped Pedro to escape, she would never forgive him and she could make the island even more unpleasant for him. The senora would be quick to take revenge and slow to understand.

That evening Senora Cosmos visited Caravetti. Her pudgy face was puffed and darkened with crying. She told him that Pedro had disappeared and left a note saying that he was to marry a girl on the mainland. "Where could he have gone?" she asked.

Caravetti felt uncomfortable with this woman of unpredictable passion. She could change from self-pity to bright anger in an instant. And yet he saw that she was really suffering and that she had loved Pedro in her flamboyant way as much as woman loved any man.

"If I knew where he was at this moment, I'd be relieved," she said. "Or even to what city he is going."

Her arms were capable of reaching half-way around the globe to wreak revenge and so Caravetti said nothing.

"I thought he might have told you," she sighed.

Caravetti stood up to heat water over the charcoal stove. "If he has really gone, you should be thankful to be rid of him. Life will be cheaper for you."

"Life will be cheap," she said dismally. "He was the only one to give it value."

Her words cut through Caravetti, giving sudden meaning to his own dilemma. He had said the same about Barbara. But, he frowned, how dare he compare their love to this sordid liaison between a gigolo and a middle-aged roué. He glared at Senora Cosmos and saw again the deep shadows under the eyes and above them the unhappiness pouring out in dejected looks. He felt split open like a walnut, as if by watching the senora he was seeing the reflection of his real self, the core of him.

The senora sighed heavily and reached inside her blouse for a hankie already soaked with tears.

The coffee was taking a long time. Impatiently Caravetti fanned the fire.

"Why did you come to me?" he asked without turning to look at her.

"Because you are the only inhabitant of this place who has the heart to know what I'm going through. Anyway, kiddo, if it weren't for my money, I'd be ostracized like you. You know that."

Caravetti watched the black liquid begin to swell and he took the pot off the stove before the coffee reached the brim.

"Besides," she continued in a throaty voice, "you can help me whereas the others cannot. Just tell me what I am to do next. I feel like drowning myself."

"Which means you won't go anywhere near the sea," Caravetti smiled.

"What's that? Positive thinking and the first sign of recovery? I admit I've been in a daze all day long. Just thinking of something definite like sinking in water is a relief."

"You really loved Pedro, didn't you?"

Senora Cosmos nodded her large head. "The damned trouble is that I knew it wouldn't last. All the time I fooled myself that he loved me though he didn't, and I knew it, but to admit it would have destroyed something that I have had rarely in my life, and you know I'm no chicken. I've had more than my share of males." She shook her head and dropped her hands to her lap. "Maybe I'm just getting old and sentimental. In the old days, I would have got over this in an hour. No, I'm wrong! This one was different, Caravetti. Maybe the hopelessness of it made me love him all the more."

"It's true that everyone loves most the thing that he can never have entirely." Caravetti handed her a cup of coffee and retired to his chair. "I guess I'm a victim of that."

"But I feel exhausted," the senora sighed. "I've come to the end, and I don't want to go on. I'm too tired, Caravetti."

"You will go on because there is nothing else for you to do. You won't kill yourself."

"Why not?" she smiled ruefully at him. "With the advances of medicine these days even cowards can kill themselves. I'm just a fat old woman with nothing to look forward to, except getting fatter and older, and dying in the end."

"But do you ever think of Pedro apart from yourself? If you did, you wouldn't be so unhappy for him."

"I have been thinking that way and that's what depresses me. Oh, I have my parties and my fun, but they don't mean anything, especially now. I thought Pedro would have my money when I died but with a rich senorita he has both wealth and beauty. I'm boring you, aren't I?"

"No, you are not, because you are bringing me to the answer of a problem which has been torturing me for a long time. How much of one is left with a great experience and how much of one is left over to go on with?"

"Not much is left over," she said.

"Pedro remains and so do you. Perspective is what you need to keep this love in its proper place. Let it stay there. Why should it belong to your life now or bother you at any time in the future? The past is not really as strong as all that. It need not control the present if you don't allow it."

"You mean there are more Pedros in the sea?" she snorted, but her eyes were gleaming with the hope in his words.

"There may be but what does it matter? Your love for Pedro belongs only to the time you were with him. The rest of your life belongs only to you. If you can enjoy it as yours completely, you can come to enjoy even the tragic moments in it, even your one-time love for Pedro." Caravetti paused to ponder over his words with an increasing awareness that he could have been speaking to himself. "Your love becomes an experience and as you can carry on living you leave your love behind." He looked sharply at her. "It has taken me a long time to discover the truth of that."

“Stop thinking about yourself and think of me for a moment,” she glowered, but then broke into a smile. “I feel better already, kiddo.”

“I'm recovering too,” he said. “All I need is some help to launch me into the present and I think I’ll stay there.”

A knock sounded on the door. Caravetti called out for the visitor to enter and the priest from South America appeared on the threshold. "I hope I’m not intruding. Good-evening, Senora. You may see your son tomorrow, Caravetti. Maria asked me to tell you. Ah Senora, not very happy this evening?"

Caravetti’s thoughts whirled so that he could understand none of them. He was not overjoyed, merely dazed. He heard the priest speak with the senora while he tried to find some definite response within himself. All he knew was that he had found his way into the present.

"Good-night, Caravetti." Senora Cosmos held out her hand and tossed her pony tail. "You’ve consoled me more than you can guess. You have a persuasive manner about you," she rolled her eyes, "and you’re damned sincere. I feel wonderful. Though it won’t last. I’ll break down in the middle of the night." She walked ahead of the priest and then turned round in the doorway. "I think I’ll send Pedro a present when the wedding announcement appears. His statue. Do you want to go halfers?"

"Senora." Caravetti swallowed. "I have a confession to make."

"If it’s about rowing Pedro, don’t bother. I saw it all through a looking-glass from my front porch. An old fat woman knows when she’s beaten." She held up her hand to stop Caravetti’s protest. "In that fight, but there’s always another, n’est-ce-pas?"

After they had gone, Caravetti breathed deeply, then undressed and tried to sleep. He could hardly wait for morning when he would return to his home and family even if it were just for a visit. He could almost sense life wakening his interest in that ephemeral feeling he called the present.

10.

Caravetti watched the dust pile thickly on the tip of his sandals. He stomped his feet to shake it off but made clouds of dirt which enveloped his legs and stuck to his ankles. Gratefully, he turned from the road onto a path where the slope and the rocks made it difficult for the sand to collect. Grape vines, loaded with blue and yellow bunches, stretched along the walls on either side of the lane. The bunches on the outside were covered with dust which floated on the skins like specks on water. The lane mounted. Weeds and tufts of grass clung to it by hiding at a base of a rock or by wedging themselves against the walls. From it, one could see the large white houses fringed with porticos: the houses of the rich which sat far back from the lane surrounded by greenery. Caravetti passed several estates before he came to the house of his parents which was now the house of his wife. He unfastened the gate and slowly walked to the front door. The maid answered his knock. Apologetically, she allowed him to enter the hall. She remembered hitting him with a broom, and she knew he would not have forgotten it. She led him to his son’s bedroom.

Maria was there. She looked at him with tired eyes and said nothing and implied nothing. Caravetti went to the bedside to look at the sleeping boy. A tortured look played upon the boy's features. The wrenched state of the bedclothes added to the tale of suffering. Caravetti could not remember his son's name for the moment.

"How is he?" he asked.

Maria turned down the corners of her mouth and shook her head.

Manuel! That was his name! Caravetti wanted to see how it sounded in his mouth. He wanted to prove that he had not forgotten it. "How are you, Manuel?" he softly asked the sleeping figure. "Manuel, my son." He patted the counterpane as if comforting it and then turned a serious face to Maria. "I'll watch him now," he said. "You sleep."

She made a motion as if to refuse and then, obediently, she left him. By allowing him into the house, she had lost her prerogative. While he was there, he gave the orders; she obeyed them.

The room was the one in which Caravetti had slept when a boy. The white iron bed was the same he had slept in. The dark brown cabinet with the two cubby-holes on either side where he used to keep his secrets, was still there. The small table and chair used to be his property. He remembered sitting there and pasting stamps in a big album. At first he had glued them until he discovered that one had to use hinges to keep the value in the stamp. The pictures on the walls had not been changed. A vivid scene in which the armada was colourfully victorious had been taken from a magazine and put behind glass in a picture frame. A comic relief showed a small dog barking at a boy with big boots who was about to march through a puddle. The boy could not see the puddle for the rain hat that had fallen over his face. And there was a small landscape painting that Caravetti had done when he was nine years old. The red curtains on the window were different. He wondered what the garden looked like.

A little girl was playing in a sand box set in the centre of the grass by a small fig tree that grew there. She had built a large Arabic-looking castle. Turrets had been made more credible with sticks. Outposts had been staggered at intervals along the walls. With pieces of wood she had erected pillars and constructed arches entering to the gardens. Pieces of grass lay about imaginary fountains. Although the façade was crude, the design was brilliant. She stood gazing at it. She was a little girl in a dirty blue dress regarding the creation of men who had lived centuries before her. Her foot swung into the centre of the castle and the sand collapsed into the hole she had made. Finishing the destruction with the palms of her hands, she smoothed the sand level and began to build again.

Caravetti turned round to look at the boy. He wished he knew him. The sleeping form had some resemblance to himself. The eyes and the mouth were his. But aside from a slight paternal feeling, he knew no sympathy for the boy's personality. He felt sorry for a little boy who was approaching the climax of his sickness, and he liked being near his son. But he was not distressed as he should have been; he was not like Maria.

A sense of responsibility had brought him to the house to watch over the child. Maria doubted Caravetti's responsibleness. She thought that he would be careless, that the child would be safer if under her care all the time. But the doctor had convinced her to allow Caravetti to help with the nursing of the boy.

The doctor had argued for Caravetti because the boy's condition was serious, and he wanted a man's judgement to support his own. The specialist had told the doctor what to do for the kidney ailment and that if the sickness got worse, an operation would be necessary. As the loss of one kidney would seriously limit the life span of the boy, the doctor was against operating until the last possible moment, which might be too late. He asked Caravetti whether they should risk the boy's life to save the kidney and the artist agreed to it. The boy's fever was high, and the doctor was worried. Caravetti's presence would be a comfort.

This was Caravetti's first visit to the house since he had left it for Paris. He was not curious as to how the rest of the house looked. He considered himself figuratively as remote as he ever was. As a guardian of the child, he had the privilege to go into the kitchen and drink a glass of water, but that was all. He was pleased, however, that Maria had obeyed him without resisting. Although she was tired enough to give into him, the flash of resistance in her eye was not lost to Caravetti. She had accepted him in his position as head of the house. He wondered whether she would ever accept him as a husband again. A chair by the bedside offered a seat. Caravetti sat down and folded his hands on his lap. He watched the boy's face, flushed with red patches, and he listened to his son's breathing, unsettled and throaty.

An hour passed. Caravetti found some paper and a pencil in the drawer of the small desk. Some of the boy's crayoning books were there. He looked at the outlined figures coloured with the boy's imagination. Then using one book as a smooth support for his paper he began to sketch the boy's face. He drew many poses and then he sketched objects in the room. It was late afternoon when the doctor arrived, and Caravetti had used up all the paper in the drawer, the backs of the crayon books and the notepaper that the maid had been able to give him.

The doctor shook hands cordially, looked at the boy, and took Caravetti into the hallway. As he closed the door of the bedroom, he smiled at Caravetti. "When did you come?"

"This morning."

"Maria sleeping?"

Caravetti nodded.

"I came now because I want to give him these pills and more shots." The doctor held a box in his hand. "He ought to be coming out of the sleep soon."

"Do you think he'll be all right?" Caravetti asked to assure himself.

"I don't know. We will know very soon though. If his temperature does not drop by tomorrow evening, then I'll operate." The doctor frowned as he thought of the operation.

They heard a short cry from the bedroom. The doctor opened the door and they entered quickly. The boy was coming out of his sleep. His face was livid with pain. The doctor ran to hold him from twisting out of bed. The boy woke up staring at Caravetti. He groaned and lay back on the pillow. To Caravetti his face looked so different now than it did when he was sketching it. The mouth that Caravetti had recognized as like his own was open and agonised. The boy's eyes burned with fever.

The doctor let go of Manuel to look in his bag. Caravetti approached his son. He wished that he could give him courage; he began to wish he could take some of the pain himself. The doctor put a needle in Manuel's thigh, and, after a moment, the groaning stopped. Manuel looked sleepily about him. He stared at Caravetti, and Caravetti stared at him. Manuel did not know the artist, nor did he seem to want to know him. He asked for his mother.

Quickly the doctor gave him the pills. As Manuel swallowed, his eyelids drooped. The doctor put a thermometer in his mouth. Gradually the boy fell into a peaceful sleep again. His temperature was higher.

The doctor left saying he would be back that night. Caravetti was left alone again. There was nothing for him to do except to sit and watch. He remembered that some of his books might be in the house,and he asked the maid to look for them. She brought him two: one which he had read, and luckily one which he had always intended to read. Settling comfortably in his chair, which he had placed near the window, he read away the afternoon and evening. At seven o'clock the maid brought him tea and sandwiches. He had not eaten lunch so that he welcomed all food. At nine o'clock, he noticed that Manuel was beginning to stir. Suddenly the boy screamed; his arms thrashed about him; he dug his finger nails into his face. Caravetti jumped to him, seized his arms, and pinned him against the bed. Gradually his movements slowed, his screamings became sighs, and the pain was dulled in sleep.

Awakened by the cries, Maria ran into the room as Caravetti came away from the bed. Her hair was uncombed and her face was strained in worry.

"He's sleeping now," Caravetti said softly. "He was delirious."

Maria put her hands to her face in relief. She had slept long and soundly but she was still exhausted. She had gone two days and nights without sleep while Manuel was passing through a crisis.

Caravetti put his arm about her shoulders and led her to sit in his chair. He enjoyed his role of comforter and so he did not take his arm away but kneeled beside Maria when she sat. But Maria glared sternly at him so that he moved to a standing position by the bed. He would have been hurt by Maria's look if he had not known that he could expect nothing better.

"You can go," Maria said plainly. "I'll watch him tonight."

"The doctor came this afternoon." Caravetti employed her tone.

"Is Manuel better?" Her eyes raised hopefully.

"Worse." Caravetti tried to sound undramatic.

She looked at the boy and then closed her eyes. Caravetti saw her lips moving in prayer. He listened carefully to her lispings to see if he could recognize the prayer she was saying, but although some of the words were familiar, he had forgotten them. He had ceased to believe in praying, but he felt more easy about the boy after Maria had said her prayer.

"Don't you think he should be operated on?" she asked.

"The doctor says he thinks he can save his kidney," Caravetti replied doubtfully. He narrowed his eyes at her. What did she care about his thoughts? "I don't know," he said. "But I'll stand behind the doctor."

"We must pray that he will be right," she advised.

"Do you think that helps?" He knew it was a foolish question to ask Maria, but he wanted to remind her of his views.

"Try it," she smiled sadly. "And see."

That was the first time Caravetti had seen her smile since he had returned. He was surprised at more than that. The smile was one that remembered him as he once was. Intuitively, he sensed the reference of Maria's thoughts. He wanted to be sympathetic to her. "I'll try," he smiled in return. "If you're sure it will do some good." He felt guilty when he saw Maria's face light up with gratefulness. He disliked obligating himself, especially to other people's whims. But then Maria was an exception. Maria with the cupid face now that she was smiling.

Caravetti promised to come in the early morning. As he walked to the gate, the doctor opened it from the other side. They greeted each other in passing but hurried on; the doctor to save a life; Caravetti to eat his dinner

11.

When Caravetti knocked the next morning it was Maria who answered the door. The distrustful look had been replaced by a hopeful one. Her eyes glistened and she smiled with the corners of her lips. It was a smile that had to remove an obstacle before it could know completeness. She took him to Manuel's room. The boy was sleeping. The bed sheets were crumpled worse than when he had left; the boy had passed a delirious night. Maria put her fingers to her lips and motioned Caravetti to sit down. She was gone a quarter of an hour before she came back with a breakfast tray. Although Caravetti had made himself a cup of coffee earlier, he took the coffee she offered him, and he ate the jam rolls with her.

They ate silently. They either stared at the boy or they glanced about the room. Caravetti fixed his eyes on a corner of the bed. Maria spoke first.

"The doctor came after you left last night. Manuel's temperature was the same," she whispered.

"When will he be here again?" Caravetti looked into her black eyes weighted with rings of sleeplessness. In the frankness of her grief, she asked pity from him. He hardened his voice to keep his heart from sliding into it.

"Late this morning or early this afternoon." She answered as if time had no meaning.

Caravetti swallowed his coffee and took another roll. At that moment he sensed the peacefulness and some of the sweetness of a feminine companion, of a sorrow that he shared with her. He watched an emotion play across her face and fade out as if she were about to speak and then decided against it.

"He had a rough night," Caravetti nodded toward the bed.

"Caravetti," Maria spoke suddenly. "Why do you want to help nurse him?"

Surprised, Caravetti muttered the first thought he had. "I want to see him well again." He spoke defensively.

"But why do you?" she insisted.

"Because I want to love him and I want to love you." His words tumbled unexpectedly from his mouth so that he was surprised at himself for saying them.

She sat back in her chair and twisted her fingers with her hands. She wanted to believe him, but she wanted a basis of truth.

"Don't you love me now?" she asked knowing the answer.

"Now? No, I don't love you."

"Why do you want me?"

"I want you because I need you," he said. To him it sounded like an over-familiar phonograph record. But he had not said it from habit; he was sincere.

She shook her head briefly in disbelief. "Then why did you leave me?"

"To find that I wanted you." Caravetti looked sadly at her. He knew he was helpless to convince her.

Maria stood up and gathered up the breakfast dishes to carry them to the kitchen. She was obviously thinking of what he had said. "I need you too," she said. "But if you come back, how will I know that you'll stay?" Her need was a family need; Caravetti thought that she did not love him. But he saw a hole opening to him. He would settle in the family; he would be father to the children; he would play husband to his wife; but all the world would be a stage.

"Have I proved nothing by constantly trying to gain your forgiveness?" he asked somberly.

She nodded slightly and looked at the floor. Still looking down she asked, "Did you pray last night?"

He wanted to say yes, but a lie would gain him nothing. "No." His tone softened to intimacy. "It's useless for me to recite prayers like a Catholic because I've lost the fervour; and I can't make up prayers like the Protestants because I can't believe that someone is listening."

She carried the breakfast tray to the kitchen. When she came back her face was drawn in determination. "If you would believe in prayer, I would believe in you."

"In other words you want me to return to the Church."

"Yes," she said.

Hypocrisy opened its sleepy jowls and yawned at him. "Why do you think the Church would help me to become a better husband?" he asked sincerely.

"It helped me to keep going when you were gone," she said.

"Did you have any lovers?" he asked in reply.

She looked at him, and swallowed. "Yes."

"Don't you think they helped?"

She did not answer. The logic meant nothing to her.

"I thought," she said, "that if you prayed for Manuel too, he would be cured. My prayers are not enough. We need you to help us." Maria believed in what she said.

Caravetti frowned. He sat in silence as he puzzled his situation. If he did not believe in what he was praying, then how could his prayers do any good? Yet if he prayed he imagined he would make Maria happy. But then that would be pretence because if Maria really knew that he was pretending to pray, she would not be happy. Although he was offered this easy solution to all his strivings to win back his social position, he felt that he needed something else to stabilize him; otherwise he would still be striving for an added something that he could not name. But there seemed no other way. To win back something he wanted he had to give himself to things he did not like. It was paradoxical! To win his peace he had to give up his freedom.

"Please." Her face begged him; her hands reached out to him.

Could he ever love her again? he wondered. He came from his chair to take her hands in his, and, kneeling beside her, he took her in his arms and kissed her. He smelt a sweet scent of desire.

"Yes," he said. "I'll pray with you."

Her breath coursed down his neck, her arms were about him. She embraced him until the shock of passion subsided into an agreement between them. They knelt at the bedside of the sleeping boy. For a moment Caravetti felt awkward, but his sense of self was swept away by the sincere incongruity of his actions. He was conscious only of kneeling with Maria at the bedside of their son.

Closing his eyes he listened to her begin a familiar prayer. His voice would echo her words, then join with hers as he remembered a phrase, then echo again and sometimes die out to come back in tune with hers. Slowly, a calmness descended on them. He was comforted by Maria's presence and by her belief. When she came to the end, they continued to kneel in silence. Caravetti rose and Maria followed him. She looked assured, and he was happy for her.

"Now," she smiled, "he'll get well." She kissed the boy's cheek.

Caravetti had no faith in the prayer. He had no conviction that the boy would be better or sicker. But his interest in the boy had been deepened. For the first time he was a member of the family. He was the slower moving cog in Maria's wheel of emotion. Coming from behind her, he placed his hands on her hips. "You're tired," he said. "You should sleep now."

"I want to stay with you until the doctor arrives," she spoke softly.

Caravetti walked to the window. The little girl was playing in the garden again. She was sitting on the grass and laughing. The maid stepped into view, and rolled a ball toward the little girl. It bounced against her feet, and she had to stand up to reach it. When she turned to throw it back, the maid was no longer there. The child's face was swamped with disbelief, and then with disappointment. She took the ball to the sandbox where she tucked it in one corner, and she wandered to another part of the yard. Standing at the window, Caravetti tried to symbolize her movements. He hoped that Maria would not be disappointed too. He began to love her.

"Is that our child playing out there?" he asked. He wanted her near him.

"Yes." She came to take his arm and to watch the little girl with him.

From the time he left Paris, he dreamed of this moment. Although he had fought for it, argued for it, persevered for it, the winning of it was not a result of his efforts. Circumstances had pushed him into it. He was a chess man who had been advanced on the board after a long wait for an opening. "May I come back now?" he asked. It was too easy.

"No," she said. "Not yet."

"Why not?" Stepping away from her he began to think she was playing a game.

"Wait until the doctor has come and then we can talk about it."

Disheartened, Caravetti could see the parable of the little girl, the ball, and the maid that disappeared all over again. When he was rejoicing in what he thought was certain, he found that the stabilising part, without which the rest was useless, was no longer there.

"You never will love me, I know," he groaned.

"I can love you," she answered. "But this time I want to make sure of your love. You must love the same things I love. And then if you leave me, you will leave more than my love."

Caravetti stared at her. The years of their separation had changed her from an obedient bride to a bargaining realist. Life with her would be more of an adventure. He smiled gratefully at her. "Love is such a temporary thing. It can turn to hate in a moment. One cannot promise to love, because one should know that love is either the most pleasing result from a number of comparisons or the temporary surrender to an overpowering desire. One's love may be beaten out by a lovelier comparison or by a stronger desire." Because her eyes showed that she did not understand him he added, "I can respect the things you love, but I cannot promise to love them."

"But spiritual love," she protested. "I want you to love the Church first."

"And second?" he asked. He wondered how people loved the Church. By fearing it? He supposed so. He refused to love through familiarity.

"The children. And the others will follow after them."

"What about you?" he queried. "Wouldn't it be wiser to love you first. Because without you the others have no value for me." Caravetti knew as he was talking that he had been taught to express his feelings that way. And he was fighting against the thought that Maria was a replacement for Barbara.

Her eyes loomed in surprise. "Do you think you could?"

He embraced her and kissed her. He kissed her again. Only a knock at the front door separated them. A moment later the doctor appeared from the hallway. The older man noticed the flush on their cheeks. Smiling, he reached out to hold a hand of both of them. He needed no words to express the gratification in his eyes.

"Well!" he exclaimed. "Look who's awake and watching."

They turned to see Manuel, his hands propped on the pillow, looking at them steadfastly. The boy's eyes flamed in sickness. Swirling about his head in twisted strands his hair crowned him like winding thorns. Caravetti stepped guiltily to the bed. He felt that his son was accusing Maria and himself for leaving him to forward their own interests. "I'm sorry, Manuel," he muttered.

The doctor was beside the boy before Caravetti saw whether his son had understood him. Feeling the patient's forehead and holding his wrist, the doctor brought all movement to a standstill. After a moment, he went to his bag where he found his thermometer. He put it in Manuel's mouth. "Well, our sick boy is not so sick today," The doctor regarded Manuel with a benevolent smile. He patted the pockets of his suit coat and reached in one of them. Bringing out a package of strong cigarettes he offered them to Maria and Caravetti. When they shook their heads he took one himself, carefully closed the package, and put it back in his pocket. He then patted the other pockets of his suit, but in vain.

Caravetti, who had been standing as if caught in a beam of searchlight, broke from his freeze and thrust his hand into his pocket. He lit the doctor's cigarette but the doctor had to hold Caravetti's hand to keep the match steady.

Puffing with pleasure, the doctor took his watch from his pocket, put it back, and walked slowly to the bedside. Caravetti tip-toed behind him, ready to peak over his shoulder when the thermometer would be in his hands. The doctor took the thermometer from Manuel, read it, and turned a bright smile at the parents. "He's much better. Last night must have been the highest point of the crisis."

Maria ran to the boy and kissed him. Tears were in her eyes when she turned to Caravetti. Her lips moved at him in gratitude.

"But he's not well by any means," the doctor frowned. "I'm afraid he'll have to stay in bed for a while yet. We have to watch that kidney if we don't want it to flare up again. Maria, when he can eat I'll give you a diet I want him kept on strictly until I let you know when he can eat other things. Do you hear?"

Maria nodded her head. In her happiness she retained his words to comprehend later. She looked at Caravetti, and she loved him. God had answered their prayer; he had meant them to live together again; and He had brought Caravetti to a state of religious realization.

But Caravetti thought differently. To him the change in Manuel was not owing to the prayer; it was circumstance, that chameleon of human fate, that accounted for the boy's drop in temperature. Tomorrow, his temperature might unexpectedly rise again. No, he could not believe that prayer had saved Manuel for him. Perhaps it had worked for Maria. But Caravetti knew that prayer was no aid to him. He sensed the workings of fate as surely as he sensed himself. Many times as a boy when he had prayed for something and his prayer had been answered, he acknowledged the strength of God. But when he had suffered as a man, when prayers refused to help him, he had given them up, not because he was against religion but because he could not endure more disappointment. Without a God he could not be betrayed by his own wants, he thought.

The doctor injected a medicine into Manuel's thigh. He did not give him more of the sleeping drug because most of the pain had gone. After patting the boy on the head he motioned the parents to walk ahead of him into the hall. When they had entered the sitting room, the doctor set his bag on the floor and sat down. While Maria perched on the arm of a chair, Caravetti sunk into the seat of the same chair.

"Manuel's sickness has brought you two together again I see." The doctor looked sternly at them as if he were about to lecture.

"It's a miracle," Maria said.

The doctor nodded his head as if what she said might be true. "Whatever it is," he continued, "it has happened. Now I don't want you to let this opportunity slip." He beat the first two fingers of one hand on the palm of the other. "We in this town have been concerned about you two long enough. We don't want to see you both living on as separate people. We want to see you happily together. Caravetti has proved his devotion to the family, Maria. That should be enough."

Maria nodded in agreement. “Yes, doctor. We’ve decided to live together again. Haven’t we Caravetti?” Her eyes shone at the artist.

“Yes,” he smiled back at her. “We’re together again.” He sensed the lack of conviction in his voice. The restoration of his old status as head of the family made no impression upon him. It was not titular recognition, he desired, rather a peace within himself. His year of striving suddenly seemed spent in vain. He had thought that if he were reunited with Maria his despondency would be cured, but now he doubted it. Now that he had the opportunity to love Maria again, he was uncertain that it was she whom he wished to love. When the doors to his house, to his family were open, he doubted if he had the right house. He understood only one thing; that he had arrived at his destination. There was no turning back and there seemed to be no going ahead. He was in limbo.

The doctor stood up. He looked about for an ash tray. Maria scooted for one and held it while the doctor stubbed his cigarette. “If I were you, Maria,” he advised, “I would arrange with Caravetti about annulling the separation terms.”

As if he were about to tumble headlong down an interminable flight of stairs, Caravetti rose to his toes in fear. The separation terms were priceless to him. Destroy them and he would have no reason for living. They had been procured for Barbara’s sake and he strove to cancel them for Barbara’s sake too. But he felt that his separation from Maria made Barbara more real to him because Barbara’s spirit worked with him on his slow, painful pilgrimage back to Maria. With the separation annulled, however, he feared that her spirit would leave him. With the battle finished, he had nothing more to win. There was a vapid end to his striving ‘for Barbara’s sake’. He sensed a vacuum opening before him. If he stepped forward, he would be lost, while behind lay the comfort of familiar reality. But his fear was not logical, he realised. He could not understand it.

Maria and the doctor were staring at him in surprise. Smiling he walked to them and put his arm about Maria’s waist. “I'm sorry,” he apologized. “I had a terrible thought but it amounted to nothing.” He looked at the doctor. “About the terms of separation. I think that until we can do something about them that I should live outside the house.”

“But why?” Maria asked. “Once I've broken them, they’re broken legally too.”

“I know,” Caravetti frowned so that his skin folded thickly in horizontal lines across his forehead. “Still I'd prefer it to be done properly by you.”

Maria kissed him. “Caravetti, I can’t believe that it’s you who’s talking.”

“Paris changed me.” His voice sounded deeply.

Before the doctor left, he looked in on Manuel to find that the boy was sleeping soundly. Caravetti saw him to the door.

“Now don’t let her get away from you this time,” the doctor warned him. “This is your one opportunity.”

When Caravetti closed the door, he leaned against it as if he were holding out an evil demon which threatened to break in and distrub the household. Circumstance like a magnetic needle had pointed out the direction he was to take, but something was trying to direct the needle from its true course. The idea that he should rebel against his situation knocked softly at his conscious self, but he had kept the door closed. When he returned to Manuel’s room, he found Maria looking out the window. When he turned her about, he saw that she was worried too.

"You will do what we agreed?" she asked.

"I'll love everything connected with you," he smiled. "But you go to bed now so that you can watch this love tonight." He nodded at Manuel.

She nodded. "When are you moving in?"

"When I legally can. It's better that way." He owed it to someone, he thought.

"Will you forgive me for the way I treated you?" she asked.

He smiled with his eyes and brought his hand softly down her cheek to clasp her chin. Maria had thrown off her witch's mask to reveal her womanly traits. Although he knew that she needed security and a father for their children, he did not doubt that she loved him. Her love was bound up with security, family and church. If he failed any of these three requisites, he would lose her love. He felt as if he had stepped into a box, suffered the lid to close over him, and heard the key turning in the lock with a fatal sound.

Maria's brightly shining eyes searched his face for signs of happiness. Small lines of sorrow told her of his suffering. With a sign of remorse she brought herself tight against him and rubbed her forehead upon his shoulder. The firm warm clasp of his hands tenderly carressed her, and she moved away contented with their powerful confirmation of his love.

"I'll send the maid in with your lunch," she said.

12.

The walls of the studio juggled the rays of the morning sun. Paintings had been taken off them and laid at their base. The room began to have a lonely look that houses know when the occupants are moving. The backless chairs stood in their customary places, but it seemed that no one would ever sit on them again. In one corner the easel, folded into a thick rod, lay against the wall. Canvases were tied together and were lying near by. The door stood open to the kitchen as if no one would ever close it again.

Caravetti put his hands into his pockets and looked at the room. He had spent over a year in that studio. He had finished a few paintings and tried to do some street scenes. Walking to the window he looked out on the street he had tried to paint. Strangely it seemed flatter than he had thought it. The crampness and the crookedness of the buildings had gone. The street appeared straighter without any particular distinction to mark it from hundreds of other streets. The view was plain and rather quiet. He turned away to begin picking up the framed pictures he had taken down from the walls. The design Barbara had left him looked up with its funny side. He recognized the chemist with the glasses. It was clearly himself.

As he put the paintings together, he thought of Barbara's portrait. He found it among some canvases. A glance was all he needed to make sure it was still there. He could not afford to forget. It was more than a keepsake. It was a memory. A fluff of dust clotted his coat sleeve. He flicked it off, took off his coat and went to look behind the kitchen door. He took down his turtle-neck pullover and hung the coat up in its place. The sweater had lasted him all through his time in Paris. Barbara, he remembered, had loved it. She used to hold it up in front of her and say she was going to take it back to the States with her. And she would make him take good care of it. If he dropped paint on it, he had to clean it off at the end of the day. Although that made him wear it less, when he did, he liked spotting it for the fun of having her make him clean it.

As he pulled the sleeves over his arms, he noticed the mending of a long rip near the elbow; it was one of the last repairs she had done for him. He remembered catching the sleeve on a nail in the small room he used as a workshop in Paris.

"Look, Barbara, I'm wounded." He showed the gash.

"Oh dear, more work."

"No," he protested. "It's perfect like this. I just wanted to show it to you."

"Caravetti, you can't paint with a rip like that in your sweater."

"Why not?" he laughed. "I don't paint with my sleeve, although it might seem like it."

"You take it off and put it on the arm of the chair this minute. It's about time I started to do some sewing. Everything's beginning to pile up again."

Caravetti laughed and patted her head.

"This one I'll do myself, just to show you how well I can mend," he said. "You get your sewing basket."

Smiling under the humour of his pat, Barbara stood up from his chair and kissed his cheek. Caravetti watched her walk from the room. Two months had passed since she told him that she was pregnant. The change in her figure was not really noticeable. The experience was different with Barbara than with Maria. He loved Barbara's child before it was born. And Barbara told him that he would never see it. She could be rather obstinate, he thought.

Pulling off his sweater, he put it on the arm of the chair and sat down. Barbara, her blue eyes twinkling, brought the small wicker basket to him. Her eyes were always happy, he thought.

Searching amongst the clutter of sewing equipment, he asked, "Is there the right colour of thread in here?"

"Navy blue," she murmured. "Yes, here it is."

The more he recognized Barbara's adeptness at finding things, the less adept he became. "Is that the right colour?" he inquired suspiciously. He held it against his sweater. "I guess it'll do."

She sat down on the other arm of the chair and watched him try to thread a needle. "Lick the end of the thread," she said.

He licked the thread and slid it through the eye. He brought the sweater to his lap. "Now to do a smooth-looking job."

"Put your hand in the sleeve so that you have a smooth level to sew on," Barbara said. "You can also see the rip better."

He worked his hand in the sleeve until he could see the white skin of the palm peek through the rip. Holding the sweater more into the light and farther away from Barbara, he ducked the needle through one end of the tear. As he drew on it he noticed that he had pulled the thread right through the sweater.

"Knot the end of the thread," Barbara said.

Pulling the thread farther through the eye until he had two lines of equal length, he tried to tie the ends. His thumbs slipped just as he had one end ready to slip through the loop of the other.

"Try licking the ends," Barbara said.

Caravetti licked the ends. The threads pointed stiffly into the air. He managed to tie a knot but he left long ends.

"Never mind. You can cut them when you've finished," Barbara said.

He looked up ready to defend his intelligence when he saw that she was crying. Dropping his needle on the floor he held out his arms to receive her against his chest as she slipped down from the arm of the chair.

"What am I going to do without you?" she said.

"You aren't going to do without me." In the softness of her body Caravetti could sense his love for her. He put his cheek against her ear and then he buried his nose in her hair.

"We have so little time left," she murmured. She was talking aloud to herself; Caravetti was there as part of her thought.

"We have the rest of our lives." He slid his hands along her back. The movement comforted them both.

"Oh darling! I don't want to leave you?" Barbara turned her head so that her lips rested against his neck.

"But you don't have to."

Barbara sat up against the chair arm. She smoothed her hair and found a hankie in her sleeve. Wiping her eyes, she stood up. Saddened, Caravetti watched her.

"Tears never did anyone any good," she said.

"Except to show them how foolish they are when they torture themselves unnecessarily," he answered.

"Darling," she turned distressed features to face him. "I'm not being foolish. Don't you see we both have a conscience. There was a time when I didn't think I had one. But I know that if we left together for America instead of separating, as we owe to your family to do, we wouldn't be able to live happily together."

Caravetti smiled sadly. "Barbara darling, you know what our conscience is as well as I do. It's what we've been taught before we could think for ourselves, and from our subconscious it comes out periodically to mix up our own thinking."

"It doesn't matter what it is, or where it comes from, subconscious or unconscious; it's there," she said.

"Yes, but if we do what it tells us we'll always be doing what other people tell us, and never what we want to do ourselves. Don't you see? If we don't have the courage to strike out on new paths, we'll only know our own little encampment," he argued.

"We can strike out on new paths anyway," she said. "By following our conscience we have a chance to refind happiness. By going against it we'll never be happy again. We're like slaves, darling." She knelt on the floor beside him. Her hand held his knee in a grip that transported her unhappiness.

"Slaves to our past," Caravetti snorted. "This is one time I wish I'd left that philosophy alone."

"It's impossible for anyone to go against his conscience. Everyone's after his own happiness," she added.

"Still, we can find our happiness together. If I divorce Maria, everything'll be all right."

"But divorce isn't recognized in Spain, Caravetti. I know that. She won't be able to marry again and she has two children to support. Somewhere back in my past I learned never to cause unhappiness like that, and I can't do it now."

Caravetti hung his head. He wondered if he could ever love Maria after having loved Barbara. He doubted it.

"Think of our unhappiness," he said.

"It'll only be at parting." Her voice tried to console him, tried to console herself. "After we've lived through that, a few months, perhaps a year, then the times we had together will be happy memories. You know what they say: 'it's only through grief that one finds solace'."

Their smiles tasted the bitterness of that irony.

The apartment bell rang twice. Barbara went to answer it. Caravetti heard her talking to a man at the door. She came back with a large box, set it on the table, and tried to break the string from round it with her fingers. He broke it for her.

"Now turn around. I don't want you to see this till I'm ready," she said.

When he heard her pack the wrappings back into the box, he stole a glance at her. She was wearing a long dress with a flower design on a black background. It looked Chinese to Caravetti.

"What's the idea?" he cried.

"It's for the expected," she said. She stretched the front far out from her waist. "See?"

Laughing, Caravetti held out the dress. "There's enough room in there for me too," he said.

"There won't be in a few months."

Caravetti put his arms about her shoulders, and, holding himself straight beside her, he waved his other arm in front of them. "Past, present, and future; subconscious, unconscious, and self-conscious, I give you the prettiest girl in the prettiest dress that you'll find anywhere. And she's not married too, so think that one over."

"That's the trouble," Barbara groaned. "I can just see them thinking that one over."

"There's another argument in my favour," Caravetti intoned. "With me beside you, no one will be able to point at you, except to say, 'Look at that crazy girl, marrying a Spaniard!"

She smiled and put her arms about his neck, "They'd say, 'Lucky girl, and he's a painter too'."

Caravetti grew serious. "Won't you give in now?"

"No, darling. I'll have my baby in Paris and I have enough money to keep me for a year after that. I might model again and not go back to the States for years. It'll be easier to bring up a child here. I'd hate to go back and live on one of those 'Main Streets'. And then, too, I could find a husband easier here, I think."

"You won't get rid of me. As long as you stay in Paris, I'll be here."

"That's sweet, dear."

"I mean it," he frowned

"But you won't be accomplishing anything." She dropped her arms to her sides and walked to the mantel for a package of cigarettes. "When I and the child go back to the States, you won't be able to come."

"Sure," he smiled. "I'll sneak across the border like the Mexican farm labourers. But I'll have persuaded you to marry me by then in any case. And when we do get married, I'll take you to Spain where we can let the old States go drown."

"I wish we could live in Spain together," she sighed.

She lit a cigarette for him and one for herself. When she handed the smoking white roll to his fingers, they both sensed the end of something. They saw it in the smoke of the cigarette, and they saw it in the eyes of the other.

"I guess I'd better get the sewing done," she said.

Barbara took an ashtray with her to the easy chair. Leaving her cigarette in it, she found the needle on the floor and picked up the sweater to begin mending the sleeve.

Caravetti crossed over to sit on the arm of the chair. Placing his arm along the back of it, he held himself steady while he watched the needle go in and come out of the wool. The movement was as old as man.

"Hurry, darling, or we'll be late."

Maria was standing in the doorway. He looked about the studio. He had done nothing but day-dream, save to finish putting on his sweater. Taking it off, he exchanged it for his suit coat. He went up to where she was standing. "Didn't get much done. I'll finish moving things later."

"I'll help you pack." She smiled to show him she was happy to be his wife. "You could carry some of the things in the wheelbarrow."

"Yes, I could," he said.

Maria saw that he was dreaming. In the first years of their marriage, she had learned to stay quiet while he thought so that now she walked silently beside him. Although she was womanly-curious, her intuition told her she would not understand if she knew what he was thinking. She found enough satisfaction in being able to walk with him.

They climbed the hill until they came to the cathedral. It was the late morning Sunday service. People were behind and ahead of them. Maria felt their eyes looking at them. She smiled at their good-will. So many mornings she had been alone. The pitying looks had driven her into herself. But she went to the earliest service to escape the crowds so that she never missed a Sunday.

This morning was like a prayer answered. She was sure that Caravetti would belong to her for always. He had been tamed from his wild ways by a year of penitence in the town. For most of the year she was determined that he was going to suffer as she had suffered, but the sickness of Manuel made her remember that one suffers enough from natural causes without having to undergo afflictions from others. And then too, Caravetti loved her, she thought. He had the quiet air of a person who is willing to settle in his life as he finds it. Caravetti appeared content to finish his life with her.

They climbed the cathedral steps and entered the nave. The darkness was dispelled by lighted candles standing about the altar and about the several chapels along the sides of the nave. Maria stopped by the water font and sprinkled herself. Caravetti followed her example. His face was a mask of white stone. She led him to a bench half-way up the aisle. Caravetti made the sign of the cross and followed her into the pew. They stood with heads bowed as the organ soared. He smelled the incense and looked at the altar to see that the service was already in progress. Maria was kneeling beside him. People about him were moving their lips in prayer. Where had the time gone? He followed the words of the prayer with his mind. With the sharpness of nail ends each word cut into his forehead. He did not try to understand them. The pain was too demanding.

Kneeling beside Maria he folded his hands in front of him and pressed his thumbs against the flesh of his forehead. He winced. The low mumblings of a priest forced their way into his thoughts. A deep voice vibrated with the very soul of the man so that it sounded unnatural; it seemed to come from the bowels of the earth; it stomped on Caravetti's senses with the heavy ankle boots of a stable worker tainted with the smells of dung and wet hay; a deep voice carried his spirit in prayer. He prayed for Barbara.

As his thoughts floated to her on the base of the deep tones, the chilly dampness of that day enveloped him once again. It was several days after she had mended his sweater. Fawn coat, brown hat, new shoes, she was smartly dressed for fall weather. Off to visit a friend in the American residence at the Cite Universitaire, she kissed him, took up the parcel of books she was returning, and laughed cheerily when he waved to her from the window.

When the police summoned him to identify her body, he went to see her brown hair curled just below the ear, the high curve of her lips, and the whiteness of her noble brow.

She had been killed instantly when attempting to cross the road from the metro to the Cite Universitaire. During rush hours, the auto traffic raced at top speed at that point. The crowds from the station could force their way through the traffic sometimes, but usually a lone person had to wait for a chance to risk a dash to the cement stand in the middle of the street and then chance the rest of the distance. Barbara had slipped on the wet road when she was running with three other people. A French-Canadian girl had been killed on the same spot two weeks earlier. Barbara was merely another victim of that crossing. And Caravetti was merely another mourner.

He notified her parents in the States, and he had her cremated at their wish. When he was packing her belongings to send to her home, he came across the sketch that she had done of him in the rowboat on the small lake in the Bois de Boulogne. He struck a match and touched the flame to one end of it. Carrying it to an ash-tray he watched it burn to cinders as a symbol of the last rites of his features. Barbara was to have them for all time.

After her death, there was little to live for. He stayed one more month in Paris, and then he knew he had to live with his family again; he had to love

Maria, because it was what Barbara had wanted, and because it was what circumstances had decreed.

A canting of voices blended with the bass of the priest. Caravetti shifted so that his shoulder rested against Maria. His heart moved in sympathy for her. The pain in his head faded away. When he stood up, he knew he had been accepted back into the Church.

At the close of the service, he walked with her into the sunshine. On the steps the people congregated to chat with friends before going to their homes. Caravetti saw some relatives smile at them. Maria started to go to them but paused to give Caravetti time to go with her. He hesitated. The people had not spoken to him since he had come back to the island. Yet they were beaming smiles at him. He walked beside Maria to them. They were as friendly as they would have been if he had just returned from Paris that day. Other people spoke to him for the first time in three and a half years. Somberly he nodded and mumbled greetings in return. The hypocrisy of society had never reared an uglier head at Caravetti as it did then. But he had been bitten by it, and he succumbed to its poison. He began shaking hands with the men who had snubbed him. He was accepted.

The priest who had returned from South America spoke to him. Caravetti recognized the sincerity in his eyes in contrast to the others. "I'm happy to see you made it to the top of the steps," he smiled.

"I'm glad too," Caravetti said. "It'll probably be the last great experience of my life."

Maria came to take his arm and as they walked down the hill, she asked him if he were happy. He smiled a 'yes' at her with his eyes. He remembered it was one of Barbara's tricks.

Bonassola, Italy, 1955

ADAM

1.

Rat-a-tat-tat, Rat-a-tat-tat, Rat-a-tat-tat-tat-tat-tat. Knuckles against hardwood table(?) Adam rolled onto his back and stretched his ribs up out of the night's cramp. He opened his eyes straight into a sunray, blinked, ducked away and sat up in the shade. The sun sparkled on tiny wire squares at the top of the screen. Bright. Smell of chlorophyll, rich green leaves thickening in the heat, verdured vapours.

Rat-a-tat-tt-tt-tt-tt-tt-tt-tat.

Scarlet necktie, blue comb bristling, Robespierre rapping on doors. Insistence! Must be insistent to succeed. Make him yield to you. Ruffle of wings, direct catch in the heart under a wing-spread, transition.

With his eyes Adam caressed the firm muscles of the wide chest beside him. He followed the contour of the figure nicking in above the hip bone, planing sheer across the femur, scissoring apart in long hairy limbs. An hour earlier, he threw off the sheets. Eight-thirty the clock had read.

Snug here, secure, a Muskoka fort. Drowsy like everyone for the first days. He just can't wake up.

The penis long, circumcised. He lifted it gently on his finger tips. Just a piece of flesh. (Hey, young fella, why don't you put up your umbrella? Da da da dee dee). Stale now, though there was a quiver, a pull, pulling harder. He has a bus to catch.

Adam took his hand away and planted it flat upon his chest.

Send him back to Manhattan.

He studied the penis from a distance. His own began to swell. Shades of Michaelangelo and his dainty little acorns.

I'll smack him.

A high swing, roundhouse on the ass, delicious crescendo.

The sting spreading into his wrist warned him he had struck too hard.

Blue eyes flew open. Crooked capillaries bulged in the rusty-tanned brow. (Why in heaven's name did he use that lotion? Cheapening.)

'Ow! For the lord's sake. Adam!'

Weak little mouth pouting.

'I don't think you're the slightest bit funny.'

High raspy voice belonged to a tit-mouse. Well, I've had him - good - over the weekend.

'Toronto bus will be here in thirty-three minutes.' I'll hold this frown a little longer.

'Dear me! I won't be ready on time! What shall I ever do?'

'Get dressed. I'll make us breakfast.' He knows he has to go. Watch him squirm.

'Really, Adam, I'm not a quick-change artist. I can't be expected to....'

'Shut up. Four days of your complaining is all I can swallow.'

'I'm sorry to hear you say that. I thought we were....'

'Close your ass and get up.'

Whine, whine, whine. He walked naked through the living room to the kitchen. Air felt fresh to the skin still.

'I'm going to tell the boys at the theatre how you've been treating me.'

A warning shout from the bedroom, a cry from the past, a Chippewa under the oak seen from the kitchen window. He wasn't worth answering. The boys would laugh.

The day smelt sweet through the open window. A day of departure and of new beginnings. Gentle Muskoka enticed the mind back over its lakes and streams to the sombre phantom of an Algonquin Indian (Chippewa tribe) and his enigma.

<The petrographs discovered north of Lake Simcoe are said to date anywhere from 350 B.C. to 500 A.D. There are logical arguments for both dates.>

Long, thin figures, plasticine men. Something mechanical about the heads, serrated like watch wheels. Something mechanical about America even then. The psyche of the continent imprinted its future on those rocks. Elongated breasts splayed to either side for fertility, procreation. But not one phallic symbol, unless you considered the many representations of arrow heads as an inhibited expression along that line.

Unless you considered them a design for patio chairs.

He smiled slowly. A Franz Marc ambiance on the porch. Instead of horses, there'd be humans, staring out of triangles with that "rump" look. Wonderful! But tomorrow, save it for tomorrow, and maybe the idea won't sound so good.

The coffee perked. He dropped two eggs into water. His arms dangled listlessly. Fat, getting fat. Yokes gave stamina.

'Well, Adam, where's my breakfast?'

His bedfellow, whining. Cherry shirt, close-trimmed blue trousers, slick dark brown hair, sportsman. Who would guess he was an impoverished actor?

'You look good.'

That saucy look, rolled eyes, tongue bunched up at the side of his mouth and rear end in extensio. Sickening! Couldn't he grow up?

'Can't you grow up?'

'Oh, so you don't think I'm a big boy yet. I'd take a look at yourself if I were you. Not even in Hollywood do hosts parade around naked.'

Screeching laughter, a hyena-bird, Muskoka loon. A week-end of it had dispelled the guy's charms. A finely rounded arm reached up for the dish towel, Achilles reaching for his scabbard.

Adam thought of moving away. A white streak flipped, stung low. He doubled up, turned away. His guest sniggered; an Iroquois with a tool of torture. The cloth snapped at his rear. He grabbed the towel and fastened it in his hands. Frightened, his guest dropped an end, and fled.

Wrapping it about his waist, he strutted smilingly by the chair behind which his adversary refuged.

'Watch the eggs while I dress.'

The laugh of the loon followed him to the bedroom.

Loons have been chased into lesser lakes. Haven't seen one on Rosseau or Joseph this time. But in fifteen years a lot of people can take the place of nature.

Dusk rolled down like blinds on the shores of the lake as he pointed the bow at the floating bird and paddled swiftly. Down it ducked as the canoe coasted over a glassy surface. Light sky, shrouded shore and tranquillity of eventide silhouetted the solitude of his person. Twelve years old, long paddle resting on the gunwales.

Up popped the loon fifty yards to his right. Its small black head held high, it looked as if it were about to laugh. A faint tinkling alarmed the atmosphere. He had to return to camp and leave the bird in peace; he watched it snobbishly ignore him; further pursuit would mean loss of canoe privileges for a week. Regretfully he headed for the wharf. On the way, he saw three more loons, as unattainable as the first and as smugly aware of his harmlessness.

White ducks were a bit soiled. Was it in Cuba or California that he acquired the habit of wearing white always? Mother and California were born synonymous. Her letter! I must answer today, or maybe tomorrow when I'll have more to say. Mother and California, warmth and heat, copulation.

'Breakfast is ready, dear Adam.'

'All right, I'm coming.'

I'm not sure that I want him to go. Nice fellow. Pleasurable. Didn't I invite him for a week? Aw, but he has to return for rehearsals. Why? I don't know. Always bit parts.

The handsome sheen of forehead, hairline arrowing back, tall, svelte figure: he caught his breath with a flood of remembrances. Manhattan Indians had become nauseatingly civilized. In sneakers they walked dogs on the hunt. Sophistication garbed them in pseudomorphism.

"It" was finishing breakfast when he entered the kitchen.

'You could have waited.'

'I've got no bloody time.'

He watched "It" swallow coffee.

Strange how excited one grew at departure. The old was being forgotten; the new waited around the corner. Mother disappeared with her paramour into Europe; he turned to Cuba and furniture design; hot, lascivious Cuba and the smooth touch of finished wood.

"It" spoke with mouth stuffed. 'Toast in toaster.' "It" dashed away to pack.

Athletic men gyrated muscled arms; he watched the Cubans swing luggage onto the back of a camion. Later, brown-skinned boys moved lithely ahead of him. Ah hell!

A robust wallop with the spoon indented the egg with a squirt. He gave me the cracked one; that proves he's selfish!

Yelping, the bus raced down the road like a moose in heat. (Take my faggot-bit. He's just the same as when he came.)

'Hey! That's your bus, man!'

He had to catch the damn thing and remove his illegal charms across the border.

Scrambling shoes, rustling papers, and the retort of a fallen chair preceded, as expected, a round of tearful cursing. Signs of temperament at the moment of stress indicated why our friend played bit parts after ten years of theater experience.

He glided happily to the bedroom threshold and seized the overnight bag.

'It'll wait a minute. Good-bye. Remember me to whomever remembers me.'

The deep blue eyes revolved round at him. Lips pressed upon his mouth and strong arms clutched his back as if cradling him. He clamped one hand to the upper arm and felt the hardened muscle with his finger tips. Gradually the grip was relaxed. The blue eyes trickled with tears.

'Thanks, Adam. You were swell to me. And I was good to you, wasn't I? I did everything you wanted me to.'

A white handkerchief on the bureau top felt cool to the hand. 'Here. Take it. Blow your nose. Maybe you'll visit me again this summer. I've let the house for two whole months.'

'I'd love to, Adam. If you were closer to home, just think. Northern New York State, for instance.'

Get this pseudo-sentimentalist outside. Let him stall now and he'll stay all summer.

'Come on.'

He ran to the front porch and handed him his case. 'Run for it.'

The broad cherry shirt and the sweet blue behind wiggled rapidly down the garden path and disappeared under the foliage. Great green spreading maple, obliterate my sins.

A motor churned ominously through the trees. Too soon! Oh no! Wait for him!

A shout sounding as if it came from his own throat rang out. The motor cut and the bus halted in the stretch of roadway before the house. Cool gray and blue, a clipper ship, it fronted Lake Rosseau rippling and twinkling under the sun.

The cherry shirt waved. Grinning, he stretched his arm up in an energetic hail. A valiant good-will gesture.

The bus drifted noiselessly away. Lake Rosseau twinkled vacantly. Silver birch stood in Indian file along the shore. The solitude had returned.

Stillness dominated the kitchen. He listened to the coffee pour into the cup. His egg was cold, but edible. The toast sitting half-out of the toaster had gone stiff. He snapped a piece in two and gathered in the marmalade.

A breeze scrapes the leaves against the window screen. The wilderness of Canada encircles my waist and weighs down my limbs. This great erasing atmosphere accepts my memories while the Cuban noons merely intensified them.

"Dissipation truly means relinquishing the spirit to past and future. Invade the leafy forest with cottages, churn up silent waterways with motorboats, but you can never frighten away the Muskoka gods who call on Winter to drive back the white destroyer and preserve the gentle identity of an ancient land. Give your soul to these gods and, like me, you will have to contend with yourself no more."

The breeze has dropped away. The silence mesmerises. Relief from the bing, bong, bong of juke box and the omnipresent serenading. In fifteen summers, though, there have been inroads; changes of scene, fashioned by the white race trying to become red-skinned in the sun.

<Nineteen twenty-three dated the official purchase of Muskoka from the Chippewa nation by the Canadian Government. The Mississagas also signed the treaty because they were the branch of the Chippewas who steadily moved south into these lands between the lakes which the Iroquois were maintaining as their Beaver Reserve.>

The shell of the egg, hollow like a white amphora had been emptied of its golden nourishment. The vitality in homo sapiens came from a boiled egg, an embryo, the supersession of races.

<Thirty thousand years ago, the earliest civilization in this area, indeed on this continent, was based on Manitoulin Island in Georgian Bay. Frankly we do not know how many races intervened between that time and the arrival of the Indian.>

Adam felt that his Being melted into the northern quintessence of nomadic man whenever he dreamed in Muskoka. He sauntered to the front door and bolted it. Through the clearing in the trees, he spotted a sailboat on Lake Rosseau. An awareness of subtle change nurtured his mind. The sailboat blinked out behind a leaf. He stared at the patch of steel-blue and remembered that scenes on becoming over familiar depressed him. (Its tortoise-shell form in light wood under a picture window, say, as a coffee-table.)

He slipped the lock on the back door as he went out. He was fortunate to rent a modern bungalow. These rustic Canucks were backward creatures; American enterprise spent thousands of dollars in advertising annually to encourage them to a higher standard of culture.

The path led him into the cool of the woods. Catching sight of the young boy from the neighbouring cottage, he stopped. The boy knelt several yards off the pathway. A square of earth had been plowed up and heaped, as if covering a small grave. A wooden cross made from shingles, it seemed, angled from the head of the spot. The boy kept his eyes closed and whispered to himself.

The transience of nature making its grief known in the soul of the young and beautiful. The peace in that picture is marvellous. It urges me to pass on and forgo the pleasure of speaking to him.

Growth, sex, decay: stages in development.

Soft sinewy limbs bulged through the ground of the trail. Step carefully by them. Mottled toadstools stood guard over black rocks, motionless like sheep,

Long grass nodded above the gluck, gluck of water along the shore. Beware of broken slats, I'll fix them tomorrow. Manjana.

Canoe painted red so that it could be seen by sleepy drivers of motorboats. Light grained rib-work reminded him of a certain stateroom on the Hudson and those week-end-stags. The exhilaration of being only amongst men whose restraints had been cast off like ballast the moment they stepped aboard.

<Dip, dip, the song my paddle sings = Pauline Johnson.>

Water was warm, like mucus, reminiscent of hot beds on the Hudson. (Marston would make a good hot bed.)

Yesterday Adam had been reclining in an orange canvas chair on the verandah of the Lodge when Marston appeared before him. Since that moment all his effort had been aimed at dismissing his house guest, a jealous encumbrance in matters of the heart. Moreover, he had never seduced Canadians, never having had the opportunity, although, by God, his country had been trying for two centuries.

Islands rich with trees gave Lake Joe a fiercer aspect than Rosseau. The sun beamed off spiring treetops that cast an impenetrable shade along the shore line. He glanced at the shore he had just left. A dead tree leaned on a forty-five degree angle over the water. Thicket surrounded its base on the bank. Healthy young trees backed up the shrubbery.

Age being pushed overboard by youth.

Its gnarled trunk and desiccated bark reminded him of his step-dad's face. The old man with the money was also leaning toward water with plenty of Scotch in it.

Liquor kills the sexual impulse. Who's afraid of the big bad wolf?

<Edgar Allan Poe was dragged in an alcoholic stupor from one poll booth to another before his tormentors hurled him into a ditch to die. He was travelling south to marry a wealthy widow.>

The canal sides at Port Sanfield showed themselves as white spots astern. With a slight turn of the paddle he brought the bow in line with the tip of the cape ahead.

He remembered his camp master under the awning of the mess tent. Hair glossed his long arms and bristled along his fingers. The arms reached out and snatched him. Squirming, he tried to wrestle out of the embrace, all the while feeling embarrassed because the kitchen help had stopped work to watch. Like a puppy dog being fondled by its master, he was afraid to bite sharply. He pushed against the man's chest, turned, but was swept back; strong black stubble scraped his cheeks and his ears resounded with a deep bass chuckling.

Released, he jumped clear and stood shyly back. The heavy brow of the camp master fell darkly. Then smirking, he returned to his cabin for a shave.

Marston had observed the action. Fearful, he sat motionless on a bench, one hand gripping the edge of the table behind him, the other clenched by his chin. The kitchen help returned to their work, cleaning pans in the morning sunshine, while Marston and he ran down the hillside toward the sounds of shouting.

The clean-cut jaw, the high hair-line, the habit of narrowing his eyes when he reflected, these particulars had helped him place Marston at once. He had not forgotten Marston's handsomeness, not in fifteen years; it had been buried in his subconscious like many other things.

From this verandah, he could view the lake for a wide expanse, for the Lodge was built on a hilltop high enough to see over the silver birch lining the shore.

<It has been a matter of dispute whether birch bark canoes derived from canoes made of animal hides used by Esquimaux or from the longboat used by the Iroquois. The question is important because it deals with the cultural influences upon this area, whether the influences came from the north or the south. Certainly the northerly nations of the Algonquin hunted in canoes of animal hide fashioned after the manner of the Esquimeau, making it probable that the southerly nations also inherited Esquimeau knowledge.>

The white-birched craft skimming over the lake and the strong red arms pumping in unison: Indians racing canoes at Port Carling.

He could observe the white passenger ship from the porch. It landed guests at the dock just before lunch and moved on to the next resort. (Sometimes there was only the mailbag to be picked up.) Adam's eyes always scanned the passengers as they climbed the walk from the dock to the Lodge steps. He was on the look-out for compatible companions.

Sounded like a motor launch behind - sinister as a shark. A party of men and women were taking a tour of the lake. One of the men extended his arm ahead and all the women shielded their eyes like sea captains.

The roll of wave mounted in a blue ridge approaching from the distance. It would hit astern; no need to alter course.

Money to buy a motorboat, sports car, clothes - instead, I get small cheques in the post from mother. Maybe I should accept that offer in New York - can't stand that ugly bastard who'll be wanting to do me all the time.

The canoe lurched up and along with the wave. Adam missed a stroke with the paddle to maintain his balance.

Crowds of Manhattan, Los Angeles, Chicago - faces and shoes moving through gray troposphere; humidity soaks the skin; dirty air and the roar of exhausts; work begins at nine and lasts into infinity.

The sky was turning bluer as the sun climbed. Faint skeins of cloud hovered on the horizon. Their distant appearance enhanced the serenity by implying that trouble was brewing elsewhere. There was no movement, no sound about the cottages along the shore. The lodge nestled quietly on its hill cap. Bathers were tanning on the big dock in front. Turning the bow, Adam paddled for the small dock in the cove.

Mrs. Ashburton, widow of a naval commander (Her Majesty's Royal One, don't you know) was seated on a deck chair and knitting. She had taken off her shoes and was tanning her feet in the sun.

Approach with a silent dip.

<Indians went night-fishing by torch light. Paddling without a ripple they drifted towards their quarry and raised their spears.>

Swinging the bow round sharply, he coasted alongside the dock. Mrs. Ashburton, startled, looked up and frowned. She regarded him suspiciously (although she had observed him often in the past month) and resumed her knitting.

He tied the painter to a ring, and smiled to himself. Mrs. Ashburton had just given him a Canadian welcome.

Young ladies were descending the path to the dock. In bathing suits, they held in their tummies and stuck out their cones.

Enough pine trees in this part of the country.

<Woman is a catchment of wire traps and lethal connivings. Predatory, she functions comparably to a spider which also procreates.>

Whatever you do, outsmile them. Give them no cause to bitch.

'Hello, Adam.'

She grinned, unattached, husband-hunting, light-headed naive.

'Oh, hello!'

Hand in pocket, one foot up on step: hold it!

'When are you going to keep your promise?'

That moment of bravado: Verandah sitters had stopped conversing to listen to them - it had been an excellent chance to illustrate his manliness. Go for a canoe ride?

'Ha, ha, oh yes! Whenever you're ready.' Wink at the girl behind.

'Oh, this is Debbie Harkness. Adam Crowfield. I think you know the...'

'How do you do, Debbie. Yes, I believe the girls tried to convince me to take Canada Dry instead of Coke - the other day at the ...'

'Yes.' They laugh amiably.

'Such nationalism really!'

He laughed with them and noted with concern that his voice sounded nervous, too high, shriller than the laugh of the girls. He glanced round. Thank God, no males to detect it.

Debbie elbowed into fuller view. 'Are you staying at the Lodge?'

'No. I have a house down on the lakeside.' Said with a slight elevation of tone.

'I wondered.' Big bright smile; gorgon's teeth. 'I haven't seen you around.'

Nod, smile briefly and take a step away. Seconds of awkwardness force the girls into moving onwards. They smile back.

'Come down for a swim if you haven't anything else on.'

Smile. 'I will.'

He watched their backs. The single piece suit with the oval cutout in back looked rather lovely. Some bathing costumes were simply hideous though.

The flat alternating sounds of tennis caught his attention. Behind slim tall trunks lay a clay court fenced in with chicken wire, at least fifteen feet high all around. Two youths were rallying and a younger boy reclined on the grass at the side. He advanced to a spot behind the lone spectator, who was in his early teens, and surveyed the sprawling figure. The boys glanced at him with disapproval. They implied that he was intruding on their privacy. He stood looking on, trying to appear disinterested. They soon forgot him and he could regard the figure and profile of the boy on the grass with no fear of being caught.

Must have a long tool: long-legged lad. Wonder if I should sit beside him, make conversation - on what? Tennis?

A rock to one side of the boy offered him an excuse to be seated near him. When the boy's head turned in his direction, he tried to catch his eye with a smile. Ignoring him, the boy continued to watch the play.

He glanced round to make certain that he was not being observed. A splash followed by laughter sounded from the small dock.

<Oscar Wilde was accused of transferring cherries from his mouth to the mouths of the young men assembled at his private party. In England at one time the penalty for <u>suspected</u> homosexual relations was death by execution. There are on official record whole housefuls of young men and boys sentenced to decapitation.>

He riveted his eyes on the neck of the boy in an effort to make him return his look. The boy glanced nervously at him and away again before he could make friendly contact.

'They are good players, aren't they?' he asked too late as the boy quickly turned his head.

An uneasiness numbed the atmosphere. The boy sat up with his back to him and watched only his side of the court. The players began to miss shots and hit the ball long. One of them jumped up to smash down a lob. He struck the ball with the wood at the top of his racket and looped it over the fence.

Adam watched the boy jump to his feet and run to retrieve it. Shaking his head with shame the player retreated to the base line. The accident dispelled the tenseness for it called attention away from Adam for the moment.

Play continued. The white costumed opponents moved gracefully as if in ballet. Their naked legs spun, pivoted, sprang and stretched in long strides.

The boy returning from a search in the long grass sat down in the sun at the far end of the court and waited until the play was over before throwing in the ball. He had drawn away at least ten yards.

<Americans have been rejected in almost every foreign country. Why is this?>

Adam silently stole up the hill. The shade from broad-leafed trees covered the ground to the edge of the clay court, which lay cracked and mirror-bright in the sun.

With its settled, comfortable appearance, the wooden lodge reminded him of a broad dowager solemnly intending to spend the remainder of her days enjoying a good view.

He walked by the back way and entered the lobby. No one in sight. He left a nickel in a box on the counter and took a newspaper: *The Toronto Evening Standard* it read; two days old.

Marston is probably swimming down at the big dock. I'll sit on the verandah and wait.

Picture of a movie actor on the front page: "Marriage In Rome". The unintelligent reproduce.

A slight breeze lifted the undersides of trees by the lake. Flower stalks in the rockery swayed as if nodding past the lawns and hedges to some mysterious presence by the water's edge. Wicker and canvas chairs gaped vacantly. A sharp clatter of dishes reached his ears from the dining room behind the window screens.

'Hello Adam!'

He wheeled round, heart palpitating. Marston, legs crossed, slouched in a chair by the wall of the verandah. He was grinning.

'I thought you'd be swimming.'

'I will after my breakfast settles. Do you want to come?'

Adam smiled simperingly. 'I'll watch you. I'd like that.'

'I'll lend you a suit. I brought two.'

The two of them changing into bathing suits in Marston's room.

'Okay. I can't resist the temptation. You'd look good in a bathing suit.'

The slight frown on Marston's brow warned him to desist making overt remarks for the present. This Canadian came from a society reared on taste and principle. Vulgarity is permitted only in the bedchamber.

(At the end of summer camp, Marston invited him to spend a few days with his family before he continued home to New York. Mother was pondering marriage at the time so that he refused any offer of hospitality that would delay his reaching her side. He wished he had accepted the invitation now. He was curious about what it was in the society of the Canadian that made him more reserved than his American neighbour.)

'Adam, you know, if you hadn't introduced yourself yesterday, I would never have remembered you. You must have a wonderful memory.'

'For some things.'

A quiet smile and a tender look.

'Well, I think I'm a couple of years younger than you so that's why I probably wouldn't remember as well.'

'Age is immaterial to me. And by the way, I've stopped having birthdays. They're disillusioning.'

Marston laughed. 'You can't be over twenty-seven. What are you worried about?'

'Senility.'

'-!'

'Youth is life. The rest is really death. In fact, the minute we are born, we begin to die.'

'Nonsense, Adam. That's when we begin to live.'

At cross-purposes already? <Baudelaire struggled with his psyche and rolled defeated in the gutter.>

How bright and beautiful are his eyes! Sensitive and alive. The counterpart to death, my counterpart (?)

A tall, heavy-set man stepped onto the verandah with a thump. They paused and turned. He smiled at Marston and approached, hand outstretched. 'I didn't find out who you were till this morning. I'm an old friend of your dad. George Ornweddy's my name. How is he? Haven't seen him for donkey's years.'

'He is very well, thank you. Do you know Adam Cornfield, an old friend of mine?'

'We met. Yes, indeed.'

Cold appraisal solidified his weak smile. Was it because he was a stranger or simply strange that he was not welcome? No one could have guessed his secret. He had been scrupulously careful which was difficult after spending years of undisguised hedonism in Cuba.

Ornweddy's thick features disturbed him. He carried the single-mindedness of the small businessman into his conversations. Now he was pumping Marston about his home life to the exclusion of all else.

Adam watched Marston smile, elude personal queries and encourage Ornweddy to talk about himself.

<Indians pow-wowed while the great lone wolf looked on from the snow-capped rocks.>

Fifteen years ago he had been extremely fond of Marston but he had not known why. Sexual experience came later to inform him of the reason for things. Attraction at that age was... what would one say? spiritual? yes, was intensely spiritual. They slept in different tents because Marston was in a lower age group, but they met at the early morning dip and managed to stay together for most of the day. At evensong he lay in the dark and watched the firelight waver upon Marston's handsome features. Shadowed by the black spirits of wood and lake they followed the paths to their tents in a state of happy peace. Whenever he was alone, he had time to realize that he was not homesick. For the first time in his life he had not missed Mother.

Through the years the remembrance of this summer subconsciously grew with him and now culminated on his return to Muskoka. His love for Marston had become the spirit of his existence. His life's aim seemed concentrated in this spectre from the past which engendered meaning into his every act. All his lovers had been mere intermediate steps to the supreme representation of that young manhood which he watched converse in half-interested tones before him.

'Will you excuse us, Mr. Ornweddy. Mr. Cornfield and I are going for a swim.'

Ornweddy's polite smile and jagged teeth prefigured his nod of approval as he accepted being thrown back upon himself. (Chief Woebegone solemnly overlooked the departure of his council).

Walking beside Marston he sensed the unconscious strength in the tall slim young man. He let Marston lead the way upstairs and climbed close behind him.

'Do you remember swimming together at camp?'

'Yes,' Marston said attentively, as if expecting him to relate an amusing incident.

'We could go in the nude every morning then.'

'Oh yeah.'

A cautious response - doubtful how to interpret the remark.

Before I make my intentions obvious, I've got to discover how square a square he really is.

Their footsteps boomed along the wooden corridor. Marston opened a door and entered a square room. Bed, cupboard and rug - the essentials for a holiday. Instead of running water, there was a long-necked jug and a basin. On the bureau he glimpsed the title of a paperback: *American-Canadian Relations 1918-1939.*

'It's history you're teaching, isn't it, Marston?'

'I tried it for a year. Can't say I enjoy teaching it. I'd rather read it.'

'Your months of travel in Europe must have helped you understand history.'

'In the summer, Adam? You can't absorb atmosphere in three months. You need three years.'

'You're right. I spent six in Cuba. All of them in pursuit of dissipation.'

'This ought to fit you.'

There was a monogram of a diver on one side which he supposed designated the front. He fingered it as he carefully regarded Marston strip off his clothes. The beauty of physique struck rapid responses in his heart. If Marston had not turned his back to him, he would have betrayed his excitement. His knees like loose elastics and his body weak from desire, he sank onto the edge of the bed and closed his eyes.

'What's wrong, Adam? Feeling sick?'

He swallowed hard and found his voice. 'Just queasy. It's nothing.' He opened his eyes. Marston stood in his bathing suit - strikingly desirable. The bulge in his crotch sent shoots of pain through him.

'Come on, get changed,' Marston urged.

He couldn't let Marston see him naked - not yet.

'You go on. I'll join you in a few minutes.'

'Hey. What's the matter?'

Marston's hand shot out and a warm palm clamped his brow. Swooning, he pushed Marston's arm away.

'I'm all right. Go on. I'll catch up.'

Taken aback, Marston stared in surprise. 'If you're sure you're okay.' He stepped out for the door. 'Remember, it's the front dock.'

The door closed softly. Footsteps passing out of hearing. Silence. Self. <Marcel Proust enclosed himself in a room sealed away from the noise and the actuality of the everyday world. He was attended only by his housekeeper and her husband.>

Difficulties of life: how to scale a mountainside, how to make a living, how to match furniture to the colour of a rug, how to lay Marston.

<The early Algonquin killed deer by chasing them into an area fenced to make a narrowing lane leading to a sudden drop into a ravine whence they struck them with clubs and spears. In the deep snow of winter hunting was easier.>

The approach must be subtle and gradual although it's going to exhaust my disciplinary powers. Then all of a sudden, I shall take him.

Adam took off his shirt and regarded his torso in the mirror. Still attractive - little pouchy here and there, and these stomach rolls are showing up before their time. God! I must be aging.

He inspected his hair for bald spots. Thinning in front. Getting old before I've really lived!

(Narcissus horrified at his own reflection.)

He folded his trousers and put them on the bed. Gingerly he picked up the bathing suit and slipped it on, experiencing a lascivious thrill from the thought that it had been worn by Marston.

2.

It was strange to meet Adam after all these years - faint resemblance to what he looked like then. The black eyes and hair as always gave him a startled look, which grew melancholy as you got used to it.

Marston caught sight of Mr. Ornweddy lying in wait for him on the front verandah. Retreating up the stairs, he took the side exit.

But stranger than meeting Adam was Adam's behaviour. The unnecessary compliments about his physical build sounded peculiarly pointed as if Adam were obsessed with the male form. The unexpected shrill notes that crept into his speech indicated a nervousness in spite of his languorous way of moving which was obviously meant to show others that he felt at ease. By frowning, he effectively warned him to end his series of physical allusions until the next occasion when it seemed he was unconsciously driven to repeat his performance. (You'd look good in a bathing suit. You have nice legs. I want to watch you swim. You must do it very well). Could it be that Adam was a fairy?

He shivered convulsively and stopped on the crest of a rock rounding into the hillside between the driveway and the lawn. The crusted surface of the rock revealed tints of green in its dress of flannel gray. Below him stretched the dock in an 'L' shape to the left. Swimmers bounced on the diving board. The blue of heaven and sea revolved into the memory of a furlough from the navy in Los Angeles, cadet's treat after a summer's cruise.

Three in the morning. Women with huge round breasts, thin blue sweaters tucked over them, were serving a mob of cars at a Drive-In, smiling through mascara, and holding out Hot Dogs as if offering up sex. Glitter and tinsel drove him away from the other fellows. He was alone in the centre of Hollywood. He saw the car slow up in the road and the fellow pointing ahead.

'I'm going to Long Beach,' he had shouted at the occupant and shook his head. 'It's too far for you.'

The car braked. A voice spoke from the dark interior. 'Aw, that's all right. I'm just driving around. I'll take you. Hop in.'

Although the stranger's face was always cast in shadow, Marston perceived that he was middle-aged. He spoke in a pleasant voice about philosophy, religion, his singing career, Hollywood celebrities, his mother.

'It's too bad you have to get back to the ship. You could've put up in my apartment for the night.'

'Thanks, but five o'clock's the deadline.'

They reached Long Beach easily but could not find the docks which seemed odd because aside from amusement grounds and oil derricks, the docks were the important feature. They drove through side streets and came to a halt by several small wooden sheds. Marston looked across the rough grass of the city outskirts and saw a bridge leaping like a sky-way.

The fellow opened the door. 'Have to take a piss. How about you?'

'No. I'm fine, thanks.'

Sitting in the car, he listened to the susurration of water upon the damp earth. He felt uncomfortable amidst this desolateness. The fellow returned, his face still concealed in shadow, and they drove into the city.

'You want to drive around for a bit?' he asked.

Loneliness cloaked block after block of pavement.

'Sure. Okay.'

They came to the bridge, turned and shot up it. Within moments Marston saw that they were returning to the sheds. The lights of the bridge twinkled far away.

'Sure you don't have to get out, stretch a bit?'

Under the casual tone of invitation, Marston recognized an insistence that puzzled him. He watched the fellow go behind the car and piss a second time. Gradually, he suspected that the action disguised a sexual impulse. Tense from fear, he wondered if he was about to be murdered.

Help was out of the question in this deserted area in the dead of morning.

After dallying about behind the car for awhile, the fellow crept into the front seat. Slipping his arm along the back of the seat, he gently squeezed the back of Marston's neck.

'Do you like having your neck massaged?'

Marston stared straight ahead, too frightened to react. The palm of the stranger's hand felt paper-soft and unclean.

'I do,' the fellow said, and taking away his arm he tried to prove its harmlessness by awkwardly rubbing his own neck.

The silence condemned him to start the motor. They drove into the city.

'I've gotta get some gas.'

When they parked by the pumps, the unholy colour of the station light silhouetted the rough outline, the protruding lips, glassy eyes, thickly wrinkled cheek of the dissipated driver as they stoically waited on the slugs of the bell.

They drove again. When they were approaching the bridge, the voice beside him asked cautiously, 'Still want to drive around.'

'I have to get back to the ship,' he answered firmly.

They passed by the bridge and continued along the wharf front.

'Have you had experiences with women?'

Shocked rigid, Marston sensed a relationship between fornication and the ostentatious behaviour of this man. So this was a homosexual.

'No,' Marston muttered at last.

'Why not?'

'I've always respected them too much.' Immediately he felt embarrassed because that wasn't really true, although he had meant it to be.

The fellow glanced sharply at him, startled.

They pulled up outside the dock gate.

'How old are ya?'

'Twenty.'

'You should've,' the stranger said. 'I had my first woman when I was eighteen.'

They shook hands. As his heels clicked over the sidewalks, wet with the sea air, he watched the car swoop away in the night like a black comet returning to another sphere.

It seemed incredible that Adam could have developed into a lover of men. But his behaviour appeared to follow the pattern of homosexual approach, which he learned to detect after his frightening experience at Long Beach. The surfeit revealed in Adam's physical aspect belied the hungry intensity of his spirit. Like a lone wolf he must be always on the search, prowling the city streets in the evening and keeping an eye open during the day.

Why in heaven's name did he come to Muskoka where he must have known he would stand out from the others? At least he had had the foresight to lease a private cottage. Lucky guy.

The wealth of the Americans fascinated him. They seemed to shoot out of a vortex into a temporary calm north of the border, acting like millionaires on a stop-over.

Their automobiles nipped in and out of Canadian traffic. They carried new gadgets that would eventually be available in Canada. They came bearing legends of fortunes won and lost and won again. Excitement from the free-and-easy land below the forty-ninth blew in with them. They even bore small American flags on the hoods of their cars.

<When Montgomery was mortally wounded in the assault on Quebec, his standard bearer fell dead in the snow beside him.>

Adam carried about the American posture of over-confidence which was mistaken in the Canadian setting for a nonchalant superiority. His white garmented appearance would have been acceptable if he acted like a college undergraduate. Unfortunately, he had the air of implying that the wearing of other apparel, such as striped sport shirts, was old-fashioned. He had had the same knack of initiating novelty at camp. In those days, Adam wore an elastic on his right small finger with such sophistication that the other boys eagerly followed his example. He used to declare certain foods uneatable, creamed celery for instance, and influenced ninety per cent of the campers to leave them untouched. Certain passwords of esoteric meaning were originated by him and adopted by everyone who wished to be "au courant". Adam had fascinated him then. Perhaps some of the fascination had been rekindled yesterday when Adam introduced himself, for he was surprised that he couldn't sleep last night.

The fact that Adam was homosexual did not deter his affection. If anything, that trait served to emphasize Adam's unique personality.

Green of the grass vibrating with richness: bright, vicious green, come, enmesh me in your blades - clean, mint-smelling.

A girl sauntered out from the trees on the path that ran by the shore. Her bathing suit streamlined her figure, supple and firmly rounded. She walked slowly, her long tanned legs tensed to take her weight upon her toes, the cheeks of her behind like cantaloupes. Her hair was tucked into a yellow bathing cap which encircled her straight classical features.

I wish I had the courage to speak to her.

Blue sky, blue lake; feminine forms lay face down all across the dock. Unhaltered, they bared backs to the sun. Their buttocks were rounded like pleasant little knolls in a meadowy paradise of form and colour. He approached self-consciously. He disliked inserting his awkward body into a landscape of rolling symmetry. Although he had conquered his excessive shyness amongst women, especially those in bathing suits, he learned to adopt an easy manner with them only by mixing in all kinds of social groups since leaving university.

Walking through the emerald green grass - Corot's kind of sensuality, seen on exhibit in Paris, two summers ago.

The slats of the dock - thick heavy planks. Slup, slup of the water against the wood like sharp slaps for being naughty.

He was a stranger to these people. The few young men dangling their legs over the sides of the motorboat at dockside came from a different city. They "clanned". Water skis were angled in the boat. He shied away from acquainting himself with them for the moment because they appeared ready to commence water-skiing. He did not want to be involved in a sport he had never done. To make a clumsy mistake in front of all these girls would humiliate him.

He stretched his towel out a respectable distance from the group of girls and sat upon it. Some girls were sitting up, smoking, sipping cokes (which they kept in an ice-cooled case) and chatting. He admired the nimble yet careless gesture of arm and hand. The straight back and pretty features refined the somewhat sexually provoking atmosphere inspired by the reclining forms around them. Vague feelings of desire stirred through his thighs. He turned away and looked at the long shore of an island one quarter of a mile opposite. He needed "woman" - general connotation.

The sweet-bodied girl bucked when held under the breasts. Her playfulness was desperate for she was a soldier of society and had to glean enjoyment from rigorous denial.

The fellows chorusing, "Banging Away on Lulu", took courage in numbers. They roamed the streets in family automobiles as if driven by some vague design, and stopped behind parked cars and sprang on back bumpers until two heads came up in the dark interior like chipmunks to thunder.

Those petting years with their distressing denials still sent shivers of frustration through his mind. (Mother's advice to daughter: piecemeal exploration, but guard the safe.)

And what about the honest girls? Those with swollen bellies are hanging from the upturned noses of self-professed saints.

The pillars of society stand like a Roman temple, lording it over the human race burning in the hearth. He was in the flames and dancing with her, hip to hip, while she was baby-sitting.

'I wish I'd worn my thinner skirt,' suggested lips against his ear.

He spun them onto the sofa and plucking at her garments thumbed his fingers hopelessly in haste.

'Only the top.'

Severe recommendation from a voice accustomed to command.

'It tickles.'

<The goddess sat upon her throne benignly laughing at the handiwork of man.>

Humiliated, he strove against the lead-heavy weight of her body pressing upon his spirit. He rode the energy of youth until, kneeling in exhaustion, he looked up at flushed cheeks and the dark glow of mocking eyes.

'You remind me of....'

She was relegating him to the ranks.

As he trespassed through the uncertainties of teen-age, he became accustomed to refusal. He depended on it. He could pretend to be serious yet be unafraid of having to play the man. His pleas were just rallying calls and like the patriotic huntsman he won plenty of exercise without ever getting near the dreaded kill.

It was a hot August night when he called for her. The navy boots were making his feet sweat.

'Over the phone I thought it was your friend,' she said.

After they came out of the movie house, she walked him to the park. He put his arm round her and watched admiringly the way she moved. Her compact little figure drew him closer. In one desperate embrace he lost his senses and laid her on the leaves. He shot his aching self into her. Immediately his body disintegrated and his mind swirled amidst the debris.

When they came out of the park, he slunk, hands in pockets, beside her.

'Now you don't like me,' she said.

When he woke up with the bugle next morning, the fellows said he was screaming in the night.

He had a few hours Sunday so he went to see her. An office girl, shy, alone, and under twenty, she boarded in a house with many other working girls. She showed him her engagement ring kept on a thin chain in a box and a snap of a moustached army man who had written that his intestines went with a shell in Korea.

'I'd still marry him if he wanted me. But he doesn't.'

They walked in a stiff wind nodding the tall trees out on the sea road.

'I didn't think you would see me today,' she said.

He blushed and glanced down. 'Last night was the first time.'

'I know.'

They looked for a place hidden from the road. But every field was fenced off. Finally they found a good place, some club house far back from the gate where they could go over into the woods. But a sign said no trespassing, and he didn't want to go because he was wearing his white naval cap -- too conspicuous, too risky. But he really didn't want to go; his desire hung petrified in the shock of new existence.

She showed him the high rock overlooking the yapping waves where she tried to jump from several times that summer. But each time she couldn't. She just stood there, waiting, she said.

He had to be back at base early. Before he left, she stood tip-toe and embraced him in a desperate love that made his heart throb out as if it were his whole existence. He never saw her again, but he had learned that one exists only by moments. And for the first time he realized he had been in pursuit of those moments which would run him all his life.

Marston crossed from the broad walk to the pavement on the other side of the street. The bright lights from the hotel terraces tried to turn night into day for the crowd of summer strollers moving at escalator speed. He saw the dynamic carriage of her breasts and the glint in her eyes as they passed. He stopped and went back. He had never proposed like this before. He didn't know how to begin.

It wasn't that he needed her especially; he just thought that he should; experience was necessary. Anyway, she looked really hot!

She was waiting on a side street away from the lights when he caught up to her.

'Quinze cent.'

'C'est beaucoup.'

'Mais comment... c'que tu veux?'

'It's only once,' he thought.

They went back to the crowds and bright lights. He ducked self-consciously beside her as she, hurrying in rough sweater and skirt against the fine drapes of the rich, asked questions in a harsh voice, trying to make him feel at ease. On the last terrace they passed, he saw three young ladies, evening-gowned and dining at a table over-looking the sidewalk where they could play social elite to the summer traffic of fellow snobbery. He saw their faces gape in shock, and he rushed on.

He followed her down a side street, through the doors of a house, and lagged, feeling uneasy, as she hummed a high tune in a last attempt to appear young. She climbed the stairs ahead of him. The bell she rang on the first floor sprung open the door of the second storey flat when they reached it. No one was about. He followed her to a bedroom. It was too late to get out of it now.

'Hay ya! 'E wan' fiv' 'unnerd fer da room.'

He thought it was part of the fifteen hundred.

'I've only got a thousand.'

She grabbed it and was talking in the hall.

Shaking a five hundred note at him, she closed the door closeting them with the cheap fixtures of a third class pension.

'Gimme da udder t'ousant.'

'Wait!' He saw his mistake. 'Give me that and I'll pay you after.'

'Yah? Waddya wanna make a' me?'

He saw the five hundred was lost to the fierce constriction of her hands. His experience had just begun. He paid to complete it. 'Where did you learn your English?'

While standing by the chair where he laid his clothes, he watched her confront the mirror and pull at her eyelashes. The sparkle faded. He watched her undress, wondering if with the money already won, she would go through with the agreement. When she took off her brassier, she tried to prevent her breasts from dangling at her waist like huge white muscleless squibs. Coddling them, she lay backwards on the bed and waited for him.

Surprise mingled with disgust as he went to her. No man would back out, he thought. This was to prove himself.

Close-up her face lay shadowed with the misery of age, glossed thickly in cream. The bone structure of her body was hitched up one side, thin and brittle, like her jaw. He saw the pale brown flecks showing summers of Bikini wear which had long gone but which clung as a remembrance of better times to the never-washed skin. Although he put his arms on both sides of her, he could not bring them against her. He tried to kiss her but his lips refused to touch her cheek. A faint reek of decay clotted his nostrils.

She shrunk from him like an old woman from a blow. She pretended to him. But it was useless.

'Why can't I?' He was frightened of impotence. He had read about it. <A eunuch stood timidly helping the queen undress. Bakunin, although dynamic in personality.... > 'Do you know why?'

'Je n'ai pas d'hauteur pour vous,' she ventured.

Sickened with tragedy, tormented with failure, he stayed beside her hoping that time would work the miracle. She wanted to leave and unhappily he returned to his clothes. Watching her prepare for the next customer, he saw age spring into youth. He was reminded of the money he had given her, of the society in front of which she had paraded him, and of his failure.

'Une vielle femme,' he growled in small boy rebuke.

Without speaking, she left. He heard her whisper in the hall. He followed shortly after and found the door standing open. By it sat a mound of a man who pityingly watched him go.

When he stepped into the street, two grocers paused from piling up crates and looked curiously at him. From all sides there were eyes like black darts.

The boards trembled, jarring him from his dream. Someone jumped from the diving board - a flash of blue in the corner of his eyes. He looked round.

The woman of the yellow bathing cap passed close by. She smiled down at him.

'You are Marston Havers, aren't you?'

Stunned, he reacted with a smile as nervous as it was broad. Family friend? College acquaintance? He realized with a start that she was waiting for a reply.

'That's right.'

'I'm Corinne Boothby.'

Toronto. Her mother went to school with mine, isn't that it?

'Do you remember meeting me here years ago? Let me see, it must be five or six.'

Her big brother owned a motorboat - came to search for them when he paddled her enthusiastically miles too far.

'Five or six! It must be ten.'

'Ten! Goodness, how time flies.'

'Well, I can notice the difference, physically speaking.'

She laughed, swept her towel beside him and sat in a kneeling motion upon it. 'You have changed a lot too. Do you remember the time my brother had to come after us in our motorboat?'

'Sure do.'

He liked her laughter. With beautiful women of well-developed dimensions he had found laughter guttural, inclined to sarcasm. But Corinne was pleasant and relaxed.

She pulled off her bathing cap, the rubber puckering loudly, and let her brown hair fall to the shoulders.

'What brings you back after so many years?' she smiled.

The breeze caught the leaves of the birch trees and fluttered them like tiny fans: pale green memories.

'I don t know. Guess I just wanted to see what changes there were.'

'Nothing's changed, Marston. Are you married?'

'No, oh God, no!'

'Why are you so defensive about it?'

'Aren't most bachelors? Are you married?'

'No!' She laughed. 'Marston, you're just the same. You're not supposed to ask a woman if she is married. Look to see if she has the ring on her finger.'

'You could have taken it off for swimming.'

He noticed the other girls had cocked their ears to the conversation and now turned smiling faces upon them. When Corinne introduced them, he forgot their names but committed to memory the eyes, the mouth, and the physical impression of each.

<Ulysses forbade his men to stop and listen to the Sirens chanting from the rocks. The haunting melody of their voices promised idyllic delights.>

The young men buzzed away in the motorboat towing two skiers towards the centre of the lake.

If Corinne is unattached, I might be able to have some fun. But she probably belongs to one of those sportsmen out in the lake.

He gazed over the lines of her form as she lay on her back beside him. Her femininity hovered in the air as a suggestion of the maleness in himself.

'Would you like a coke, Marston?' One of the girls had taken a bottle from the container.

'Okay, thanks.'

He disliked the drink but he didn't want to refuse because the offer was in the form of an introduction into the group. The bottle passed from one person to another up to the point where he reached over Corinne and took it.

Adam sauntered down the walk from the lodge. Marston had completely forgotten Adam. It was as if he received the initial shock of meeting the man for the first time again.

'He's fallen,' said a woman looking at the water-skiers.

'Good for him.'

Satisfaction rippled through the reclining forms.

'They both have.'

Heads popped up, scrutinized the distance, and fell back again.

Adam stepped heavily over the trembling planks. His shoulders were hunched forward and he walked lazily, without spring to his muscles. He smiled uncertainly and approached.

A boyishness still shaped his features and a youthful attractiveness patterned his figure. Marston was aware that the eye of every woman watched the stranger.

Adam halted several yards from him and, cocking his thumb at the far end of the dock, said pleasantly, 'Sit over here with me. I want to talk with you.'

Marston sensed the tense reaction of the women. Rejected? They failed to comprehend. (Each one of Bluebeard's wives must have thought he truly loved her.)

Skin felt hot, rather red. 'Do you have any suntan lotion, Adam?' He strode with him to the other end of the dock.

The name "Adam" lay behind, worryingly, in the consciousness of the women. Corinne gave no indication that she knew he was departing. Corinne, get up and see me go, will you?

The American charm (course by Dale Carnegie) was personified in Adam's grin at those of the girls who took ostentatious notice of him.

<The Americans sent agents into Lower Canada with propaganda and money to persuade the French to join them against the British in the 1812 War.>

(There was always the possibility of surprise attacks from south of the border at any time during the Nineteenth Century.)

Marston could not help feeling uncomfortable upon accepting Adam's invitation to sit alone with him. There was a sense of possessiveness in the atmosphere, perhaps engendered by a quaver in Adam's voice, as if he had been terrified of being rebuked.

Adam dipped the lotion into the palm of one hand and kneeled. 'Turn round. I'll put some on your back.'

The strong prodding fingers massaged his back. They circled carefully, gently from shoulder to waist.

'There. Put some on mine, Marston.'

Adam closed his eyes and leaned into Marston's hands. Reminded of a cat, Marston expected him to purr. <It was during those years that Benjamin Franklin was Post-Master-General that the countries were united.>

'There, that ought to do it.'

'No, Marston, put more on the tops of the shoulders.'

Straining at the friction of skin upon skin, he became aware that suntan oil was not a perfect lubricant.

'Okay, is that good enough. What did you want to talk to me about?'

Corinne has turned onto her stomach. She has gone to sleep upon her hands. Some day my prince will come. He's probably in that boat buzzing back here.

Adam smiled quizzically. 'You're in a hurry, aren't you?' His expression implied that beneath his sarcasm he felt hurt. 'More interested in talking with the girls?'

Marston's face became hot, especially along the sides back from the eyes. 'Of course not. I just wondered what was so important.'

'It was a ruse,' Adam said. 'I didn't want to sit with all those females like a caliph in a harem. Do you mind?'

A trace of a plea lurked in the black of his eyes. Marston felt sorry. After all, Adam must feel lonely in a foreign country, and I am his only friend up here.

'Have you been back to Canada since that summer at camp?'

'No,' Adam sighed as if he were under the duress of heavy sorrow. 'But I am glad that when I returned, I met you again.'

He nodded amicably. 'I'm glad to see you again too.'

<Canadian reserve was formed in great part from the Tory settlers who after fleeing from the savagery of Whig mobs carried on the British Empire further north.>

Adam leaned on one elbow and placed his hand upon Marston's knee. Affection shone from those black eyes, but still loneliness lay there.

The motorboat coughed to a halt at the dockside. What if those guys should notice them posed like this? He jerked his knee away from Adam's grasp.

Those guys will think I'm a Homo too!

Some of the girls stood and gathered around the boys who clambered from the motorboat. Corinne sat up and watched with unconcern, as if she had no special friend amongst the crew. From a side view her waist curved seductively below her breasts. He wanted to reach out and take them ripe like corn from the stalk.

'Corinne!'

She turned. Radiant. Drill my tongue between those lips, taste the pollen. Queen Bee. She will sting me dead in revenge.

'I want you to meet an old friend of mine. Bring your towel.'

A shade of anger clouded Adam's brow. The corners of his eyes screwed up in wrinkles in an effort to appear pleasant. He stretched out his arm and took Corinne's hand when she reached them. Their handshake looked limp. Marston did not think that Corinne was enchanted, although she said that she was.

'Corinne is also an old friend, Adam.'

'Yes, Marston and I were young flirts years ago at this very place.'

Adam's eyes grew darker. 'Flirting is quite harmless. At that age it means nothing.'

Although the group was laughing and shouting behind them, the atmosphere seemed very still all of a sudden. Marston felt that they were trapped without a word to utter.

'You're American, aren't you?' Corinne asked.

(You drive big cars through endless, overcrowded cities, clown and spend most of your money on banana splits, don't you?)

'Yes, I am.'

(We organized the Berlin airlift.)

The men had put their arms around the women and some of them kissed in a frolicking mood.

Pure abandon - how I want pure abandon! The fear in my heart is too great.

Georgie Porgie kissed the girls and made them cry.

Spin the bottle. When I was at the age that I knew Corinne, I heard about the game from my more fortunate friends. The girl spun the bottle within the circle of boys and, when it came to a stop, the boy at which it pointed had to take the girl into the hall and kiss her. I wondered how you got invited to those sort of parties. Of course, whenever I thought of them, I always had the best-looking girl in mind.

'How did you come to stay at this lodge?' Corinne asked. 'I should have thought an American would have preferred the ritzier places further down the lake.'

Marston sensed Adam's annoyance and said, 'All Americans aren't the same any more than all Canadians are.' He spoke with a smile in order to show Corinne that he wasn't taking sides. The flesh of her legs weakened him with a spasm of desire. He could not continue.

The soft folds of woman's flesh beating a sensuous rhythm through the limbs to excite the heart. Il Giorgione's *Venus* seen on exhibit in the Palace of the Doge, Venice.

'I have a cottage near here. I just dine at the lodge.'

'Oh, you do!'

She was thinking: parties!

'I had planned to hire a chef, but it seemed superfluous for one person. And I like to cook anyways,' Adam drawled.

'I bet you cook well,' she said.

'I've been hoping to have Marston over for a meal whenever he wants to come.' Adam turned upon him full-face.

'Sure.' He tried to look interested. 'I'm always hungry for good food.'

<When the British landed at Washington, the American President had to leave his dinner of roast turkey untouched lest he become roast turkey in the succeeding fire.>

Corinne glanced back at the girls who were laughing at one of the sportsmen who seemed to be having trouble stepping into the water skis, but Corinne, preoccupied with her thoughts, was not amused.

Adam wrinkled his nose at her for Marston's observation when her head was turned away.

'Marston, I'm going in for a swim,' she said. 'Coming?'

He watched her form rise up slim and gorgeous, Venus Aphrodite, as her arms bent like wings to slip the bathing cap over her hair. She dove cleanly into the water. Before she reached the surface, he dove after her and came up just as she turned round to look for him.

It was thrilling to feel the attraction between the sexes through the seeming opacity of liquid. Drugged in her charm for an instant, he tread water faintly.

'Come on, I'll race you to the small dock!' she cried, striking into a crawl.

He saw her bright child's face challenging him to take the canoe across the lake. Fondness is an affair of the heart, I guess. She is a part of my security in the fact that her mother knows mine: her world is mine - no, was mine. Nostalgia. I want her body.

He gave chase.

The cool lake water sped past his ears and swished at the crown of his head. He dug his arms deep under him and rejoiced in their strength and trimness. He glimpsed her thrashing wildly feet ahead.

'Not the dock, I mean the rock,' she gasped.

Cheater! The rock capped the point at the entrance to the cove which was at least twenty yards closer than the dock. He laughed and gritted his teeth. Straining for speed, he felt transformed into a gyro of effort. The gray rock formed his horizon. The movement in the water beside him was like a shark to his pride. He shot ahead, vaguely glimpsed the distance for a tour de force, and reached the roughened mineral with outstretched hand.

Sitting up on the slope of the rock, he prevented Corinne from climbing beside him.

'I won,' he breathed. 'What's my reward?'

She was too out-of-breath to answer so that he let her up on the rock. She sank beside him and leaned into his arms. A shock passed through him and he started. Tired as she was, she pulled away and leaned on one arm to the other side. Her leg pressed alongside his from thigh to water's edge. He took the top of her bathing suit in both hands and rolled it down to the waist and up again. He was so shocked at his action that the beauty he had seen was lost in a white blankness of skin.

'Marston!' Corinne sidled away, eyes staring. 'Why did you do that?'

He shook his head and felt helpless. 'I don't know.'

The water moved up and down his ankles. <Victor Hugo's Etienne waited in a rock chair for the tide to rise around him and drown away his remorse.>

She looked flustered. 'But no gentleman would do that. I thought you were a gentleman.'

'I'm sorry. I just thought I'd have a little fun with you.'

She smiled and seemed to relax. Gorgeous Corinne, if only your mind were as advanced as your body. She recovered her poise in spite of the frightening novelty of being disrobed unexpectedly in public.

'Well, no one saw you, so it's all right, you're forgiven. But don't do it again, please.'

His nerves were trembling. A thick cluster of bush hid them from the view of the front dock, and a boathouse concealed them from the bathers on the small dock.

'You must have attracted me more than I thought,' he said. 'It seems incredible that you are the same pug-nosed creature I was looney about.'

'Did you like me way back then?'

'In a certain way, yes. Besides, you were the only girl my age up here, weren't you?'

'Oh, thanks a lot.' She smiled.

<Rasmussen coming out of the polar zones into balmier weather.>

'Well, I must admit, I liked you too,' she said. 'You weren't quite so impetuous then.'

They laughed. Again he remarked on the warmth and pleasantness of her laughter. There was a fine beauty in the arch of the throat.

'Who is the gang with you?' He nodded back at the front dock.

'Toronto people. I knew a couple of the girls before. Sort of fun, aren't they?'

'Look like it,' he agreed.

He wished he had not mentioned the group. Corinne meant a good deal alone like this, but, by placing her in the presence of others, he took her away from himself, as if he were fitting her into a particular society with stereotyped views and aims which were at variance with his own. (Teletype bands clicked from a machine on a stand at waist level, spelling monotony, frustration.)

If I could take her into the woods at night, maybe I would forget about her background. I love those breasts. I think I could forget that her mother went to school with mine. Would I be betraying any trust set in bond back then?

'Where on earth did you meet your friend?'

Her surprised tone implied dislike for Adam which he thought unfair.

'Why?'

'Well, he seems so strange. I thought he was angry with me for knowing you.'

'Oh no, he's not mad at you. He's moody, that's all. I haven't seen him since we were boys, but I remember his moods of despondency.'

She kicked a spray of water onto the rock. The low drone of a motor engine informed them that the water-skiers were circling in front of the big dock again.

'How long are you staying, Marston?'

'A few days. You?'

'I've been here a week. I'm going back at the end of next week.'

She sounded as if her holiday had been tedious and that she counted on him to enliven it.

'Going anywhere tonight?' He tried to sound off-hand, although the spectre of the group winnowed up to frighten him rigid. If she were going to be busy with one of the young men, then it was the end, breasts and all.

'No. Did you want to go to the dance at the lodge across the lake?'

'I'd like to, yes. Shall we eat dinner together and then canoe over?'

'Oh, we shouldn't eat at the same table. Some of mother's friends are here and might talk.' She looked askance at him.

(Now dear, if you take a girl out your intentions must always be honourable). <*Les Demoiselles D'Arles* = Van Gogh's black vision, seen as a print *ad infinitum*.>

'I guess you're right. I'll see you afterwards.'

God! We're both university graduates. Nevertheless, he could almost feel her svelte body in his arms. He laughed with happiness as if it were the spectacle of her mother's friends that he found amusing.

'Marston!'

Sharp and bitter, a voice barked at their backs. Adam stepped through the bushes and glared down at him.

'I thought we agreed to go swimming together.'

(We don't understand why you elect to remain British.)

Marston felt yanked out of romanticism into classical reality, or, rather, he seemed strangely immersed in both but owing in allegiance to the older Romanism. Adam with his black eyes reminded him of a noble Roman - the young senator, Catiline - unfortunately this time Catiline feigned to think he was being conspired against.

'Adam! Why didn't you swim after us? You used to be a good swimmer. What's the matter?'

The challenging tone worked well. Adam was non-plussed. His expression was no longer accusing. He smirked, the round lines of his cheeks becoming pronounced like the rim of an apple.

'If you had thought of inviting me, I would have tried it.'

'You're invited to race us back to the dock,' Corinne said.

A challenge spread thinly with sarcasm. (The Female Product - not American, rather universal.)

Adam's look sharpened. (George Washington at Valley Forge.)

'It's a deal, though I haven't been swimming for a long time.'

'We're worn out from our race over here,' Marston joked. 'So we're even.'

His joviality found no response in the intent faces of the others. They hardly noticed him so deeply were they involved in mutual antipathy. As Corinne stood on the rock beside Adam, he sensed a resolve form itself in the air, a resolve that extended far beyond the winning of a swimming race. He smiled at them, trying politely to sustain an amicable relationship, although he felt like a comical stooge in a tragedy by doing so.

They plunged flatly and struck out in a crawl, their arms looping out of the water like pistons on the engine of a big ship.

<Motion in space = *Nude Descending a Staircase.*>

The realization that they had left him on the rock dragged him from immobility. He gaped after them and plunged. Water tried to run up his nostrils but he blew it out, feeling cleansed through and attuned to a good race. But they were yards ahead. Valiantly he struck out until his chest burned with spent energy. His arms felt heavy suddenly and he hove to the side stroke where the scissors kick of legs could glide him in pursuit. He looked up to see Adam and Corinne reach for the ladder at the same moment. They rested at its foot and turned to find him. Lying on his back he blew out a spew of water and calmly backstroked the distance to them.

'What! Out of breath? You weren't racing, were you?' he called.

'I suppose you came behind us all the way like that,' Corinne said between breaths.

'Behind you? I wasn't concerned with where I was going - to be truthful.'

'We tied,' Adam smiled, 'but we beat you, if that is a consolation.' He looked at Corinne.

'Somehow, he seemed to have been beaten before he started,' she said quietly.

Corinne had been a smart kid in school. She could probably make some bright observations, although she might not understand them.

She clambered up the ladder. Adam followed her and he followed Adam. Three blind mice, See how they run. They were running into a mysterious presence, of which, perhaps, Adam was the most aware. There was the satanic conniving, seen in an Arnold Boecklin painting, especially suited to the wild romanticism of Muskoka.

'The others have all gone,' Corinne cried. 'The bell for lunch must have sounded.'

Adam took his arm. 'I asked my waitress to set your place at my table.'

The firm clasp claimed him.

<In 1812 when the British troops were fighting Napoleon's Army in Europe, the Canadian pioneers faced the choice of submitting peacefully to the American armies or risking the loss of all they had wrought from the land by resisting the invasion with inferior numbers.>

3.

Arms tingling with energy; the body refreshed, rejuvenated; Marston had given him life! Adam could have hugged him for that.

The girl was stooping to pick up her towel. Marston's fascination with her backside was obnoxiously noticeable. She knew her attraction; that is why she was taking so long.

Marston, stop being a fool!

He watched Marston scoop up their towels. He admired the breadth of back and the fullness of the shoulders. He would have liked to have run his hands over those firm muscles which rippled just under the skin.

Taking his lotion and towel from Marston, he tried to stall him from following in Corinne's steps. Marston frowned, annoyed.

'Let her go ahead,' Adam said.

She turned round. 'Aren't you coming?'

Marston, puzzled, cried. 'You go ahead. We'll see you in the dining room.'

Rid of her at last! That slight swing of hip is quite unnecessary. The handsome eyes shifted over his features. 'Don't you like Corinne?'

Understatement, typically British, I reckon. You know I hate her guts!

'No, I don't like her. Do you?'

He looks surprised - a Canadian being told his culture is barbaric. He's thinking: (maybe he knows that he doesn't like her, though that's too much to ask for.)

'I like her! I think she's a good sport.'

Being a good swimmer does not make a woman a good sport. The unpleasant personality of the woman reminds me of thousands of shop girls and minor career categories. Brainless, unreflective mammal, they spend their lives persuading men that they are pretty in spite of their ugliness. Rouge, paraphernalia, disguise.

<The witch doctor of a tribe performed the correct dances to exorcise the evil spirit in a sick young brave.>

They walked up the hill together. Their bare legs flashed in front of them. He felt the pain in his heart which Marston had inflicted by deserting him for the company of a female.

The verandah was empty and no wonder. Lunch was the meal that won the most response from the lodgers. Activities in the morning air abetted hunger in the frailest of beings. He sensed the sharp desire in his stomach and glanced sideways at Marston who seemed rapt in thought.

<Psychologists ascertained that the desire for food was stronger than the desire for sex - but, of course, that was in rats.>

As they passed the dining room doorway, he caught sight of the first table filled with one family who had patronized the lodge for fifteen years. The beetle look of the parents had been stamped markedly upon their children and was never so obvious as when one caught them all in a row at one glance.

Marston hung back in order to climb the stairs behind him. Adam felt uncomfortable, as if his buttocks were being scrutinized for blemishes. The door of Marston's room loomed ahead in reprieve from inspection.

Amazing how self-conscious I am! It's all my own imagination but 1 just can't seem to help myself.

He swung open the door and walked in ahead of Marston. The privacy made him feel very close to Marston. As soon as the door closed, he put his arm around his friend's shoulders and looked passionately into his eyes.

Door closing over the past intensifies the present. Fresh from a swim with bare feet on a wooden floor, and closeted in a dry room, young men experience intimacy to the depth of their natures.

Marston stepped away from his arm with an exclamation. 'Boy! Am I hungry!'

The cry was not spontaneous; it was made from nervousness. Marston was afraid of him. But that was one step towards the goal at least.

He took off his trunks and stood nakedly regarding Marston who had turned his back and seemed to be fiddling with the clasp of his bathing suit.

Marston glanced shyly back at him. He was only too well aware of his desire. The bathing suit revealed white skin unkissed by the sun.

Desire burned in his belly and shot strength through his body. For a moment he was sure he was going to leap upon him, but somehow his better sense restrained him. (A section of Canadian society was eating lunch within earshot). Red heat filled his vision, and he sensed weakness float in his limbs as if he had been cast helplessly adrift from the knees up.

Marston was saying something and smiling. He was doing up his trousers.

'Adam, are you listening or dreaming?'

'Dreaming.'

'Hurry up and get dressed. I'm hungry.'

The tone rebuked him. It was sharp and deliberately intended to reject him. Ah yes, subconscious rejection, but nevertheless.... The road to the most priceless treasure is the longest and hardest.

'I was thinking of how lucky you are,' he said.

'Lucky? What do you mean?'

'You have a beautiful physique; you are young and charming; you have all the advantages of the privileged. Imagine all the young girls whose hearts you must have broken, are breaking, and will break.'

Marston laughed loudly. 'That reminds me of German irregular verbs: brechen, brach, gebrochen. I spent a whole summer learning them.'

'You have even the supreme confidence of dismissing whatever praise I may give you.'

'I'm sorry, Adam. I wasn't laughing at what you said. It's probably quite true but I couldn't care less. You'd be surprised how wrong you are about my luck.'

'I know one thing for certain. You are capable of breaking hearts.'

Marston buttoned his shirt and answered with chin held high. 'I don't consider that lucky.'

The subject of homosexuality had to be introduced, did it not? The subconscious had to be charmed away from its reptilian concept.

He pouted. 'Do you know that you wounded me this morning?'

'When I went swimming with Corinne? Don't be crazy, Adam!'

'I like you very much, Marston. Haven't you noticed that?'

The hard glare of defense covered Marston's eyes. Yes, my dear friend, I am presuming on your person, but it's absolutely necessary that I do.

'Marston, don't look so angry.'

The loud clanging of the bell began directly beneath them. They listened to the noise recede into the distance as the waitress who rang it went her rounds. In Marston's eyes, he recognized a hostility which spoke in deep tones to his heart, while the metallic ring of the lunch bell harshly underscored it.

'The second bell,' Marston said sternly. 'We'll miss eating altogether if you don't hurry.'

Sighing, he pulled on his white ducks and squirmed into his shirt. An unhappy retreat was saved from being termed a rout by the immediate necessity of lunching. He watched Marston comb his hair and decided that a casual remark would smoothen his disturbed state of mind.

'You should grow it longer like mine.'

'Yes, perhaps I should.'

He sounded irritated, as self-righteous as a provincial Canadian. <There were sugar-coated pills meant for short tempers and upset stomachs. Absolutely useless, the United States exported them by the bushel to its neighbours.>

'Aren't you feeling well?'

'I'm feeling well enough. Are you ready?'

Oh ho, imperious now. Quickly he passed his comb through his hair and along the sides of his head so as to brush the strands behind his ears.

'I'm ready.' He opened the door for Marston and followed him out. 'Do you honestly resent my confession that I like you?'

Marston glanced around quickly as if he were afraid someone would overhear. 'Let's not talk about it now.'

'But do you?' he insisted.

'It's not that; it's something in your attitude I don't like.'

How true! He hated it himself. It was a compulsion to make his nature overt. He had seen it in many, many others and recognized the tendency growing through his own personality. He wondered if it were very noticeable. Perhaps it accounted for the aloofness of the lodgers.

'Let me lead the way.'

Marston's footsteps behind him were like a moral support as he walked through the dining room. All the lunchers seemed to look up at once, but he met their eyes with an amused stare. If they were thinking things about him, he would be showing them that the gossip of inferior beings could not touch a noble spirit.

<Roger Casement died a martyr for Ireland, yes, but more so for humanity.>

His table by the window was set for two. At first, his place had been laid in company with three young ladies who were inclined to welcome the presence of a bachelor, but after a week of escaping them by either eating earlier or later than they, he was transferred to a smaller table which had become vacant.

He took his place facing out at the other tables while Marston sat on the side. It was pleasant to be able to watch Marston in profile while he ate. The excitement of going on a canoe trip years ago was similar to the excitement he felt at having Marston beside him now. Marston figured strongly in his memories of camp life. His affection for him had finally come to mean something. By portaging a canoe on their shoulders they started a feeling of brotherhood that years of absence could not diminish. For him, that feeling had increased to love. He could not be sure how strong it was until they made love, but he sensed that they had been meant to meet. The impulse to holiday in Muskoka could be called psychic, for he was being led into the discovery of himself. What could make that discovery more complete than love. Perhaps through this beautiful friend he would find the contentment and the confidence that he desired so badly.

Mr. Ornweddy lunched silently with his wife nearby. Mr. Ornweddy looked sharply at him, as if mistrusting him. Mrs. Ornweddy appeared interested in the grandchild of her neighbours. The grandchild was naughtily spilling food over its front and giving the odd shout that bounded through the great wooden room. Its grandparents suffered stoically, having accepted their duty as part of the burden of growing old. The lean grandmother became actively interested in the child only when it rocked the wooden chair with crackling annoyance.

Great laughter erupted in the hall and a young group sallied into the room. The slap of sandals and the swinging lurch of short-panted behinds remained a recognizable trait of the women. The men having indulged more readily in the warm-up drinks before lunch spoke at the top of their voices until they were actually in the middle of thc sanctuary when the winces and frowns of the older guests intimidated them to adopt more cautious tones. He had read the dislike on the faces of some of the young men and fancied he had heard the word "fairy" whispered as he walked by them. He had not wanted to get close to their group on the dock. There was enough adversity met in life without searching it out.

The fat woman whose name he could never remember regarded him with Scottish dourness. She had taken an instant dislike to him, and he had had to suffer her slights and caustic remarks whenever they chanced to meet, or rather, confront one another. She and the librarian, Miss Renfrew, who sat on the other side of the room, were his worst enemies. If they found the slightest reason to complain about him, they would not rest until he was hounded from the lodge. Luckily, he did not sleep in the place(?) Miss Renfrew complained bitterly about the fracas made by the young people. She threatened to cut short her stay if the young people were not forced to leave. Being a librarian, she was divorced from the world of economics. The poor soul could not understand the proprietor's reluctance to do her bidding.

The soft glance of the divorcee sitting with her children calmed his worries about the lodgers. One sympathetic smile erased the bleakness of all the others. Conversations with her helped fill the vacuum in his solitude and repay her for the obvious liking she had for him. Repayment in words. But what useless things were words to a woman who wanted flesh. He should not encourage her by speaking with her. Unfortunately, he needed contact with her. He needed her voice and her smile. Oh unapproachable mother!

I wonder if she feels the same way about me as I feel about Marston. I wonder. He smiled to himself. She hasn't the depth of feeling that I have for Marston. Besides, she won't get the flesh, but I will.

He passed his hand over Marston's wrist when he pretended to reach for the sugar. Contact! Marston turned questioningly to him. Oh God, what a hard-hearted lover!

He glanced around. Mrs. Ashburton had picked up the movement and was watching for further signs. After a few glasses of gin in the evening, she would gossip. A cold shiver passed down his back as he thought of how she would report her observation. He and Marston would be mentioned together. (When you come to consider it, there's something romantic about that).

He envisioned two young heads with tousled hair paddling a canoe in the regulation blue uniform worn by the campers.

'I like your waitress, Adam. She's pretty, eh?'

'Nice girl. Not very quick though.'

Corinne swung into the room. She caught Marston's eye and held it until she was sitting and chatting with the others at her table. He had to admit that her print dress was pretty. She seemed determined to captivate Marston, damn her soul.

<The double curve motive was the basic design for the Algonquin tribes. On pottery and dress the motive was worked in with floral arrangements.>

'Marston, there's going to be an Indian regatta in Port Carling this afternoon. Will you come with me?'

Swallowing salad, Marston wore an amused gleam in his eye. 'Indian regatta? I didn't know they could get enough Indians together to make a regatta.'

There are a few in the Indian village there, you know. Most of them act as guides for tourists who fish. What do you say?'

Eyes wavered, sought out the figure of Corinne eating and returned. 'Okay, but I have to be back for dinner.'

He frowned and Marston glanced down shyly. Corinne had dated him for the evening, obviously. Empty twilight and the lonely dark channeling through sleeplessness to the ache of dawn.

'We'll be back on time. The lodge down the lake is sending its launch to pick up those people who want to go from here. I think you'll like it. Reading about Indians is a sort of hobby of mine, so I'm really looking forward to it.'

'Indians are unmapped history, aren't they, Adam?'

'For the most part, yes, but the more we learn about them I think the more easy it is for us to understand ourselves. I believe that the climate fashions the culture of a people or at least it affects their mentality. So the American today is linked psychically to the American Indian culture of yesterday as well as to the other cultures which preceded the Indian.'

Marston laughed, his pearly white teeth moving out from cherry lips, his blue eyes twinkling, his handsome features tilted back as if he were being rocketed into space. 'If you ask me, American culture can learn a hell of a lot from the Indian, especially in the way to bring up children.'

Marston's laughter was not derisive. It was good-humoured and required a humorous reply.

'Let's leave that problem to the school-teacher.'

He laughed with Marston. The warmth of their personalities suddenly broke open to one another and charged him with gaiety. People were staring. He wanted them to notice how happy he was with Marston. At least Marston now knew that he understood him somewhat.

'Talking about tying people's hands,' Marston said. 'I've read accounts of how pioneers had their wrists tied so tightly by the Indians that the circulation was stopped.'

'Plus other cruelties like skinning alive and walking on coals, but Marston, we haven't done those things to school-teachers yet.'

'You have just about stopped the circulation, boy.'

Corinne was looking at them. Her eyes waited in vain for Marston to notice her.

'If we could get back on the beam, return to the principles of North American culture as it were, we could correct all these failings. I don't really care if anything is done, but that's my philosophy and that's why I am interested in Indians.'

'How long has that been your philosophy?'

Marston's cleverness could easily be overlooked until you were caught by it at moments like this. He smiled loosely, feeling foolish but powerless to lie, really afraid to lie.

'Since I came to Muskoka this summer.'

There was again no derision, no sarcasm in his laughter, just pure fun. He loved him!

Corinne flashed her eyes resentfully at him. Perhaps he should do something. He leaned forward.

'Your girl friend is trying to get her hook in you, bait.'

Marston glanced round, smiled quickly and returned to him, full attention. Corinne appeared satisfied, the witch.

'I wonder how Indians courted?' Marston asked seriously.

'They didn't bother with girls,' he smiled. 'The woman's lot was so bad in the north that the mothers used to kill their girl babies to save them from the insupportable drudgery of life.'

Marston's expression had enough false distaste in it to be very amusing. 'I've got a better idea. See if you can signal the waitress to bring us our desserts. The boat will be coming by soon.'

The waitress, by good fortune, pushed through the swinging kitchen door with a tray of desserts. Before she reached the side-table, he caught her eye with a definite plea she could not disregard.

'The meal feels good after a swim, doesn't it? I feel ten years younger since you came, Marston.'

The mellowness in his stomach reminded him of coffee and cognac before a Havana Kiosk under the four o'clock sun, minus the invigoration of limb and mind, however.

'We ought to have a lot of fun together, Adam. It sure was a surprise meeting you.'

(You bet we'll have a lot of fun together).

'Eat your pineapple and let's go.'

Mr. Ornweddy was approaching. The man deliberately disregarded him and leaned smilingly toward Marston.

'My wife and I wondered if you'd care to come for a drive with us this afternoon.'

'Oh, thank you, Mr. Ornweddy, we already have places on the motor launch.'

'Ah, I see.' Ornweddy looked darkly over at him as Marston said "we" as if he were an intruder in the one big happy family of the lodge. 'We'll see you there then,' he smiled at Marston and went away.

The grandfather sitting next to Ornweddy jumped up from his chair and, setting his thin legs in motion, he made a swift exit wearing his usual determined demeanor which said, 'I'm going fishing whether anyone comes with me or not.'

The sharp look of the widowed Mrs. Ashburton roamed on guard.

'Look, I have to fetch my camera. I will meet you on the front dock in a few minutes.'

The beetle family had left their table and were ranged along the verandah. Rather than pass by them (he had the dreadful feeling of being preyed upon whenever he did) he went by the back door. One of the offspring, a tough child of twelve, saw him through the doorway before he reached the back hall. 'There goes the orderly,' the boy said, referring to his white clothes, and sniggered. He added a babbling of the lips to make clear to his family that he meant an orderly of the mental rather than the general hospital.

Aaron raised his ax and cleft the log with a mighty stroke. His thick hair hung over his pugnacious face.

'Ah, Aaron, I thought I'd find you here.'

'Hello Mr. Crowfield.'

The huge hands twiddled the ax handle like a toothpick. A big innocent smile overwhelmed the boy's mouth, large and sometimes cruel. A giant mule, this Cyclops who could crush me between his fingers, maul me in his arms while I like a nimble Ulysses must use my wit.

'Will you get my camera, Aaron. I'll need it this afternoon.'

'Oh, yes sir.' The long heavy body sprang up the stairs of the staff house and penetrated the room which he had visited on occasion, but only to sit and talk, to reconnoiter.

Small, with boarded walls, the pine still scenting after thirty years, the room looked over the tops of trees to the lake and islands in the north. The iron cot sank in the centre. Keepsakes cluttered the bureau top and table. Pennants of high schools and colleges let by previous occupants adorned one wall; a map of Gravenhurst and Muskoka Lakes looked out dustily from another.

'Here you are, Mr. Crowfield.' Aaron had wrapped the sling about his thick wrist and fitted the camera in his hand as he bounded down the stairs. 'I took a couple of pictures but there's lots of film left.'

'That's great! I'll try and use up the rest and then we can go to Bala and get the roll developed.'

'Gee, that'll be great,' Aaron tenderly handed over the camera as if he were the one lending it out.

'Be seeing you, Aaron,' he nodded and went.

Before he turned the corner, he looked greedily at Aaron's statuesque form posed with ax held high, and quivered with fascination at the danger he could encounter. But this afternoon he had been awarded quite a different kind of danger. This afternoon he was in pursuit of the spirit as much as the body. Failure could maim his soul with a havoc that no giant's fist could wreak. Death of the body might be unfortunate, death of the spirit was catastrophic.

He paused on the crest of the rock between driveway and lawn and looked out at the lake. Two sailboats nudged along in what seemed yards from each other. Their tall white sails buffeted against the breezes in a spirit of companionship. They tacked together.

<Watts-Dunton lived with Swinburne for years. It has been said that Swinburne would have produced very little if he had not been under the guidance of his literary companion.>

There in the distance came three canoes in Indian file. The paddlers were boy campers. The long rhythmic stroke of the canoers would last for hours, while their bodies became disciplined to the will of their minds. Plod, plod onwards into adventure. After the lake, there is a river with its bends, its herons, its kingfishers, and maybe a rapids. After the river are another lake and a town. There is an island to sleep upon, that is, there was when I was young, but the rich may have moved north with their stakes and barbed wire since those times.

The cedar and pine boughs were heaped under a tree with a bed roll resting in the middle. The fire glowing in the perfumed air of night slowly cast a charm of sleep on tired eyes as a camper draws to the close of a ghost story. 'And his wife's hair turned white like ivory.' Jolted awake by the line, the campers send terrified glances into the impenetrable darkness. They listen to the water lisping at the rocks and fall into a profound sleep.

Adventure! This afternoon offered a different kind of danger. The comparison was not flattering; it was very unkind; it might even be thought dispiriting. The subtle drone of the motor launch drifted through the slim white trunks of the birch. Adventure called. Marston was pacing the dock, probably from worry because his dear friend, Adam, was not there.

He gave a shouting laugh and leaping onto the grass, sprinted for all he was worth to where the bushes gave way to the steps leading onto the dock. Descending majestically, he found himself so comical that his slight spell of dejection forsook him. Happy with expectation, he waved at Marston. Unfortunately, as he stepped onto the dock, the three red canoes came in line with his vision. Abruptly serious, he called Marston's attention to them.

'Do you remember - not so long ago?'

'Do I! Happiest time of my life.'

The launch approached. Boyhood was the healthiest time of my life. Oh hell! Across the water the island's shoreline was lit up by the sun now.

The launch coasted in and backed up to rest against the dockside. The co-driver hopped out and fastened painters fore and aft. All of the benches in the shade of the cabin roof were occupied by guests staying at the lodge down the lake. Their apparel was crisp and smooth, undeniably of the best materials. They wore sun-glasses with the maladroitness of the wealthy, and some frowned through them, annoyed at having to make an extra stop. A brotherhood of incommunication molded them into a unit too formidable to invade. The benches aft in the sun carried younger and happier spirits who made room for the newcomers. Several middle-aged couples from the lodge were helped into the boat before he and Marston stepped in.

The motor purred and they moved away in the direction of a neck of water between an island and the mainland. By his elbow there fluttered a small Canadian flag. The red background blended handsomely with the blue of sea and water.

The division between his country and Canada seemed unnatural, more so than any other borderline in the world. When seen in proper perspective, the Great Lakes System formed the nucleus of an extraordinary waterways that must have been intended for the heart of a fabulous nation. Human beings influenced by short-sighted political ends had not envisioned the power of a single nation united about this system. The Iroquois lived south of the St. Lawrence while the Hurons and Algonquins lived on the north bank. Even when the Iroquois, having procured more firearms from the Dutch than the Hurons could acquire from the French, systematically destroyed the Hurons and then the hapless Neutrals, they retired south of the Great Lakes and left uninhabited the fertile lands which they had conquered.

'This is beautiful country, Marston.' Prosaic but true.

Marston's eyes glinted as he brushed his hair back in the wind. 'This is just the place to retire if you could stand the winters.'

'I don't know. With a good companion the winters ought to be rather lovely.'

'Were you thinking of a dog to bring you your slippers'?

He turned to look affectionately at Marston. 'No, I wasn't thinking of a dog, Marston.'

His handsome companion glanced away as if he were too shy to acknowledge the inference. He wished Marston were not inhibited. Although this show of timidity was cute, it became annoying if persisted in.

A large lawn with a two-storied boathouse at its side appeared like fairyland out of the wilderness. The lawn stretched up a hill to a white mansion.

'Look at this beautiful place. Whose is it?'

'It belongs to the Squirt family which makes the electric plugs,' Marston said. 'The family owns the island.'

The wealthy heads inside the cabin were turned in respectful curiosity as if on a march past.

--Here, my good sir, are four large rooms which absolutely must have the best furnishings you can lay your hands on. Give your creative instincts free rein and, remember, let expense be no deterrent.--

To wear white flannel on the beach. A plush violet dressing gown. Host at cocktails in the garden sunshine. Croquet to amuse the guests.

'Have you ever spent a summer in Manhattan?' Marston was asking.

'Marston, you just disturbed me from the most beautiful dream. Of course I haven't spent a summer in Manhattan. I'm poor but I'm not that poor.' (Liar)

That reminds me. I can cash mother's cheque when we reach town.

'I was thinking of taking some history courses at Columbia next summer.'

'Are you! I have an apartment in New York always at my disposal. When you've decided, let me know.'

Water sparkling to the starboard. Spray drops looked like dew on the chestnut-coloured wood. Fresh breeze. Children on swings over there. Marston looks bored.

'Tell me, what kind of history do you want to study?'

His eyes flickered with interest. Soft blue like the sky. He remembered them from camp days as if they were staring at him from the inside of his brain.

'American history, that is, the expansionist period during the nineteenth century.'

'Our sorest point,' he smiled.

'I feel a compulsion to understand why the Americans needed to invade those countries around them.'

'Simply the spirit of the westward movement, Marston. We found the Indians could not withstand us and our national ego was inflated.'

'I think it is an inverted ego, Adam. The aggressor has to gloss over his inferiority with battlefield victories. Unfortunately, he erects his national culture on false assumptions when he becomes the glorious possessor of far reaching land. Eventually, he will be led to discover that his true ego is far inferior to what he had supposed. Such a discovery could be rather disastrous; something like a dream world being made to confront reality.'

The hardness of tone made Adam shiver.

'What's wrong? Catch a chill?' Marston looked concerned.

'No, someone walked over my grave,' he smiled affectionately. 'That's a Canadian expression too, isn't it?'

Marston's smile encouraged him somewhat. They were friends surely. Marston stood before the darkness and would prevent him from drifting by. He swallowed dryly.

"You think then that an aggressor is only an aggressor because he is not being honest with himself?'

'Yes,' Marston nodded, 'which makes him dishonest in his dealings with others.'

He shrugged and looked out to the neck of water immediately in front of them. 'Everyone is dishonest, Marston. A man with integrity doesn't stand a chance in the world.'

Marston was biting his lip pensively. He looked disappointed. (The darkness rocked beneath his soul and intimated its dissatisfaction with the white bit of guilt suspended above).

He felt his cheeks redden and turned his head more toward shore.

<The court was embarrassed when Oscar Wilde admitted that he was forty, not thirty-nine as he had said.>

Port Carling was round the bend.

'It's the honest men who keep the world going,' Marston said with finality.

'The non-aggressors?' He burst into laughter. God! It felt good to laugh. 'They can stoke this globe all they want just as long as they let me enjoy myself.'

He threw his arm around Marston's shoulders and rocked him in his seat. With his other hand he jabbed him lightly in the chest. Strong and solid, the body invaded his embrace.

People were watching, amused. The young man behind them had his arms about two girls: why weren't people amused at him?

<On sporting days the young braves provided a continuous line of entertainment with their frolic.>

He rested his arm along the back of the seat and closed his eyes to feel out the soft tremor of the motor as the boat coasted slowly on the curve into the harbour. He was gliding into a new experience upon a low-throated hum that voiced its sexual implication.

Sailboats and motor boats cluttered the dock front. Space at one of the cement lees had been left for the launch which moved easily into port. He jumped out and gave his hand to Marston. The elderly rich were only just beginning to stir as he directed Marston away towards town.

The locks in great green steel strength allowed a rush of water to escape imprisonment with the monotonous continuum of a mill stream. The spirit of excitement shouted almost visibly in the air on the outskirts of town. Few people were in the main street which ran like an asphalt lane through the business area. A quiet resignation informed the ambiance and settled into the faces of those unfortunates who had to remain in their places of business such as the national bank.

'Wait here, Marston. I'll be right back.'

The marble floor cooled the inside considerably. The teller was new. He straightened his spectacles as he peered suspiciously at the cheque. With serious mien he approached the manager, a gray-haired man in his fifties who glistened with good health from his all-year-round habitation in these regions.

'Good afternoon, Mr. Crowfield,' he called affably. (Nice sort of banker). He glanced at the cheque which the teller nervously proffered. 'Yes, yes, yes, it's all right.' He smiled broadly to cover any embarrassment. 'In to see the regatta? 'Course, it's changed since the old days. Great fun, though.'

Dollars. Beige, yellow, blue, purple, green. Gentlemen, the Queen.

There are some things you cannot buy - true love for one.

The sun glistened in Marston's fair hair. Through the window he looked like a Greek God loitering on a corner in twentieth-century sports clothes. Luckily, he was just a perfect specimen of young Canadian manhood.

Dear Mother, Rec'd yr. check today. Thanks for the extra. Expenses more than expected.

'Marston, I have a favour to ask you. For everything we buy today, let me pay, okay?'

'Oh no, I couldn't.'

'I insist. It's my treat. I invited you. Now be good and don't object.'

Marston's shrug and amused smile was endearing.

I think he's getting a kick out of the way I'm treating him.

They hiked along the shoreline which curved out to form the right side of the harbour.

--Indian Village Straight Ahead--

The wide dirt trail revealed the remnants of cinders scattered to melt the ice in winter. A log cabin on the right. A wide office window in front. A counter seen through the window and maps on the walls. Signs advertising guides. A padlock on the door.

No scalping of American tourists today.

'Everyone must be watching the races,' he said more to himself than to Marston for his companion seemed absorbed in contemplation. But they didn't need to converse. He sensed their companionship.

The cabins were silent and seemingly empty. A bark wigwam at the water's edge emitted a small, round-shouldered squaw who called them hoarsely. She waved beads in her hands and rounded her large brown eyes piteously.

'Wait a second!'

He pulled a dollar from his pocket and reached for a string. The squaw shook her head, grinned toothlessly and held up four fingers.

'Four dollars?'

She nodded and proffered the beads. Something touching about her helplessness. How many more moons would she see? He gave her four dollars and took the beads. Bowing felicitously, the squaw watched him retreat to Marston.

'My present to you.'

Those blue eyes could drown you. They sparkled with surprise.

'Well, thanks, Adam.'

'Let me put them around your neck. Pretty, aren't they? You know, they are not originally an Indian art. Porcupine quills were used for centuries until the porcupine started to get scarce. Then the Europeans brought in the glass beads which were manufactured in Venice, I believe.'

Marston nodded attentively. With a subject to hold his interest, he could make a strong impression on him in the course of the afternoon, that is, in addition to the affection they already had for one another.

Indian children, pudgy little creatures, were tumbling in the dirt with a large mongrel dog. Not far away, their mothers, prettily clothed in summer dresses grouped at the shore to watch skiffs sailing round the point. The trail led into the woods from where they heard a murmur of voices. A clearing of bright green grass opened in front, swept over a slight incline and spread out to a great field by the water's edge. People lay on the ground, stood conversing in clusters, and watched the sailboats through binoculars.

'Indian regatta, did you say?' Marston queried. 'Looks like an excuse for a picnic.'

He laughed. 'There are probably some Indians in the sailboats.'

Boys carried tin cartons of cold drinks voicelessly through the crowd. Maybe they were Indians. They were cute and dark-skinned.

Crackling of a loudspeaker. 'Ladies and Gentlemen, in a few minutes the Guide Canoe Race will take place starting five hundred yards up to your right.'

'Hey kid,' he called. The boy turned a thick-lipped face to him. One cheek was scarred, but the whole facial aspect was attractive. 'Give us two bottles of orange, please.'

His lean sinewy body stretched as he pulled off the cap. His concentration was profound when he poured the orange into cups and took the money.

'Cold pop here!'

He went away screeching, having been encouraged by a sale.

Marston was sitting by the water's edge and watching the Indian guides get into their canoes. The approach had to blend consideration with steadiness of purpose. To take him by surprise would never do. But how to broach the subject? the intent? the purpose?

Ah, if I lose him I'll....

"Hey!'

'Sorry.' The woman passed on, wide of girth and poor of manner.

Almost spilled it.

Marston looked up. 'Look, Adam, let me pay for these, will you?'

'No, my treat. Take one.'

'You're going to have to let me pay you back.'

'That's the provincial Canadian in you. You're all interested in paying back pennies. It's no wonder we had to develop your oil, your iron, your gold fields.'

'And our minds.'

'Come, come, sarcasm? Be grateful for the democratic mass media.'

He sat at Marston's feet. The long legs were right beside him. Reaching out, he placed his hand on Marston's knee and rocked it.

'Why don't you backwoods people get smart and come over to our side?'

Marston's body rolled deliciously with each rocking motion.

'Which is your side?' Marston asked.

Was that a lead question? (!) Try it!

'The queer side. You'd enjoy it.'

'The what?'

Wrong lead. Marston's face was collected in a humorous frown as if he thought someone were pulling his leg.

'Republicanism, you Tory grit.'

'Much, much too liberal for me, Adam. We find that we get there just as fast by sticking to the middle of the road.'

'But get where? That's the question.'

'That's an historical question, unanswered even by trips into outer space.'

The guides stretched their long strong arms over the gunwales and dug into the water in slow time. Their broad backs gave him the sensation of riding in the canoe with them. He could almost sense the sideways slip of the keel.

A shout went up. Arms pointed out into the lake. A skiff had tipped. Black dots bobbed in the water about the hull. Already the roar of a motorboat responds to the impulse to rescue. More cries called attention to the winning skiff whose sail coasted by the finish line. The defeated wallowed in mass sympathy.

'Do you believe in fate, Marston? that some people are intended to lose?'

The orange drink tasted warm, possibly about the temperature of the water sousing those bobbing heads.

'The majority of people usually have an optimistic view of fate; they believe that they are intended to win; otherwise no nation would have the courage to start a war,' Marston said.

'Maybe, but I don't believe in winning or losing per se. I believe in disaster because it takes the situation out of the human world of little social achievements and relates it to the supernatural cosmos. That way I find more personal significance in every day happenings.'

'That is, if they are disasters,' Marston smiled.

'Right! Disaster always has meaning for me. But you're different, aren't you? I think of you as a kind of conqueror.'

Four braves to a canoe, they seemed to have reached the starting point. Men of mountain shoulders, they glared menacingly in imaginary warpaint. Their backbones were made of flint.

'Me? I don't even like fighting,' Marston said.

<Hiawatha proposed a federation of Iroquols nations within a tightly knit political organization. He foresaw that if Indians continued to war amongst themselves, they would be furthering their annihilation by continental invaders.>

'I don't mean physically. You seem to have a mental invincibility, which, of course, has nothing to do with being genius or clever clever,' he laughed. (Marston laughed, puzzled. Lovable!)

Marston pitched his paper cup at his feet. Adam picked it up and studied its white emptiness. Swallowing the remainder of his own drink, he slipped his cup inside Marston's and dropped them at his side.

'What I mean,' he said quietly, 'is that you can attract men's minds and emotions so that they fall under your influence. You have attracted me more than words could tell, Marston.' He reached over and gripped Marston's leg above the knee.

A lump rose in his throat. His whole body quivered.

'I am completely at your mercy,' he whispered.

'My mercy?'

Marston sat rigid in wondering thought. His face revealed his amazement and his sympathy.

A gunshot struck echoingly at the woods. The canoes leaped forward, their prows slicing through the water. Five vessels bore men straining with passion toward the finish line, toward an exhausted end.

'When someone is in love, he places himself at the mercy of the person whom he adores.'

'In love?' Marston wrinkled his nose. 'You don't love me! You couldn't.'

The guides paddled furiously. They splashed and rocked to avoid crashing into one another. War whoops sounded from shore.

'I do, I swear it. Laugh at me if you like but you'll be destroying me and denying life to a part of yourself.

'But we're just friends, Adam.'

That reasonable tone beat like a bass rhythm through all the excitement. Women jumped on their toes and clasped hands to their faces.

'I need you, don't you see!' He squirmed up beside Marston and gripped his wrist. 'If you deny me love, then you are denying yourself.'

'I don't understand you.'

The gasping mouths and heaving chests of the canoers breathed in his ears. Their arms thrashed out to take him.

'Just say that you understand. If you had ever been in love you would. But just say it.'

The long, hard line of jaw confronted him - line of defence.

The shouting grew louder and louder as the canoes approached, skimming a glassy surface. The canoers' faces grimaced with effort. Like pistons their arms drove at the water.

'What good would that do, Adam?'

'For me! I want you, I need you!'

He could barely hear himself above the cries of the spectators. The hollow sound of the scrape of paddle against gunwale groaned in his ears. A high piercing war cry exclaimed foreseeable victory.

'Okay,' Marston sighed wearily. 'I understand all right but....'

'Oh, Marston!' He brought his forehead hard against Marston's shoulder. Clamor throbbed in strong even concussions against the pate of his skull. His strength ebbed in a stream of weakness circling in his stomach.

A heavily resounding thud brought forth exclamations.

'Stop it, Adam! People are noticing us!' Marston's hands thrust him rudely aside. 'For Christ's sake!'

Two canoes had collided and tipped their crews into the lake. The Indians shot sputtering to the surface by their upturned craft. Then laughing at their misfortune, they slung an arm over the keel and shook their heads in despair at the spectators.

Adam twisted round to catch sight of the two lead canoes struggling for first place. Low grunts rolled upon shore where sympathisers waited with clenched fists and tightened faces. Suddenly, the outside canoe moved in front. It made its rival seem to stand still as it nosed ahead by measured feet and spurted across the line.

Forgotten in the wild sweep of rejoicing, the crew of the last canoe divided its time between paddling and bailing water in the middle of the course. Meanwhile, the shipwrecked guides were pushing their canoes to shore.

'Do you see how ridiculous defeat looks,' he said to Marston who had stood up to watch the action. 'Yet they can't prevent it. It's fated.'

'Adam, will you get off this "defeated" bit. I don't see why we can't just be friends.'

Hold hands and lets be friends - the Bobsie twins.

An overwhelming urgency to convince Marston that he, Adam, was supreme amongst mortals, that he, Adam, merited the most demonstrative affection, took a hold on him. He stood beside Marston and spoke softly into his ear.

'Our friendship can be beautiful if you are willing.'

The loudspeaker crackled. 'More volunteers for the special contest, the straddled bow race, are still being sought. Will anyone interested report to thc canoe dock.'

Marston slapped him on the shoulder. 'Let's try it! You sit astride the bow of the canoe and paddle with your hand.'

He stepped back in surprise. He saw the stern of the canoe wavering like a peacock's tail high behind him.

'We haven't got bathing suits.'

'Take off your shirt and your shoes and socks. I've got short pants and you can roll yours up. Come on, you won't tip anyway.'

Marston strode away and Adam, shaken by his abrupt mood of enthusiasm, followed.

I can't let him know that I detest these stupid contests. He'll think I'm a bad sport.

The contest official had a whistle cord wound about his thin red neck. He jerked his finger at two canoes for them to use and nervously rubbing his hands directed them to place their belongings in the care of his large wife who sat upon the grass.

Place your shoes at the feet of Buddha - and your shirt.

The old wide armchair would do for her: the kind which knights used to sit in when wearing full armour.

When he returned to the canoe selected for him, he noted with disgust that it was an older, splay-bottomed type. Marston was paddling his newer craft to the starting point twenty-five yards away. There were plenty of tourists in this race. The Indian guides who were competing wore over-serious expressions. Obviously they were out to lose yet to make the race look good at all costs.

He put his bare foot on the board floor and pushed away. The paddle felt light in his hands as if he were charged with nervous strength. He lined his canoe up between two others manned by sporty-looking businessmen in their fifties. From their faces he guessed that their rivalry was intensely personal. Marston was climbing to the bow of his canoe which lay two over upon his right. On shore the crowd was gathering to watch.

Balancing gingerly with his hands on the gunwale, he moved into position in the bow. He felt the most comfortable with his legs bent inside, his chest upon the tip, and his arms dangling over the sides. He glanced behind. The aft section rose precariously from the water but was not as high as he felt it to be.

Everyone appeared to be set. The starter called out from shore. One of the tourists, looking monstrously fat in his hunched up position, was ordered to back-paddle into position.

Absurdity. Man returns to the ape.

He took a deep breath, heard the whistle, thought of Marston in competition, and pushed at the water with cupped hands. The rear swayed, threatening to spin him around when he paddled forcefully. One businessman was turning in circles; the other, sneering gleefully, forged ahead.

Although his canoe was a heavier make than most, he found that it clung better to the water and gave him a chance to glide on each stroke if he was careful. Competition was thinning. Marston was about even with him. Marston shot him a smile. He gritted his teeth and slightly increased his speed.

The canoe on his left began heading for shore in spite of the efforts of its occupant. It blocked the paths of two others, in one of which was the businessman who had been sniggering over the poor start of his rival. He now shouted two words of anger and smashed into the offender's broadside.

He and Marston were leading the field, although an Indian was moving up quickly from behind. A motor launch passed by. He knew instinctively about the wave from its wake before he saw it. If he took it broadside, it would carry him backward. But if he turned to meet it, he would be off course. The small wall of water moved ominously toward him His heart palpitated. He swiped one hand forward and the other back to break the wave bow on. The aft swung round, tipped up as the wave lifted the canoe, and threw him forward over the prow. As if spun on roller skates, the canoe skittled on end. He struck the water face first and, gasping for breath, reared up to the surface. Something heavy smacked the side of his head.

Drifting, half-conscious, world of white spray, hands roughing his person. He choked, his stomach wrenched in constriction as if its flesh were being torn from the lining. Marston's face appeared vaguely. An arm fastened about his shoulders, keeping him from swallowing the biting water. He drifted on his back, the nap of his neck settled on a fleshy shoulder, his face raised to heaven. The lake threatened to smother him after each stroke of his rescuer. The hands of others seized him. He was borne onto the grass where he turned on his side and vomited clear, clean, transparent lake water.

When his stomach stopped trying to break free from his body, he turned on his back and opened his eyes. Marston was looking down at him.

That worried frown of Marston's - floating in the back of his mind - pleased him. His head felt detached from his body and when he tried to sit up, Marston's image spun round from a fixed center. He breathed deeply, gaining strength from each intake. Marston's voice played soothingly about his ears.

'You're feeling better now, aren't you? Just rest and you'll be all right. You swallowed a little water, that's all.'

The murmur of voices broke into his consciousness as if, after an exclamatory pause, prearranged for stage effect. He sat bolt upright, blinked, and felt uneasy in the stomach.

Men were running in sport on the field before him. The shade of a tree extended to people who were sitting with their backs to him. The sun had fallen into a late afternoon position. Time had been eclipsed.

Marston's voice reached his ears. He saw the young history teacher resting on one knee and arguing with a professorial-looking man. They were a short distance away in the thin line of spectators who were enjoying what appeared to be a lacrosse match.

Dragging himself backwards, he leaned his shoulders against the sharp bark of the tree trunk and wondered how long he had been sleeping. He was still shirtless and shoeless. His white ducks were dry, though grass-stained. Damn!

The hard knock of lacrosse sticks awakened him to the match. Some of the players looked Indian, at least as far as half-breeds can look Indian. Two men crossed sticks in his line of vision and one of them caught a blow on his skull. He threw down his stick and grappled with his opponent, but other players prevented them from fighting, and the game ran on at an exhausting pace.

<Pontiac used the game of lacrosse as a ruse to destroy a series of forts along the frontier. Braves offered to hold an exhibition match for the settlers within the walls of the fort. At the height of play, one of the players cast the ball through the passage into the inner fortifications and his team-mates led the chase in pursuit. On that signal scores of serene-visaged Indians, who had mingled amongst the people of the fort to watch the game, threw off their robes and brandished knives and tomahawks to massacre their unsuspecting hosts.>

<Winckelmann was murdered by a stranger whom he took to his hotel room in Trieste ostensibly to see his gold coins.>

Marston ought to come for dinner; he had promised him dinner and there was no time like the present.

Marston was approaching in a tall ambling stride. His handsome face grinned. 'Awake? Boy! you sure slept.'

'Did I?' His voice piped weakly. 'How long.'

'More than an hour.' Marston crouched in front of him and studied his face. 'You look fine now.'

'I don't feel it. I feel like a washed-out rag. Is there anything light that I can eat?'

'I'll get you some fruit.' Marston sprang up. 'There's a woman with a stand at the other end of the field.'

'Wait, don't go yet!' He took a deep breath. 'I owe you my life, don't I? Thank you, Marston.'

Marston burst into laughter. He seemed nervous as if the shock of the incident had remained with him. 'Don't get melodramatic. I was just the first to reach you.'

He smiled simperingly. 'Third method of rescue, wasn't it? Do you remember practicing that together?'

'Yes! Of course I do! With that instructor with the buck teeth we used to call 'Buck'. Strange that we should really have had to use it.'

'It's lucky that you were doing the saving. I remember almost failing the test because of the damned third method. The fifth is the easy one, but I was more than just a tired swimmer this time.'

'The main thing is that you're fine now, eh?' Marston backed away. 'I'll bring you your shirt and shoes. Would a melon be all right or would you like some grapes?'

'A melon's okay.'

He sank back against the tree. The lacrosse stick with its thonged basket could make a good basic design for a floor lamp.

'Oh Marston!'

Marston heard him and turned. He marveled at Marston's hearing since his voice sounded piteously feeble. 'Who won the race?'

Marston flashed a brilliant smile, his white teeth glistening. 'A guy from Texas.'

He chuckled. His stomach hurt. He must have strained the muscles. Damn!

Defeated again. The gentleman from the deep south had been merely nominal winner. Marston achieved the most significance by his heroic self-sacrifice at the expense of disaster. Marston, the hero of his dreams, stepped into reality and snatched him up in his arms for purely utilitarian reasons.

The match dwindled. The players checked themselves into temporary lethargy. The afternoon hung in a plethora of sun and shade. The loudspeaker announced Port Carling at ten points and Bala at zero; minutes of play remaining. The crowd began to disperse as thoughts of ice cold drinks coincided with the five o'clock torpor.

An Indian boy in his early teens waved awkwardly and walked over to him.

'How are you feeling, sir?'

The round innocent features inexplicably reminded him of Renaissance cherubs.

'Fine, what's your name?'

'Thomas. I live in the village over there.'

The boy pointed. His limbs were lean and straight.

'I see. Do you like milk shakes, Thomas?'

'Yes sir!'

'The next time I'm in town, I'll treat you to one. How's that?'

'That's swell.'

Marston joined them. He carried a bunch of grapes.

'Oh, this is Thomas. He has been inquiring after my health.'

'And inquiring after the blanket too, aren't you, Tom?'

'Yes sir. My mother said its all right if you still want to use it.'

Marston handed Adam the grapes and stooped down and folded up a brightly coloured Indian blanket. Adam blinked with surprise. He had not noticed that he had been lying on it. In the heavy shade he had completely overlooked it so dazzling by contrast was the bright green of the grassy field in the sun.

'So it belongs to you,' he smiled charmingly. 'We shall have to have that soda for a certainty.'

The boy laughed with delight and, throwing the blanket over his shoulder, he waved as he strode away.

'How about having dinner at my place tonight?'

'Oh no. I wouldn't ask you to do any cooking in your condition.'

'No cooking. I've cold chicken and lots of salad which needs to be eaten soon. Come on.'

Marston grinned. 'Okay, but first let's see the round dance in the center of the village. It'll start when the match is over. Say, I hope you don't mind the grapes. She hadn't any melons.'

A whistle blasted the end of the sporting activities for the day. The lacrosse players sauntered off the field and mixed with the departing spectators. He put on his shirt and socks and shoes.

He felt strange upon his feet, as if the wind were holding him up and whirling by his ears. After a few steps, the sensation passed away and he began to enjoy his experience in retrospect. Death had ridden by unexpectedly, but Marston as his watchful sentinel had prevented any destruction. Life with Marston would be secure and blissful. Unfortunately, Marston could pose as his saviour; more unfortunately, he chose to disregard the honour. There seemed no way to presume upon their comradeship because Marston would react suspiciously to any overture to a friendship closer than that which already existed.

Marston's attitude was puzzling. He stood by ready to prove the solidarity of their friendship at the same time that he resented any demonstration of familiarity. And yet, he must have known that his old camp pal had a deep affection for him that almost cried to be expressed by physical means.

They were passing through the Indian village which had come alive with voices and the sounds of cooking. In a clearing a crowd encircled a dozen Chippewas in full regalia hopping on each foot in turn as they wound back and forth and to both sides in line. The monotony of the dance intrigued him. The pounding of the feet reiterated the passage of time in the unchanging land of river and lakes. Always had the mystery been here and always would it remain. Man beat out his contact with nature on the floor of the land, and he awaited response in good signs from the skies. Controlled, the dance formed a circle and maintained its steady rhythm.

<The Siberian peasants increased the tempo of their dances until their blood was heated to an uncontrollable passion and the sexes fell upon each other in an orgiastic frenzy.>

Were there not similarities between Algonquins and Siberians? They both cooked in vessels made from birch bark set high enough from the flames to escape burning. They wrote in pictures on the soft tissue of the bark. Hidden from the public eye, could not these Algonquins have speeded up their dance to a state where the mind is completely eclipsed by sexual desire? Tradition thumped its mystic message from generation to generation and joined the races of the past to the races of the present just as it united the dancers into one spirit.

<It was the custom among these Indians to hold a ceremony known as the Feast of the Dead every eight or ten years. At this time all those deceased since the last ceremony, having been temporarily interred in graves, were brought from surrounding villages to a central spot. Here a communal burial took place following several days of ritual activity. The remains of the dead were first suspended from a scaffolding over a large pit, often lined with valuable furs; then, on the last day, they were dismembered and stirred up together in a large grave. Strings of beads, tools, pottery vessels and other articles were placed in the ground with the dead. In this way friends and relatives from many different villages came together and jointly paid their final respects to the deceased member of the tribe.>

The monotony of the dance became threatening. Shades of anxiety fell over the faces of the white spectators. Life was slowly being reduced to a simple theme which mocked those seekers after variety as superfluous to the needs of the world. The individual was, by contrast, a self-indulgent romanticist. Guiltily, he regarded Marston from the side of his eye and sensed in him the eventual defeat of his desires.

Sickness crept up from his stomach and his head spun. He put his hand firmly on Marston's arm.

'I'm not feeling well. Lets get a taxi.'

As the thumping receded, his agitation decreased. The air smelt extremely fresh, and everything about the town looked clean and inviting. The taxi stand was close at hand. He sank back in the cushioned seat with Marston beside him and relaxed in the pleasure of being moved swiftly and gently without effort.

4.

When the taxi turned toward Port Sanfield, Marston was gazing at the thick woods hemming in the road. The isthmus into which they came divided Lake Joseph from Lake Rosseau. Twin Lakes. Rosseau was the wilder-looking of the two, but it had that special beauty of independence. Now the sun was hanging low over it and encrusting its trees and islands with rosy tints.

'Say, Adam, didn't you have a camera with you?'

Adam opened his mouth in horror. 'I did but I've lost it. I think I took it off the launch but so much happened since then, I don't know where I could have left it.'

'I don't think you took it off the launch. Maybe when the people return to the lodge, it'll be dropped off for you.'

'Oh, Marston, what a stupid thing to do!'

They flashed through the village of Port Sandfield, the clank of the bridge being its most significant marking.

'I hope you are right. It's too valuable to lose.'

He smiled as he thought of excursions in Europe - tour of Rome, the square of San Marco in Venice. 'It's the first time I have heard of an American not missing his camera.'

Adam returned his smile sportingly. He leaned forward as he peered at the side of the road. 'Turn in along here, driver, at the next lane.'

They wound up the lane to a sprawling white summer house. Expensive and tasteful, but sort of presumptuous as a residence for one person.

Adam paid the driver and led Marston in through the back door.

<The underground railway guided slaves out the back door of the United States into Canada.>

As Marston entered the house, he had a presentiment of capture. Adam's pressing invitations throughout the course of the afternoon had been trying and, at times, alarming. Within the walls of his home there was more opportunity for Adam to make his demands unavoidably obvious, yet he wanted to remain true to the trust he had placed in Adam because that trust signified the respect that one man should feel for another.

He was aware that his reasoning was naive, but he preferred to risk disappointment rather than damage their friendship through a misunderstanding.

White linoleum clean upon the floor. Shining whiteness of stove and refrigerator. The dining room set out in the finest colonial style of furniture. Windows overlooking the lake - red sun balancing sharply on the horizon. Sitting room comfortably furnished with arm chairs, footstools, and a cabinet of leather-bound classics.

'How do you like it?' Adam spun on him.

'Terrific!'

'Sit down and I'll rustle us up a meal. Won't take a jiffy.'

A telephone hung in the hall.

'May I telephone the lodge and let them know that I won't be there for dinner.'

'Sure.' Adam moved away in his strange saunter into the kitchen.

When he contacted the lodge, he asked for Corinne. Luckily she was nearby. Her voice sounded huskier.

'Marston speaking. I'm staying at Adam's for dinner and I'll pick you up afterwards. How's that?'

'Oh,' she said shortly. 'Well, there's a party leaving from here. I'll go with them and meet you at the dance.'

The change of tone surprised him. 'Sure, if that's what you want to do.'

'It'll be easier like that.' Her tone softened. 'Good-bye. Don't forget to see me.'

'I won't. Good-bye.'

Fear of a woman's mind in constant change. Maybe she had replaced him with another suitable young man in the course of the afternoon.

Replacement, replacement rang ominously through his thoughts. Surely Corinne had intimated that she liked him; she could not possibly have changed her mind and be sane.

His reasoning failed to encourage him as he remembered the numerous times that girls had disappointed him in the past. True it was, that trust was only to be found in man.

Corinne's long-legged figure paraded in the nude through his imagination. He sensed the excitement of slipping his arm about her waist and gazing down upon her breasts.

I'll go to the dance and pick her up. That's the only way to find out if she really likes me or someone else.

Saxophone tones in absentia saddened his sentiment.

He strolled to the kitchen doorway and watched Adam preparing a salad.

Adam glanced at him and carried on. 'I am going to make you the best salad you have ever tasted. Now, go away and let it be a surprise.'

His fingers skipped nimbly and his swift sure actions expressed a special satisfaction from working in the kitchen.

Marston returned to the sitting room and picked up a large green book lying on the sofa. Thinking of Corinne, he leafed through the pages. Warm and sexy - full bodied love. Smell of freshly serrated pages - fluff planed from the edges - rolled like down in the fingers. He flicked on the lamp behind him and read;

"INDIAN MYTHS: ALGONKIAN"

Adam's fascination for these people of the northlands puzzled him as did so many peculiarities about Adam. Why did he not interest himself in the many Indian nations of his own country, or at least in the Totem Pole culture of the Pacific Coast? The big-boned Algonquin were continuously being chased to the non-agricultural regions of the north by the ferocious Iroquois. They were forced to trade their furs and canoes for maize and tobacco with the nations to the south.

They were almost nomadic so distantly did they canoe their trade along the northern waterways. Of course, they were inventors: snow-shoes, moccasins, birch-bark canoe. Their spiritual strength fostered by rigorous winters was phenomenal. But why did they attract Adam?

In the margin of one page a line in red ink was drawn alongside a paragraph. Spreading the book on his lap, he read the designated print with curiosity.

Wiske'djak never got married to a woman. But he pretended to get married. One time he dressed himself like a woman, with skirts, and tried to deceive a young man, so that he thought Wiske'djak was his wife. Wiske'djak pretended to be jealous of the man when he went away. The other people knew that it was Wiske'djak all the time and laughed to themselves and made fun of the pair. The young man lived with Wiske'djak for some time, thinking it was his wife. But the other people made fun of the young man so much that at last he left Wiske'djak. Several times he got young men to live with him as their wife, but at last they all left him and he went away by himself. He was a queer fellow, that Wiske'djak. He never got married because he would not be bothered with a woman as he had to be traveling all the time.

He closed the book and set it aside.

Twilight in the bay window. Fly-catchers licking up the last of their suppers in plummeting swoops. The darkening room as the outside world drew invisible shutters upon it. Adam banged a plate in the kitchen, its short sharp ring pin-pointing the somberness in the here and now.

One clung to manhood as a center of gravity. To have it taken away would free the soul into a sort of outer space forever. The heart grew cold at the prospect. He would leave the house if, by doing so, he were not shamed by his cowardice.

Adam approached bearing a tray with dishes of salad and chicken and two tall gasses of milk.

(American industry worked with Canadian raw produce.)

'Here's your plate,' Adam said, handing him a fork with it. 'And milk.'

They settled down in quiet feeding. The taste of the food awakened them to their hunger which had to be partially satisfied before they could express any emotion.

'You do make a good salad,' Marston said. 'It's not too sharp and it has a lot of flavour to it. Very, very good.'

He cut a piece of white meat in half with the side of his fork and ground its fresh fibres between his teeth.

Adam had paused from eating and his black eyes were staring at him.

'What's the matter?' He blushed. 'Don't I sound appreciative enough?'

Adam made no response but returned to his meal. The silence loomed like a great rock barrier between them.

'Is this lamp enough light?' he asked wondering if he had really done something to anger Adam or whether Adam was just pretending to be annoyed.

'It's not the light; it's you and your damned phony behaviour that I don't like.'

'Phony?' He sat up in amazement. 'How am I being phony?'

Adam's lips curled. 'You pretend that I'm giving you supper because I want you to compliment my tasty dishes.'

'Hell no! I'm being sincere when I say it's good.'

'Of course you are; it is good! But you don't have to treat me as if I were a stranger who makes you nervous.'

'To be frank with you, you do make me nervous.'

Startled, Adam continued in a milder tone. 'You are making yourself nervous, Marston. I wouldn't do a thing to hurt you. Haven't you understood yet that you are precious to me?'

'It's this constant laying claim to me that's so disturbing. Sure, you can like me and I can like you but let's not have any of these Tchaikovsky overtures, eh?'

'Why did you choose the name of a homosexual?'

'Because you are right, Adam. Tchaikovsky calls out for sympathy. He creates disaster so that he can come through with his little cry of help for the lost individual, which is always himself by the way.'

'So you think that that is what I'm doing?'

Nod as a sullen rejoinder. There was more to say but he could not. Already Adam was struggling to regain his confidence.

'You probably think of me as a case for the mental home,' Adam declared.

'Oh no, I don't. All I know is that I am not attracted physically to men. I can't like you the way you want me to.'

'Marston, listen to me. Homosexuality is natural amongst men. I know, I know, it's an old argument, but it can rely upon a lot of history for proof. All I want you to do is to just try it. Just once.'

'Why, when I know that I won't have any pleasure from it and maybe feel remorseful to the end of my days?'

'For my sake. For the sake of our old friendship and our new relationship which will certainly result.' Adam regarded him tensely.

'I'm sorry,' he shook his head. 'Sexually I like women. Anything beyond them revolts me. Even some of them revolt me.' He tried to bring a smile to Adam's face in vain. 'I wish we could be good friends, Adam, because I'm very fond of you.'

'Marston.' Adam sat beside him on the sofa and put his arm about his shoulders. The black eyes yearned for him as if trying to penetrate his mind. 'Women are cheap whores with their thoughts constantly on material goods like hardened merchants. They'll use you to marry them as a complement to their egos and then harness you to work for them while they play games behind your back.' He smoothed the hairs along Marston's arm. 'You think you're in love with a woman, but you'll find that love is the last reason why she is with you.'

'Boy! You're pretty hard on women. I admit there are some like that, but not every one.'

Adam laughed and brought his grinning mouth close to Marston's ear. 'You are an idealist, dear Marston.'

Idealism - was that the basic ingredient of Isaac Brock and Tecumseh? And what of Hull, Wayne, Scott and the other invaders - what was their basic ingredient?

'You are a pessimist, dear Adam.'

Adam pulled on his arm. 'Come, I want to show you the bedroom.'

Unreasonable to flee, unmanly to show fear. He allowed Adam to lead him gently by the arm.

<At the time of the Oregon dispute, Polk's campaign slogan was, 'Fifty-four forty or fight.'>

<The United States Government absolutely refused to make reparation payments for the series of Fenian raids on Canadian soil. Nor had the Government attempted to prohibit the raids which were organized in full view of the public.>

Adam reached in the bedroom and switched on the light. The bed was untidily made.

'I'll put on clean sheets,' he said.

Fright stuck in his chest. He was being advised to capitulate. Pulling his arm away, he retreated to the center of the sitting room, and then, noticing Adam's sardonic grin, he picked up his glass and swallowed the rest of his milk to hide his embarrassment.

'It's dark outside. I've got to be going.'

'Well,' Adam sighed. 'If you must, you must.' His eyes glinted devilishly. 'Won't you have second thoughts on staying for dessert?'

'Afraid not.' He faced Adam grimly, thoroughly shaken. 'Can you call a taxi?'

Adam became abruptly stern. 'Call one yourself,' he said sharply. 'The Elgin's a few minutes away. There may be one there.'

Harsh good-byes probably helped give expression to Adam's disappointment. Physically, he was a man, but he seemed to have developed the emotions of a woman. Or were there such things as emotions peculiar to the sex rather than particular to the individual?

"Hotels - Elgin."

He dialed the number printed in the booklet, asked a woman for a taxi, and received an affirmation. The woman's voice remained with him - soothing, encouraging. It was contact with life beyond this box.

Adam had disappeared into the bedroom. A framed reprint of Rembrandt's "The Man in the Golden Helmet" stood on a table by the radio. The sad gaze of the old guardsman spoke of countless disillusionments brought upon a sensitive spirit. A call to the sympathetic heart.

As a boy Adam had been a free spirit, how could it have come to pass that he should be chained to perverted desire? In the course of the day, he had remarked signs of the decay into which Adam was sinking: the thick look of his body about to go to fat for lack of exercise, the swaying walk like the meandering pace of cattle, the disinterested manner in which he took a refusal to submit to his wishes, his preoccupation with disaster. "In Pursuit of Pleasure" hinged to him like a name plate. What was there in life for Adam? Did the guardsman transmit the secret that uninitiated young men like himself could not read?

History channeled emotions back over the ages. It acted like a subconscious sentinel to lend support to his own emotions in the present. What was the mysterious link between historical fact and personal experience? Was it a need for that same feeling of continuity that Adam appeared to be searching for? Could he find it in the guardsman's wistful expression or would a painting such as the Mona Lisa give him an answer?

Corinne's naked body rose like a pillar to disturb him.

A horn bleated in the driveway.

Adam appeared from the bedroom. He had changed his white clothes to a red shirt and tight-fitting blue trousers.

'I'm coming as far as the lodge with you,' he said. 'I want to see if my camera has been returned.'

The back door of the taxi opened revealing the inside lit like a cubicle by a solitary bulb offering monastic haven from the darkness round about. They sat in and drove in silence. The road wound them by the black wall of forest and past gaps of lake coves achromatic like slate in the dim light from the stars.

Marston sensed a vacancy of feeling which appeared to belong to this unresponsive landscape. Amicability would only have increased his sense of loss and incriminate him for some unexplained crime, his judges being the trees indistinguishable in the mass.

'Stop here, driver.' Adam's voice belonged to a stranger.

'No, Adam, we'll drive in and drop you off.'

Adam opened the door and stepped onto the road. 'I prefer the walk.'

'It's not far,' he protested weakly.

Adam slammed the door. The taxi started up, gravel knocking upon its fenders until it regained the asphalt highroad.

The thought of Adam's fifteen-minute walk along a deserted side road passed a sense of loneliness into him. Beside him, the seat spoke of a presence forsaken.

He noticed that his hands trembled, and he clasped his kneecaps to tighten the muscles of his arms. The wholeness of his body took physical shape in his mind, as if he were seeing a consummate figure from a Matisse drawing. He felt preserved as an entirety somehow. Adam had threatened his autonomy. When he rejected Adam, he had kept that essence which he had been able to recognize as himself throughout his life so far. Recognition of his essence entailed recognition of Adam's essence as well; and so from the start he must have been instinctively aware that they were not duplicates.

But what am I? What does Corinne mean to me? Will she mean as much as Adam means to me?

The lights from a corner gas station cast a lawn of star dust over the turn-off. Music drifted in the window: a trumpet blasted out a refrain, tonally charged with narcissistic glory. Rows of long, sleek-bodied cars were parked in evidence of the popularity of the dance which drew young people from both sides of the lake.

He left the taxi at the side gate of the hotel and followed a cement walk to the casino which was suspended over the water. Couples were wandering hand in hand along the dock. The music stopped and the chatter of voices carried up the front lawn.

He stepped through the doorway into the convivial lighting - "Gentlemen Must Wear Coat and Tie."

(General Wolfe arriving on the plains at Quebec without his sword)

'I'm sorry, I can't admit you without proper dress.'

The ticket-taker was a chubby-cheeked young man with an imposing jawbone. If discovered in thirty thousand years what species would he be aligned with?

'Please excuse my barbarity, but I have come a long way.'

'Those are regulations.' He flicked a fistful of tickets with his thumb.

Corinne had her back to him. She was sitting with a happy-looking crowd. Perhaps he should not join them and upset the party.

'Look, I just want to speak with the group over there,' he nodded.

The ticket-taker slowly looked round. The group seemed to pass his inspection. 'Which person do you want?'

He designated Corinne. The ticket-taker left his post to notify her of his arrival. Corinne came all smiles to him.

'What took you so long?' she cried.

He remarked the note of impatience.

'I can't get in. Will he let you out?'

The ticket-taker framed a superior expression and turned away.

Corinne laughed lightly and took his arm. Tender clasp.

'Come on, I've had enough anyway.'

'What about your friends? (Not that I give a damn).

'Oh, they know I'm with you now.'

So there was no rival for her affections - at least on the scene.

She led him onto the dock. A breeze was blowing off the water.

'Those dances bore me stiff,' Corinne said. 'Year after year the faces may change but the people are always the same.'

'I know what you mean. After a while there's no more fun to be had.'

'Unless,' she interposed, 'you're with a special person. I guess that's where the difference lies.'

He looked at her. The breeze had blown some tresses of hair across her face. They clung to the corners of her mouth. She made no attempt to remove them so he brushed them back to the side of her head and smoothed her cheek.

'You feel lost without some guiding mate, do you?' he smiled.

(Awfully charming that smile. If it didn't come naturally, I wouldn't dare try it.)

'Mate?' She reared back. "Well, you might call it that though it sounds as if I'm looking for a Tarzan.'

'He got married in the end.'

She smiled. She did not think it humorous. She may have lacked a broad sense of humour but that could be easily overlooked when you considered the rest of her.

The band struck up a lively old tune - old, the late thirties.

'It's surprising how they fit a few oldies into an evening,' he said. 'Hut-sut Ralston on the Rilawah....'

'Oh, don't sing. It's so nice and peaceful here.'

They had reached the end of the dock. The lake lay like a bed of pitch under the light from the beacon beside them. He wondered if he should put his arm round her.

'It's funny meeting you again after all these years, Marston.'

'It is strange,' he said, putting his arm about her waist. Her body seemed to float beside him. She turned her face to him and he brought his lips upon hers.

They took breath and kissed in soft pecks at lips, cheeks, and neck.

She put her hands on his shoulders and gently forced her release. With his passion aroused, the need for a woman raced through his blood. He gazed at her breasts, full and round under a white sweater.

'Let's go someplace where it's more private,' he suggested.

She smiled at his tone of urgency. 'Not now.' She held back his hands as they reached out to caress her. 'I'd like to get back to our own lodge, but I have to wait for the kids who brought me in their boat.'

The light from a motorboat passed over them and they blinked. The boat sputtered to a halt at the dockside.

'I think that's Mr. Ornweddy,' Corinne whispered excitedly. She ran on tip-toe toward the boat.

The droning voice of an elderly gentleman thanked his host as his thin shape moved onto the dock. He was holding fishing poles in one hand.

'Hello, Mr. Ornweddy!' Corinne's voice rang young and cheerful.

He could not hear Ornweddy's reply, but he knew that Corinne had got them a lift. He walked towards them. Corinne beckoned him to follow her on board. She sat between Ornweddy and him.

'Well, well, Marston,' Ornweddy chuckled, barely visible in the dark shade from the dock.

'Didn't see you at the regatta,' he said quickly.

'An old friend arrived at this lodge and wanted to go fishing. So I didn't want to crowd my day. How was it? Plenty of people?'

'Yes, pretty crowded.' He settled back.

The motor made too much noise for them to converse for which he was thankful. He put his arm around Corinne's shoulders to protect her from the cool night wind.

The prow moved over murky depths. Buoys to be avoided.

They picked up speed, the wind whipping their hair. One lone light signalled passage home. Corinne moved warmly against him, but not obviously, for fear that Ornweddy would notice.

In less than three weeks I return to the grind. New smiling faces will be positioned behind polished desks. They will ring out the gamut of human emotions before the year is out, and I, exhausted, where shall I lie fallow for a summer season? Europe again, maybe. But my need for woman is becoming unbearable. A schoolteacher cannot afford marriage, of course - but, then, what man in my generation can?

I must lay Corinne tonight - I must or I am not a man, nor is she a woman, nor are we anything but prey to other kinds of sex.

Three light bulbs designated corners of the front dock. A string of coloured lights trailed up the front walk to the sombre lodge, indiscernible atop its hill.

Corinne drew away slightly. The motor slowed, it's echo beating off the wooded shore. Ornweddy steered his boat to the small dock, where a beacon light illumined the approach, and coasted it to harbour.

Seconds of non-motion rooted them to their seat. Marston flung out an arm mechanically and climbed onto the dock. He helped Corinne out and moored the boat while Ornweddy drew a tarpaulin over its top.

'That's all right,' Ornweddy said. 'Don't wait for me. I want to check a few things.'

(Mother and child)

They walked by the tennis court. He wanted to lead them to the path at the far end, but Corinne stopped just short of it.

'Let's sit down here,' she said.

He could barely discern her profile. They sat side by side on the grassy slope. He brought her onto her back, kissed her, and ran his hand over her figure.

Delight, delight, screaming delight!

He brought his leg over her and they embraced tightly. Her lips became a drink which momentarily drugged the chisel-sharp desire working his thighs.

'Let's go to my room,' he suggested.

She tried to sit up, but he held her down.

'What's wrong with going to my room?' he frowned. (Not again, no, no, no, defeat, surely not again!)

'Let me go and I'll tell you,' she spoke away from him.

Hopefully, he allowed her to sit up.

"First of all,' she said, 'I am not going to anybody's room.'

'You don't want to make love,' he said acidly.

'Not until I am married.'

'Corinne, look, you don't expect us to pet as if we were frustrated teen-agers. I'm too old for that stuff. I need to make love.'

'Then find a prostitute if you want to make love.'

'Where would I find a prostitute up here? And what gives you the right to connect money with physical love? Any love I know has always been a combination of both the physical and spiritual in spite of what Puritan ethics want us to believe.'

'Then you should get married.'

'Are you mad, Corinne? Do you honestly believe at the age of twenty-some-odd that marriage is the answer to the problem of desire?'

She stood up abruptly. 'Since you can't talk reasonably, I'm going in.'

'Corinne, don't leave me. I want you, I need you terribly.'

'I'll stay only on condition that you promise to behave yourself.'

Anger mounted in his temples. It burned into the flesh of his head. 'You don't really give a damn then, do you. You were just out for a little night-time frolic on the grass. What I'd like to know is just what do you do for sex?'

'I'm going in, Marston. Good-night.'

He watched her fade into the blackness, her white sweater resembling a fleur-de-lis before it disappeared.

<Bishop Strachan strongly opposed the union of Upper to Lower Canada on religious grounds.>

The air was cold to the skin. His brain clouded. He lay on his back and tried to reason away his dejection.

Dull, sombre, sick, unhealthy energy overlaying my body like a huge black canker.

He stood up and slowly climbed the hill to the back of the lodge. So as to escape meeting anyone, he took the outside stairs to the second floor and reached his room unnoticed. He flopped onto the bed.

The scent of Corinne's soft skin and the touch of her fine strands of hair against his cheeks invaded him immediately. He fought to concentrate on school, swimming methods, Indians, anything, but, slipping helplessly into the embrace of invisible Pygmalion, he began to rub the heat into her veins.

The room closed on him in the shapes of women he had seen and known. Remembered sights, imaginings filed in the mind flipped to the surface, re-lived enjoyment from provoking postures, her! no, no, her, her, that, yes! no! her, her, beautiful her, now her, better, perfect, stay there... the long legs... the breasty curves, her of the flesh conjoining, lost! bolt of red fire, Her!... Heat of the unconscious slowly slipping into the dull weight of dead limbs. Hot, hot desire drifting from off the body as if in vapours.

He sat up.

(Constant practice makes for efficiency: another test tube sterilized)

The trees dimly reflected the verandah light upon the window. The house was deathly still - not a voice to be heard along the draughty corridors.

Marston stepped to the basin, picked the jug up from the floor, and, grasping it by its neck, poured out a measure of water. The sweet sickening smell of him clogged his nostrils. He dropped off his clothes and kicked them across the room. Applying the cold water, he washed himself thoroughly.

His spirits began to revive. He could not stay in the room. He had to roam; he wanted contact with people.

I wonder if Adam is around the lodge somewhere.

<After denying entry to American vessels in the maritime fisheries for many years, Canada tendered suggestions for reciprocity.>

He switched on the light - dim and yellow, probably not as bright as the gas which came out of that pipe in the wall at one time.

Let's see, a clean white shirt for the ladies, my summer suit and a tie with a conservative stripe. Slow labour of doing up buttons.

'What am I dressing up for anyway?'

He moved his shoulders comfortably inside his white shirt and light-weight coat. He slipped on a pair of easy shoes, opened the door and carried the basin across the hall to the men's room where he dumped the water in the toilet and flushed it. He rinsed out the basin and returned it to his bureau. He clicked off the light.

As he was descending the stairs he caught sight of Adam strolling with a woman on the verandah.

Ruth someone or other wasn't it? Her husband had either divorced her or left her - proper status had not been established.

He stepped onto the verandah and saw that they had stopped strolling to look over the railing. He stood at the top of the steps where Adam would see him and invite him to join them. He waited, hands in pockets, and stared at the triangle made by the lights on the front dock.

Adam appeared to be ignoring him. Perhaps Adam was interested in the woman: she was very pretty and probably accessible.

He heard her voice. 'There's your friend.'

He turned and approached them. 'Hello, Adam, Hello, Ruth.'

Adam nodded stiffly, making him extremely nervous, unwanted. But Ruth smiled as if she welcomed him.

'Did you find your camera, Adam?'

'Yes,' Adam said. 'It was returned to the lodge. I should go and check on it.' He smiled at Ruth. 'I'm looking forward to pursuing our conversation tomorrow.'

He left without so much as a glance at Marston. Through the window opposite them, Marston saw the older lodgers reading newspapers and magazines in the lamp-lit sitting room.

He doesn't want to know me. I can't blame him.

Ruth was wearing shorts. Her tanned legs were well-formed, attractive. She was smiling at him.

'I'm going for a walk,' he said. 'Do you want to come?'

'All right. Where?'

'I think there's a path leading off this side of the verandah.'

Their heels resounded on the boards. He felt the trembling of the wood up the backs of his legs. They reached the start of the path.

'It leads by the back, down to the water and around by the tennis court,' he said.

'Fine,' she smiled. 'On the third time around, you might hold my hand.'

He laughed. He held her hand.

The woods gave way to a small clearing from where they saw the back of the staff house. A frame of window was lit up on the second storey. The pyjamaed form of the lodge handyman appeared momentarily in the frame.

'That's Aaron,' Ruth said, shuddering.

'What's wrong? Don't you like him?'

'Brutes like him frighten me. Come on.' She glided ahead.

A movement on the ground caught his eye. Adam walked into a patch of light and peered up at the window. He shifted nervously. He seemed to want to attract Aaron's attention but was holding back as if afraid. He fingered a pebble, hesitating to throw it against the pane, his face pallid, terrified.

Adam! Adam! For Christ's sake, Adam!

Ruth was whispering for him to hurry along. Soft sibilance from the dark. He moved his feet in her direction, his legs like cords of wood.

(New York City, 1961)

AFTERWORD

"Caravetti" is taken from my first unpublished novel, a long interwoven enquiry into various aspects of love after the fashion of Andre Gide's *Les Fauxmonnayeurs* and Aldous Huxley's *Point Counter Point*. It was 1955 and I returned from Italy to London hopeful that I would find a publisher. I gave the manuscript to John Guest, the distinguished editor of Longman's for many years, who, after he read it, took me to dinner and kindly suggested that I write from a point of view. When I quoted Flaubert that the artist should not enter more into his work than God enters His, he smiled dismissively and said that Flaubert said many things. Guest's advice was good for writers expecting to publish with English-language publishers, but I had knocked about the Continent long enough to catch glimpses of the truth that art could reveal. Bertrand Russell perceived philosophy in the same way: that the philosopher had to cut into the darkness on a sense of adventure and follow his reasoning where it took him; in that light, Thomas Aquinas was not a philosopher because he posited a point which he called God and arranged his argument to arrive at that point; that seemed a good example of "point of view." I thought the difference had great significance for the arts. An editor of another House whom I met at a party asked me to let his reader see the manuscript, and it was this reader who suggested that most of the novel was too "advanced" and that the conventional "Caravetti" section might make a book on its own - advice that I, being an impressionable young man, followed to no avail.

"Adam" is a spin-off from that first novel, comprising a Gidean hedonist and the Julian Green-like inhibited Marston, which I first recast in a novel set like the first on the Balearic Island of Ibiza. The late novelist Angus Wilson read it and suggested that, since stories of northerners losing their inhibitions in southern climes had been overdone, I should set it in Canada, and, thus, something very different emerged.

"Helen" looks at another aspect of love, which I did not address in that first novel, but which I was interested in exploring back then. Millard Lampell, the New York writer, kindly encouraged me to rewrite my first draft into that which I gave you here.

DRB